Running With Grace

Wings of Faith Series Book 3: An Inspirational Love Story

Barbara Jane Oliver

Synergistic Connections, LLC

Paperback ISBN: 978-1-968938-05-5

E-Book ISBN: 978-1-968938-04-8

Beta Reader: Kate Marie at Beta Reader Bookings, LLC

Book Cover: Miblart Book Cover Design

First Edition 2026

Visit the **Author's Website** at https://barbarajaneoliver.com/

Published by Synergistic Connections, LLC

Also By Barbara Jane Oliver

ALTHOUGH THESE NOVELS ARE part of a series featuring inter-connected characters, the main romance centers on a unique story-line with its own arc and resolution. Each book can be enjoyed as a standalone novel, making it a pleasurable independent reading experience.

WINGS OF FAITH SERIES

- Before the Blessing: A Bristol Heights Novella (Colton & Nicole): Download FREE When You Subscribe to My Newsletter

- Renewing His Hope Book 1: Daniel & Samantha

- Soaring in Faith Book 2: Aaron & Meghan

- Running with Grace Book 3: Brandon & Grace

- Walking in Love Book 4: Julian & Lyndon: TBA

BRISTOL HEIGHTS SANCTUARY SERIES

- Sanctuary in His Arms Book 1: Joshua & Simone: TBA

- Sanctuary of Truth Book 2: TBA

Dedication

I dedicate this book to my Lord and Savior, Jesus Christ. Thank You for giving me life, breath, and your everlasting love. You are always with me, walking beside me and guiding me through all the pathways of my life. I am eternally grateful. It's all for Your Glory! Amen!

Inspirational Scripture for Wings of Faith Series of Books

Isaiah 40:31: But those who hope in the Lord will renew their strength. They will soar on wings like eagles; they will run and not grow weary, they will walk and not be faint.

Acknowledgements

I WOULD LIKE TO express my heartfelt gratitude to my husband, Ronald. I appreciate your unwavering support, strength, and love. Thank you for consistently being present in my life. I hold you in the highest regard. Furthermore, I extend my appreciation to my daughter, Erica, for enlightening me on the existence of living miracles. You genuinely fill me with cheer! Additionally, I wish to thank my parents, Mom and Dad, as well as my brother, Willie Jr. There are no greater cheerleaders in this world than you. I cherish each of you deeply!

To Page and Michele, my Mastermind sisters! Thank you for showing up faithfully every Monday on Zoom, for cheering me on, and for sharing your wisdom so generously. Your encouragement, honesty, and support have been such a gift on this author journey. I'm deeply grateful to walk this path with you both.

I extend my sincerest gratitude to Beta Reader Bookings, LLC for your insightful and thoughtful feedback on this narrative. You have offered candid reflections, and your diligence in detail has significantly enhanced the quality of this book.

To my friends and family, the members of my church, my ARC readers and reviewers, and every person who shared a note, a call, or a message of encouragement... THANK YOU! Your support, prayers, and kindness carried me through this journey more than you know. This book exists because of you.

Contents

Running With Grace

Wings of Faith Series Book 3: An Inspirational Love Story

Barbara Jane Oliver

Synergistic Connections, LLC

Chapter 1

THE X-RAY OFFERED NO clarity. Eight-year-old Gabrielle Miller's lungs appeared clear, yet her breathing told a different story. Her chest rose and fell in shallow, labored hitches, each breath a question without an answer. The bloodwork didn't help. It only deepened the mystery. Elevated white cells. No infection. No obvious source. Her fever continued to spike, undeterred by the cocktail of medications Dr. Brandon Lawson had ordered.

Brandon stood alone at the radiology workstation, arms crossed, the glow of the monitor reflecting off his face but illuminating nothing useful. Twelve years in emergency medicine should have given him the tools to solve this. But tonight, all his training had met its match in an eight-year-old girl with eyes too tired for her age.

The ER buzzed behind him. Nurses called out vital signs, and stretchers rolled in with the clatter of a world teetering between disaster and rescue. The rhythm was familiar. Predictable, even. Except for Gabrielle. She didn't fit any pattern he knew.

"Dr. Lawson, we need you in trauma two." Jessica Whitaker's voice cut through his concentration. The auburn-haired nurse appeared beside him, her usually calm expression drawn tight. "It's Frederick Brooks from the I-185 accident."

Brandon's jaw set. The sixty-three-year-old construction worker's pickup truck had collided with a semi during the evening thunderstorm. The preliminary report included internal bleeding, blunt-force trauma, and likely head injuries. Frederick survived the impact, but barely. Brandon suspected he wouldn't survive the night.

"Vitals?" Brandon asked, already moving toward the trauma bay.

"His blood pressure is dropping fast. Dr. Martinez requested a surgical consult, but..." Jessica's voice trailed off.

Frederick Brooks was dying.

The next forty-seven minutes blurred into a frenzy of adrenaline, orders, and increasingly desperate measures. Brandon worked alongside Dr. Allegra Martinez, doing everything their training allowed. The man's body fought, just like his weathered hands had likely fought to build half the bridges in this county. Brandon's own father had been that kind of deliberate, hardworking, sacrificial man. It was hard not to see him in Frederick's still form.

At 12:34 AM, the monitors flatlined.

Brandon stood motionless as the last tone echoed, long and final. Dr. Martinez placed a hand on his shoulder, her dark brown eyes reflecting the grief they all carried when medicine reached its limits.

"We did everything we could, Brandon," she said.

Brandon nodded, not trusting his voice, and stripped off his gloves. His movements were detached, almost mechanical. Frederick's family waited in the consultation room, expecting some version of hope. He would have to walk in and dismantle it.

Where is God when children suffer? Where was He when Frederick's truck hit that guardrail?

The bitter thought surfaced on its own. He stopped praying the night Dr. Stephanie Whitmore died. Her faith stayed intact even as cancer consumed her body. If God wouldn't heal someone who dedicated her life to serving others, who believed without wavering, then what hope did any of them have?

He had once believed God met him in these moments. Now, he wasn't sure God showed up at all.

Brandon walked toward the break room, bone-tired in a way that had nothing to do with the hour. The hospital's organized chaos surrounded him. Monitors beeped and the staff moved with purpose. Families waited in plastic chairs, praying for outcomes that medicine couldn't always guarantee.

"Dr. Lawson?" Hanna Vaughn intercepted him near the nurses' station, her salt-and-pepper hair escaping from its clip after hours of constant motion. The veteran nurse had mentored half the staff at Lakeside Hospital. "Frederick's daughter wants to speak with you."

Brandon exhaled through his nose. These conversations, the ones where he watched hope leave a person's face, never got easier. "Alright. Give me five minutes."

He entered the break room, needing a moment before facing Frederick's family. The fluorescent light felt too harsh, too clinical for the raw human cost that defined his evening. He rubbed his face with both hands, trying to collect himself and do the thing Gabrielle Miller still couldn't do. Breathe without effort.

He couldn't stop thinking about that little girl. Her brown eyes were too big for her face, and her chest heaved with every breath as if her body was working double shifts just to keep the air coming. Her parents sat in the waiting area, praying, pleading, clutching each other's hands as though faith were something they could physically hold on to.

"Dr. Lawson's been incredible with the tough cases." Jessica's voice drifted from the hallway. "And the chaplain supervisor? She's been lifting everyone's spirits. She brought cookies last week and sat with the Calloway family the whole time their son was in surgery."

Brandon's lip curled. Another chaplain, full of good intentions, offering hollow comfort and well-rehearsed platitudes about divine will. He had no patience for people who spoke of God's love while children suffocated and good men bled out on operating tables.

"False hope," he muttered, pushing himself to his feet.

The one place in the ER where he knew he wouldn't be disturbed was the supply closet. Brandon slipped inside, surrounded by boxes of gauze, IV tubing, and sterile equipment. These were the tools of his real faith. Science. Medicine. Human knowledge pitched against chaos and death. He leaned against the metal shelving and closed his eyes.

Footsteps echoed in the hallway outside, mixed with the low hum of voices. He could identify the rhythm of his colleagues' discussions, the familiar tempo of a hospital that never stopped. Somewhere down the hall, Gabrielle's monitors beeped on, marking the medical mystery that refused to yield to his expertise.

Jesus wept.

The scripture surfaced from somewhere deep within his memory, a remnant from his childhood faith that he had buried alongside Dr. Whitmore. John 11:35. The shortest verse in the Bible. It once brought him comfort. Now it struck him as mockery. If Jesus wept over death and suffering, then why didn't He prevent it?

His pager buzzed against his hip, but he ignored it. Frederick's family could wait a moment longer. He needed to compose himself back into the doctor they needed before telling them their world had just shattered.

Footsteps passed in the hallway, then faded. The automatic doors at the main entrance hissed open and closed as someone entered the department. A woman's voice, warm and unhurried, spoke to the nursing staff, but Brandon paid little attention.

He closed his eyes and focused on his breathing. Soon, he would walk into that consultation room and deliver the words no family was ever prepared to hear.

The supply closet door remained slightly ajar, a thin line of fluorescent light cutting across the dim space. Brandon stayed in the shadows, listening to nothing but the hum of the ventilation system. Until the creak of the door hinge told him his solitude was about to end.

Chapter 2

Grace Winslow sat in her parked car for a full three minutes before she made herself open the door.

The engine ticked as it cooled. Through the windshield, Lakeside Community Hospital glowed against the April night. Every lit window represented someone in pain, someone afraid, someone praying for a phone call that would change everything. She knew the math of this place. More bad news than good. More questions than answers. And still, she came.

But tonight, getting out of the car felt harder than usual. She had spent the evening at home, alone again, eating leftover soup at a kitchen table set for one, watching the chair across from her collect dust and silence. Five years since Anthony's death, and she still caught herself listening for the sound of his key in the lock. Not every night. Just often enough to remind her that faith didn't cancel out loneliness.

She pressed her forehead against the steering wheel. *Lord, I'm tired. Not of You. Not of the work. Just... tired.*

The prayer sat unfinished. She didn't know what to ask for. She never did, on nights like this.

Grace grabbed the two cardboard trays of coffee from the passenger seat and the bakery box tucked beneath her arm, nudged the car door shut with her hip, and walked toward the entrance. The scent of fresh espresso and cinnamon rose from the trays. By the time she reached the main corridor, the antiseptic tang of the hospital had replaced it.

Her heels clicked against the polished floor as she headed toward the emergency department, weaving past drowsy visitors and janitors with their rolling carts. This late-night ritual had become sacred over the past few months. Coffee for the night shift. Snickerdoodles from Willow Barnes. Handwritten notes tucked between napkins and sugar packets, each one prayed over before she sealed the envelope.

These were her way of saying: *I see you. You matter.*

And if the giving kept her from sitting alone in that kitchen, well, she tried not to examine that too closely.

At the nurses' station, Grace set everything down. "Fuel for the faithful," she said, managing a smile that felt almost real.

"Grace!" Jessica looked up from the computer, her ponytail barely holding on. "You're a gift from heaven. I was telling Dr. Lawson earlier how much everyone appreciates these visits."

Grace waved that off. She never needed recognition, but words like that, especially on a night when her own house had felt too big and too empty, reminded her she was where she belonged. This hospital and its needs weren't just a job. They were her calling. Her role as the chaplain supervisor bridged Cottonwood Faith Community Center, New Hope Baptist Church, and Lakeside Hospital. Here, where life-and-death decisions played out by the hour, she was most aligned with God's purpose.

At least, that was what she told herself. Most days, she believed it.

"How's the night been?" Grace handed over a cup and scanned Jessica's face. The strain around her eyes told its own story.

Jessica's smile faded. "Rough. We lost Frederick Brooks... the man from the I-185 accident. Dr. Lawson did everything humanly possible, but..."

Grace closed her eyes for a beat. "I'm so sorry."

"And there's a little girl... Gabrielle Miller. She's eight years old, and she can't breathe. No diagnosis. No answers."

An ache settled behind Grace's ribs. She had walked through too many hospital corridors not to recognize the particular helplessness that came when answers refused to show up. "Sounds like a heavy night."

Jessica nodded. "Dr. Lawson's taking it hard. He always does, but lately..." She shook her head. "He's carrying too much."

Grace had heard about the ER physician who pushed past the limits of human endurance, who ran toward crisis with a focus that bordered on obsession. She had noticed him from a distance over the past few months. A tall, lean figure with dark hair silvered at the temples, moving through the department like a man with no intention of stopping. But they had never actually spoken.

"Where is he now?" Grace asked.

"Probably off somewhere decompressing. When he's processing a difficult case, he tends to avoid... people." Jessica's expression held both affection and concern. "He's an incredible doctor, but he's built walls as tall as a fortress, if you catch my drift."

Grace understood walls. She built her own after Anthony's death. Intentional ones, constructed with care. The difference was that her walls had windows, places where God's love could pass through to others. Some people erected fortresses without a single opening.

Or so she told herself. But on nights like tonight, sitting alone at that kitchen table, she wondered whether her windows were as wide as she pretended.

"I'll pray for him," Grace said. The words came automatically, the way they always did. She meant them. She also recognized the limits of them.

She continued her rounds, stopping to chat with night-shift nurses who reached for Willow's snickerdoodles with grateful hands. She caught bits of conversation that flickered between medical jargon and personal worry. Everyone here was giving everything they had. Grace understood that kind of giving, the kind that left you hollowed out by morning.

Near the supply area, she noticed a door slightly ajar. Light spilled from the crack into the dim hallway. A tug in her spirit. That inner nudge she had learned not to ignore.

"Hello? Is someone in there?"

A pause. Then a man's voice, rough with exhaustion. "I'm fine. Just taking a moment."

Grace stepped closer. "I'm Grace Winslow, the chaplain supervisor. I brought coffee from Heavenly Delights. Would you like some?"

The door creaked open another inch. Dr. Brandon Lawson stood inside, leaning against metal shelving stocked with medical supplies. Up close, she could see the toll the night had taken. The deep lines carved around his eyes. The tension locked in his shoulders. The way he held himself rigid, as if relaxing might undo him entirely.

His eyes met hers. Dark, watchful, and stripped bare in a way she doubted he intended anyone to see.

She recognized that look. She had worn it herself in the months after Anthony's funeral, standing in the grocery store aisle, forgetting why she was there, forgetting how to want anything at all.

"You're the chaplain supervisor," he said, a thread of wariness beneath the professional tone. "Jessica mentioned you."

"And you're Dr. Lawson. She mentioned you too." Grace held up a coffee cup. "She said tonight's been... a lot."

Brandon stared at the cup as if weighing whether accepting it meant accepting more than caffeine. Then he took it. His fingers brushed hers in the exchange. Brief, incidental, the kind of contact that happened a hundred times a day in a hospital and meant nothing.

"I don't need prayers," he said, his voice clipped.

"Good thing I'm offering caffeine and not prayers." Grace leaned against the doorframe and folded her arms. The supply closet smelled of latex gloves and antiseptic, a far cry from the cinnamon still clinging to her jacket.

Brandon regarded her with the attention of a man accustomed to reading vital signs. "I thought chaplains were supposed to offer some sort of spiritual comfort."

"Only if it's welcome. I've found that sometimes the best thing I can do is just sit with someone in the dark."

His expression shifted, as though she had answered a question he hadn't expected anyone to understand. "Most chaplains I've met come armed with verses and a five-step plan for grief." He paused. "No offense."

"None taken." Grace tucked her hands into the pockets of her jacket. "I buried my husband five years ago. I know what useless comfort sounds like."

The words came out steady. She had said them enough times that the sentence had worn smooth, like a river stone, the sharp edges of the grief underneath hidden by repetition. But tonight, with the kitchen table still fresh in her mind, the steadiness cost her more than usual.

Brandon looked at her directly then, his gaze stripped of its professional distance. Grace held it. She was used to holding people's pain. That was the job.

"It was an IED," she continued. "He was with his medical unit in Afghanistan. He believed in protecting people who couldn't protect themselves."

Compassion crossed Brandon's face, unguarded and clearly surprising to him. "I'm sorry for your loss," he said, and meant it. She could tell the difference between politeness and sincerity. She heard both often enough.

"Thank you. I share that because I know what it's like to feel responsible for people you can't always save. Anthony carried that weight, and it sounds like you do too."

Brandon lifted the coffee cup, steam curling between them in the fluorescent glare. "Medicine used to feel like a calling. Now..." His voice trailed off.

"Now it feels like fighting a war you can't win," Grace supplied.

"Exactly." He glanced at her, curiosity replacing some of the wariness. "How do you do it? How do you keep believing when..." He gestured toward the emergency department beyond their small refuge.

The question deserved better than a rehearsed answer, so Grace took a moment. "I don't know if I've an answer that would satisfy you. But I've learned that faith isn't about understanding God's plan. It's about trusting that love still matters, even when the outcomes break your heart."

She let the words breathe, then added a scripture she had leaned on herself. "*'Cast all your anxiety on him because he cares for you.'* Not because He'll fix everything. But because you don't have to carry it alone."

Brandon rolled the coffee cup between his palms. "I used to believe something like that. Before..." He stopped himself, jaw tightening as if he said more than he intended.

"Before you lost someone who mattered," Grace finished.

His eyes cut to hers, and the pain in them was unvarnished. But instead of going further, he pulled back behind the clinical composure she imagined he wore like a second skin.

"It's not important," he said, though his voice betrayed him. "What matters is that medicine has limits, and sometimes those limits aren't enough."

Grace recognized the deflection. Self-protection. She had done the same thing in those early months after Anthony's death, sharing just enough truth to acknowledge the wound without exposing the depth of it.

She wanted to press. That was the old instinct, the social worker in her who believed the right question at the right moment could crack a person open and let the healing in. But she had learned that people didn't heal on someone else's schedule.

"I wish I had better answers for you," she said. "But I've never believed that doubt and faith can't share the same room."

They stood in the cluttered supply closet, surrounded by IV bags and boxes of nitrile gloves, two people who understood loss occupying the same small space. Grace noticed the way he gripped the coffee cup. He wasn't drinking from it. He was just holding it, as if the warmth in his hands was enough.

"I should let you get back to your patients," she said.

"Gabrielle Miller's parents are probably wondering why their daughter's doctor hasn't come to speak with them," Brandon agreed, but he made no move toward the door.

"The eight-year-old with the mysterious symptoms?"

"You know about her case?"

"Chaplains hear things. If her parents would like someone to sit with them, I'm available."

Brandon considered this. "They might appreciate that. They've been holding on by a thread."

Grace nodded. "Prayer and panic often go hand in hand. Sometimes a thread is enough to hold a family together."

"You believe in what you do," Brandon said. It was a statement, not a question.

"Most of the time." She handed him a snickerdoodle from the bakery box. "The rest of the time, I show up anyway."

He looked at her as if recalculating an equation that had just introduced a new variable. "You're not what I expected in a chaplain."

"What did you expect?"

"Someone who'd have tried to pray over me by now."

Grace's mouth curved. "The night's still young, Dr. Lawson."

For the first time since she opened the supply closet door, Brandon laughed. The sound was brief, surprised, almost rusty, as if it had been stored away for too long. "Fair enough."

"I should go check on the Millers." Grace stepped back from the doorframe.

"Chaplain Winslow." Brandon's voice caught her at the threshold. "Thank you. For the coffee. For..." He paused, turning the cup in his hands. "For not trying to fix anything."

The words landed somewhere deep. That was the aspect no one warned you about regarding ministry. Seminary didn't teach that the moments that mattered the most were often the ones where you did the least.

"You're welcome, Dr. Lawson."

She turned to go, and she was halfway down the corridor when Dr. Martinez's voice cut through the hallway behind her.

"Brandon, we need you in trauma two. An eighty-two-year-old woman with a suspected femur fracture from a fall. She's showing signs of an embolism."

Grace heard the shift before she saw it. The sound of his footsteps changed. What had once been loose exhaustion was replaced by purposeful determination. She glanced back. Brandon was already in motion, his stride locked in, his focus absolute. Whatever weariness had filled that supply closet, he had shed it like a coat at the door.

She watched him disappear around the corner. Then she kept walking.

The Millers' consultation room was at the end of the hall, its door closed. Grace paused outside it, one hand raised to knock, and for a moment her composure wavered. She thought of the kitchen table. The empty chair. The prayer she couldn't finish in her car.

Lord, I don't have enough tonight. But You do. Let that be enough.

She knocked, and when a woman's tear-strained voice called out, Grace opened the door and stepped inside.

Chapter 3

THE OVERHEAD LIGHTS IN the hospital garage buzzed as Brandon swiped his badge and pushed through the exit turnstile. Thirty-six hours ago, he walked through the same doors, thinking only about medicine. Now, Grace Winslow occupied a corner of his mind that he hadn't offered her.

He could still see the way she leaned against that supply closet doorframe, one shoulder braced against the metal, holding out coffee like it was the most natural thing in the world. The way she told him she had buried her husband, voice steady, eyes clear, no tremor in her hands. He kept circling back to that image when he should've been circling back to Gabrielle Miller's bloodwork.

He checked his phone for overnight updates. Three texts from colleagues. Two missed calls from Sebastian. Nothing that required his immediate attention. Still, the quiet unsettled him. When emergencies weren't shouting for his attention, his mind turned on itself.

The drive through Brookside's neighborhoods offered little distraction. Early joggers moved along sidewalks still damp from the dew. Victorian houses stood over gardens heavy with azaleas and dogwood blossoms. Spring in Georgia didn't announce itself. It simply arrived, lush and unapologetic, as though winter had never happened.

New Hope Baptist Church appeared ahead, its white steeple sharp against the pale morning sky. Brandon's foot eased off the gas before he registered why.

Dr. Whitmore's voice. Clear as though she were sitting in the passenger seat.

Medicine and faith aren't enemies, Brandon. They're dance partners. Sometimes one leads, sometimes the other, but they both move to the same music.

He had been twenty-seven when she said that to him, standing in the hallway outside the pediatric ICU at three in the morning. She had just lost a patient, a toddler with an undiagnosed heart condition, and she was the one comforting *him.* He remembered the coffee stain on her white coat, the reading glasses pushed up on top of her head, and the way she pressed her palms together when she prayed in the waiting room with families. She never hid that part of herself, and she never forced it on anyone. She simply lived it, and people leaned toward her because of it.

And God had let her die anyway.

The church's stained-glass windows caught the rising sun, throwing color across the sidewalk like confetti. He accelerated past the building. Twelve years had passed since Dr. Whitmore's death, and the sting of it hadn't dulled. It had only changed shape.

At his apartment complex, he parked and climbed the stairs to the second floor. The hallway carried the scent of carpet freshener and someone's homemade bread.

Inside, he dropped his keys on the counter and stood for a moment. The apartment looked the way it always did. Beige walls. Clean counters. A leather couch angled toward a television he rarely turned on. Medical journals covered the coffee table in neat stacks, each one bookmarked and annotated. The only photograph in the room sat on the bookshelf. It was him at his medical school graduation, flanked by his parents. His mother's hand rested on his shoulder. His father stood at attention in his dress uniform, proud and rigid, the way he stood for everything.

No throw pillows. No art on the walls. No evidence that the person who lived here did anything besides work and sleep.

He powered up his laptop and opened the hospital's secure portal. Gabrielle's test results filled the screen. Elevated white blood cell count, but no identifiable source of infection. Breathing difficulty, but clear lungs. Neurological symptoms that surfaced and vanished with no connection to any treatment plan.

He pushed back from the desk and rubbed his temples. Nothing in her chart followed a recognizable pattern. The puzzle contradicted a decade of emergency medicine training.

He pulled up research databases and began comparing her symptoms to rare genetic disorders. Mitochondrial diseases. Metabolic conditions. Autoimmune presentations in pediatric patients.

Every avenue closed before it opened. The medical literature described similar cases but offered no definitive answers.

Hours bled into one another. His eyes burned from the blue glare, but the need to find an explanation drove him forward. This was the place where he felt competent. Facts lived here. If a person was willing to sit with them long enough, the mysteries of diseases could be solved here. If he could identify Gabrielle's condition, he could treat it. And if he could treat it, he could save her.

But somewhere between articles and acronyms, his thoughts slipped sideways. To Grace. He hadn't meant to let her in. But the woman had stood in a supply closet at midnight, handed him coffee, and made him laugh. A real laugh, not the polite exhale he offered colleagues. He couldn't remember the last time that had happened.

The night's still young, Dr. Lawson.

He shook his head and pulled up another database.

His phone rang. Sebastian Reid's name lit up the display.

"You sound terrible," Sebastian said, by way of greeting.

"I'm just getting off from a thirty-six-hour shift." Brandon held back a yawn. "I'm fine."

"That's your answer for everything. You could be on fire, and you'd tell me you were fine." A child's voice shrieked with laughter in the background, followed by a dull thud. Sebastian's voice moved away from the phone. "Rachel, we talked about throwing the basketball inside the house. Use your words, not your arm." He came back. "Sorry. My daughter just tried to take out a lamp. So tell me... when is the last time you took a day off?"

Brandon rubbed his eyes. Two weeks? Three? Time blurred when every day followed the same rhythm. Work. Research. Sleep. Repeat. "I don't need a day off. I need answers."

"The Miller case?"

"Among others." Brandon minimized the research windows on his monitor. "Kids don't get sick for no reason, Sebastian. There's always an explanation."

The line went quiet. Six years of friendship had built a kind of shorthand between them, and Brandon knew Sebastian was choosing his next words the way he chose his instruments before surgery. Carefully and with intention.

"You know what my son asked me last week?" Sebastian asked. "He asked me why God lets pets die. He was talking about that hamster funeral we had in February. And I sat there at the kitchen table, looking at this fifteen-year-old kid with tears running down his face over a hamster named Professor Whiskers, and I realized that my honest answer to a teenager was more truthful than anything I'd have said to another adult."

Brandon waited.

"I told him I didn't know. I told him that I pray before every surgery, and sometimes children still die on my table. And I told him that the not-knowing is the hardest part of believing, but it's also the part I refuse to let go of."

Brandon stared at Gabrielle's test results, at numbers that refused to arrange themselves into anything useful. "I'm not sure I can live like that."

"You already do." Sebastian's voice carried the matter-of-fact warmth of a man who had watched his friend wrestle with the same questions for years. "You walk into that ER every shift not knowing if your patient will live or die, and you show up anyway. That's not so different from what I do before I scrub in." He paused. "You know I'm here if you need to talk."

"I know. I appreciate it."

"One more thing." Brandon could hear the shift in Sebastian's tone, lighter, the voice he used when he was about to enjoy himself at Brandon's expense. "Grace, the chaplain supervisor, stopped by pediatrics yesterday. The nurses in my unit haven't stopped talking about her."

Brandon took a slow sip of cold coffee he didn't taste. "She seems capable."

"Capable." Sebastian laughed, a rich, low sound. "Please. The nurse supervisor called her a *breath of fresh air,*' and that woman hasn't said anything positive about another human being since 2019." He let a beat pass. "But sure... capable's a good word to describe her... if that's what we're going with."

Brandon said nothing, which was itself an answer, and they both knew it.

Another crash sounded in the background. "Rachel! I said no basketball! Brandon, I've got to go before my daughter demolishes the living room. Get some sleep."

The line went dead.

Brandon set the phone down and let Sebastian's words about Professor Whiskers circle in his head. He turned back to the research, but it had lost its pull. The numbers and acronyms blurred together, offering nothing.

A knock at the door broke through. Brandon glanced at the clock and realized the afternoon had disappeared without his notice. He crossed the room and opened the door to find his neighbor, Vivienne Frost, standing in the hallway. She twisted her wedding ring, and the lines around her mouth had deepened since the last time he had seen her.

"Brandon, I hate to bother you, but Mitchell's been having those chest pains again." She pressed one hand against the doorframe. "He's convinced it's just indigestion, but he's too stubborn to go to the emergency room, and I thought maybe you could take a look."

He was already reaching for his stethoscope before she finished the sentence.

He followed Mrs. Frost into an apartment that smelled like cinnamon and old books. Forty years of marriage filled every surface. Framed photographs crowded the mantel, each one a chapter in a shared life. Ceramic figurines from vacations lined the windowsill. A patchwork quilt, faded and well-loved, draped the back of the sofa. The apartment was the opposite of his own in every possible way.

Mitchell Frost sat in his recliner, scowling at the interruption but too winded to argue. He waved one hand toward his wife. "She's making a fuss over nothing. I ate too much pot roast, that's all."

"Let me be the judge of that." Brandon pulled up a chair and conducted a thorough examination, checking vitals and listening to heart sounds. He detected minor irregularities, a murmur that he had flagged on previous visits, but nothing that suggested an emergency.

"See?" Mitchell folded his arms across his broad chest. "I've survived forty years of Vivienne's cooking and two knee replacements. Takes more than a little heartburn to put me down."

"Keep an eye on the pain," Brandon advised, writing down warning signs on a piece of paper. "If it gets worse, or if you have any shortness of breath, call 911 right away. Don't wait for it to pass."

Mitchell took the paper with the reluctant compliance of a man who had been outnumbered. "You're worse than Vivienne, you know that?"

"I'll take that as a compliment."

"You're an angel, Brandon." Mrs. Frost walked him toward the door. "Mitchell and I pray for you every night. We know how hard you work to help people."

Brandon paused, his hand on the doorframe. "That's kind of you, Mrs. Frost. But the prayers aren't necessary. I'm just doing my job."

Her gaze sharpened, though her voice stayed even. "Everyone needs prayer, dear. Whether they think so or not."

He didn't reply to that. He couldn't think of a response that would be both honest and kind.

"I want to tell you something," Mrs. Frost said, lowering her voice as though sharing a secret. "Mitchell's been having the most interesting encounters at Providence Park. He sometimes meets a silver-haired gentleman there, an older man with a walking cane. He says the man has a way about him. He has a weathered face, as if he has lived through things most people only read about. And every time they talk, Mitchell comes home changed. More hopeful about the things he can't control."

The skin along Brandon's forearms prickled, and the sensation had no rational explanation. "What kind of man?"

"The kind sort." Mrs. Frost's face brightened at the memory. "Mitchell says he never asks anything personal. He just seems to know what a person needs to hear."

The conversation continued for several more minutes, but Brandon heard little beyond the description of the mysterious stranger. When he stepped back into his own apartment, the emptiness felt louder than it had that morning.

Who was this man at Providence Park? And why did the description, a silver-haired stranger who said exactly the right thing at exactly the right moment, leave him reaching for a rational explanation he couldn't find?

Brandon went back to his desk, but his hands hovered over the keyboard without typing. He read the same paragraph three times and retained nothing. Finally, he closed the laptop and stood at his living room window, staring toward the distant tree line where Providence Park lay hidden among Brookside's older neighborhoods.

Medical school had taught him to see coincidences for what they were. The brain's attempt to find patterns where none existed.

Random events dressed up as meaning by a mind desperate for order.

But Grace showing up at that supply closet door with coffee at midnight hadn't been random. And Gabrielle's case refused to follow any logic he knew. Now, a mysterious stranger appeared in the park with exactly the right words for an old man with a troubled heart.

It was too much. Brandon walked to his bedroom. Forty-two hours without sleep had burned through every reserve he had. What he needed now was rest, not speculation about silver-haired strangers and spiritual coincidences.

He lay down fully clothed and was asleep before he could pull the covers back.

Sleep would restore clarity. He would wake up, dive back into the research, figure out Gabrielle's illness, and keep his distance from Grace Winslow, no matter how easily she moved into his thoughts.

You don't have to carry it alone.

He didn't believe that. But some part of him, the part he kept locked behind the research and the routines and the long shifts, wanted to.

Chapter 4

Sunlight poured through the tall windows of Cottonwood Faith Community Center, casting gold across the scuffed hardwood floor and the worn spines of theology books lining the walls of Pastor Scott Wilson's office. Grace sat across from him, her palms wrapped around a mug of chamomile tea that had already gone lukewarm. The familiar leather armchair squeaked as she shifted her weight, and she realized she had been stalling for the better part of ten minutes.

Pastor Wilson waited. That was the thing about him. He never rushed a conversation to its destination. He let it arrive on its own, the same way he had been letting people arrive at their own truths for over thirty years of ministry. His silver-rimmed glasses caught the light as he watched her, his expression patient and unreadable.

"The emergency department presents some unique challenges," Grace began, watching the steam curl from her cup. "The traumas go beyond physical injuries. The families carry as much pain as the patients. And some of the staff..." She paused. "Some of the staff carry more than they should."

"You're worried about someone."

Grace traced the handle of her mug. "Is it that obvious?"

"You didn't drive out here on a Tuesday morning to talk about hospital policy, Grace." His voice carried a familiarity earned over years of knowing her. "Who is it?"

Grace looked down into her mug, watching the last wisp of steam dissolve into the air. She had practiced this conversation on the drive over. But now, with the chamomile bitter on her tongue and the afternoon light slanting across the floor, all that preparation felt like cowardice.

She let out a slow breath. "Dr. Brandon Lawson. He's the emergency physician who treated Gabrielle Miller, the little girl I mentioned on Sunday. He's incredibly skilled, and his dedication to that child's case goes well beyond what's expected of an ER doctor." Grace turned the mug between her palms. "But whenever faith comes up, even in passing, he shuts down. Not in an angry way... more like someone touching a burn that never healed."

Pastor Wilson nodded. "Sometimes, when people experience profound losses, especially those who once held faith close, they can develop what I'd call an *allergic reaction* to anything that reminds them of their former beliefs. The very thing that once comforted them becomes the thing that hurts most."

"So how do I reach him?" Grace set the mug on the side table. "If he's closed off to faith, to any of it, do I just leave him alone?"

"Your job isn't to fix him, Grace." Pastor Wilson removed his glasses and cleaned them with a square of cloth, a habit she watched him perform a thousand times. "Your job is to trust God with the rest. You live the truth. Let your life speak louder than any sermon you could preach."

The words were right. She knew they were right. But they landed the way sermon notes sometimes did, clear and reasonable and just short of touching the real wound.

"What if it's not just about ministry?" The question left her mouth before she had fully decided to say it. She looked at the bookshelf behind him rather than at his face. "What if I'm concerned about him in a way that I can't quite explain? He's a colleague... and a skeptic. He's someone I barely know. And yet I keep thinking about him, and I don't understand why."

She didn't want to say the word *'attracted.'* She couldn't. Not yet. She wasn't even certain that was what this was. But Brandon Lawson had taken up residence in her thoughts, uninvited, and no amount of prayer or professional compartmentalization had removed him.

Pastor Wilson put his glasses back on and regarded her with the look he reserved for moments when someone was circling a truth they weren't ready to name. "Tell me more about your late husband."

It had been five years since that name had meant a living person instead of a memory. It still reached into her chest and squeezed. The ripples never stopped.

"Anthony died while serving in Afghanistan." Her voice held. It always held. That was the problem. "He was a medic. We had talked about starting a family after his deployment. I was thirty-four when I got the call."

She wrapped her fingers around the edge of the armrest. "After he died, I threw myself into social work, then into chaplaincy. I told myself that God needed me to be fully available for ministry. That seeking happiness for myself was selfish. I felt that if I kept busy enough, the loneliness wouldn't catch up."

"And has it?"

She looked at him. "I went home last Tuesday after a fourteen-hour day at the hospital. I heated up leftover soup, sat at the kitchen table, and... and I couldn't pray." Her fingers pressed harder against the armrest, knuckles straining beneath her skin. "I sat there for twenty minutes with my hands folded, and nothing came. And it's not because I don't believe. It's because I'm so tired of being the person who always has the right words for everyone else. Sometimes it seems as if I've nothing left for myself."

She hadn't said those words out loud before. Not to her friend and coworker Carmen Delgado, or anyone else. Hearing them in this office, surrounded by the theology books she had studied and the faith she had preached, made the words real in a way that frightened her. The woman who sat with dying patients, grieving families and struggling doctors couldn't find her own way to the throne of grace on a Tuesday night in her own kitchen.

Pastor Wilson leaned forward. "Grace, do you believe that God wants you to be holy?"

"Yes... of course."

"Do you believe He wants you to be happy?"

The question sat between them. She opened her mouth and closed it again.

Pastor Wilson reached for the worn Bible on his desk and turned to a page he clearly knew by heart. "*'He heals the brokenhearted and binds up their wounds.'*"

He closed the book. "Grace, Psalm 147:3 doesn't say that He heals the brokenhearted who have earned it. It doesn't say that He binds the wounds of people who never stopped praying. It says that He heals the brokenhearted. Period."

He looked at her over the rim of his glasses. "You've spent five years binding other people's wounds. Have you considered that the verse might also be about you?"

She twisted her hands in her lap. "I want to believe that."

"Denying your own heart isn't holiness, Grace. It's fear wearing holiness as a disguise." He held her gaze. "The question isn't whether you're allowed to feel. The question is whether you're willing to trust God with your whole self, including the parts of your heart you've hidden away."

She stared at the bookshelf. A copy of Oswald Chambers sat next to a volume of Henri Nouwen, the spine cracked from years of use. She had read and taught from both. She counseled others using the principles in both. And sitting here, she wasn't sure she believed any of it for herself.

"I don't know how to do that," she said.

Pastor Wilson nodded once. "That is the most honest thing you've said all morning."

The pediatric ward at Lakeside Community Hospital operated with a different energy than the emergency room. Bright murals of forests and ocean scenes covered the walls. A play area near the nurses' station held bins of stuffed animals and coloring books. The fluorescent lights had been fitted with warm-toned covers, and someone had taped construction paper butterflies to the ceiling tiles above the hallway.

Grace knocked on the door to room 314 before entering. Gabrielle Miller lay propped against pillows, her color noticeably improved from two nights ago. Her dark eyes, though still circled with fatigue, carried the lively curiosity of an eight-year-old who had grown bored with hospital television. Her parents flanked the bed. Tobias Miller sat near the window, his large hands clasped between his knees. Denise perched on the edge of the mattress, her fingers absently smoothing the blanket.

"Grace!" Denise stood and pulled her into a hug that lasted a beat longer than courtesy required. "Thank you so much for coming."

"How's our girl feeling?" Grace smiled at Gabrielle as she moved toward the bed.

"Much better." Gabrielle's voice was small but certain. "The nice doctor with the beard said I might get to go home tomorrow."

Grace recognized the description of Dr. Sebastian Reid. "That's wonderful news. Have you been able to rest?"

Tobias spoke from his chair. "We've been taking turns sleeping. The nurses have been incredible, and Dr. Reid has been very patient with all our questions."

"And Dr. Lawson?" She kept her tone professional, the same even cadence she used with every family. "How has he been with Gabrielle's care?"

Denise exchanged a glance with her husband. "He's been very thorough. Very professional. He seems to take Gabrielle's case personally, like he can't rest until he has every answer." She hesitated. "But he's..."

"He looks sad," Gabrielle said. Her voice cut through the adult conversation with the blunt clarity that only children possess. "It's like he's carrying a heavy backpack that he can't take off."

In all her years studying the language of unspoken pain, she had never heard a more precise diagnosis. Gabrielle just summarized Brandon Lawson in a single image more vivid than anything in a psychology textbook.

"Dr. Reid mentioned that it's unusual for an emergency physician to follow up so closely after a patient transfers to another department," Denise continued. "He said Dr. Lawson has checked on Gabrielle every day."

A man who couldn't let go of a case and followed an eight-year-old girl's recovery as though the outcome were his personal responsibility. Pastor Wilson's phrase returned to her. *An allergic reaction to faith.* But also, perhaps, an allergic reaction to powerlessness.

"Would you like to pray together?" she asked.

The Miller family formed a circle around the bed, hands joined. Grace bowed her head and opened her mouth, and for three full seconds, nothing came out. The kitchen table. The empty prayer. The silence of last Tuesday night pressed against her, and she felt the terrifying possibility that it would follow her here, into this room, in front of this family who needed her.

Then Gabrielle's small fingers tightened around hers, and Grace found her voice.

"Lord, we come before You with grateful hearts for the healing we've already seen in Gabrielle's body. We ask for continued strength for her and for wisdom for the doctors and nurses who care for her. Comfort this family, Father. Give them peace that passes understanding. And be with every person in this hospital who carries burdens they were never meant to carry alone. In Jesus' name, amen."

"Amen," the Millers echoed.

When Grace lifted her head, she sensed someone in the doorway. Brandon stood there, a medical chart in his hand, his expression carefully neutral. The sleeves of his white coat were pushed back to his forearms, and a pen was clipped to the chart with the same deliberate order he brought to everything. She didn't know how long he had been standing there or how much of the prayer he had heard.

"I apologize for the interruption." His voice was formal and measured. "I wanted to check on Gabrielle's progress before my shift ends."

"Dr. Lawson!" Gabrielle's face brightened. "Look, I can sit up all by myself now."

Brandon moved to the bedside, and the shift happened right in front of her. The rigid formality loosened. His hands, checking the monitors and adjusting her pillow, moved with a tenderness that went beyond clinical protocol. He crouched beside the bed rail so he was at Gabrielle's eye level rather than looming over her, and he explained each part of the examination to Tobias and Denise without a trace of impatience. This was who he was when he forgot to guard himself.

The realization landed in a place she had been trying to keep sealed shut.

"Her blood tests continue to show improvement," he reported. "Dr. Reid will make the final decision about discharge, but the indicators are positive."

As he turned to leave, Denise caught his arm. "Doctor, we can't thank you enough. We know you didn't have to keep checking on her after she transferred out of the ER."

The muscle along Brandon's jaw flexed. It was the same tell she noticed in the supply closet, the one that surfaced whenever someone got too close to what he was protecting. "I just want to make sure she gets the best possible care."

"We've been praying for you," Tobias said. He delivered the words with the plain sincerity of a man who meant them without calculation. "Gabrielle told us you look like you could use it."

Brandon's hand tightened around the chart. Grace watched his face, the way gratitude and resistance fought for the same space behind his eyes, neither one winning.

"I appreciate that," he said. His voice had gone low, almost rough. "Take care of yourselves."

He left the room without looking back. She didn't chase him or follow with a kind word or a well-timed scripture. She let him walk away because Pastor Wilson was right. It wasn't her job to fix him.

But the raw honesty in his voice when he said *I appreciate that* had given him away. He wasn't angry at the Millers for praying. He was afraid of what it would mean to let them.

She spent another twenty minutes with the Miller family before heading toward the elevators. The afternoon had given her more to sit with than she expected, and the weight of it pressed against the back of her eyes like the beginning of a headache.

The elevator doors opened, and Sebastian Reid stood inside, a paper coffee cup in each hand and a stethoscope draped around his neck like a scarf he had forgotten to take off.

"Grace." He grinned and held out one of the cups. "I grabbed an extra. It's hospital coffee, so lower your expectations accordingly."

She stepped in and accepted the cup. "Thank you. How are the Millers looking from your end?"

"Gabrielle is rebounding faster than any of us expected... which is either very good news or the kind of medical mystery that gives me an ulcer." He took a sip of his coffee and grimaced. "My daughter Rachel keeps telling me I should switch to green tea. She's thirteen and has apparently decided that she is responsible for my cardiovascular health." The elevator began its descent. "How was your visit?"

"The family is holding up well. They mentioned that Brandon has been checking on Gabrielle daily."

Sebastian nodded, his expression turning thoughtful. "He has. And before you ask, the answer is *yes*. It's unusual for an ER physician to continue checking in on an admitted patient. But Brandon doesn't do halfway. If a case gets under his skin, he'll chase it until he has an answer or until it drives him half out of his mind." He paused. "Gabrielle's case has definitely gotten under his skin."

"Do you know why?"

Sebastian looked at the elevator numbers ticking down. "He lost someone important during his residency. Her name was Dr. Stephanie Whitmore. She mentored him and taught him everything about treating patients as whole people instead of just symptoms. She was a brilliant physician and a woman of deep faith. Brain cancer took her when she was thirty-four." He glanced at Grace. "Brandon was with her at the end. I think he's been fighting God over that ever since."

The elevator reached the ground floor, but neither of them moved. The doors slid open and then closed again when no one pressed a button.

"How do you manage it?" Grace asked. "Working beside him every day, with your faith, and his resistance to it?"

"I don't preach to him." Sebastian pressed the button to hold the doors open. "I just try to be someone whose life makes sense to him, even when my beliefs don't. Last month, he walked past my office while I was praying before a surgery. You know what he said?" Sebastian's eyes crinkled at the memory. "He said, *If that makes your hands steadier, I'm not going to argue with it.'* And then he brought me coffee." He shook his head. "That's the closest thing to a compliment Brandon has ever given about faith, and I'll take it."

"Sebastian, can I ask you something?"

"You just did, but go ahead."

"Everyone I've talked to today has told me not to make Brandon a project. My pastor said it. You are saying it. Even the Millers said it without knowing they were saying it." She looked at him. "But what am I supposed to do when I can see that someone is drowning and I've spent my whole life learning how to throw ropes?"

Sebastian seemed to consider this as he held the elevator door with one hand and his terrible coffee with the other. "You know what I tell my kids when they want to help a friend who's going through something hard? I tell them that sometimes the bravest thing you can do is sit on the same bench and say nothing." He met her eyes. "Brandon doesn't need a rope, Grace. He needs to know that someone is willing to sit on the bench."

He stepped out of the elevator. "Get some rest. You look almost as tired as he does, and that is saying something."

She walked to her car with Sebastian's words turning over in her mind. Sit on the bench. Say nothing. For a woman who built her entire career on saying the right thing at the right time, the advice felt like being told to fight with her hands tied.

But underneath the resistance, a harder truth was working its way to the surface. She sat in Pastor Wilson's office and confessed that she couldn't pray at her own kitchen table. She stood in Gabrielle's hospital room and felt the words dry up in her mouth before a child's hand brought them back. Maybe the reason she kept trying to fix other people's faith was because it was easier than sitting still long enough to examine her own.

She started the engine and pulled out of the hospital parking lot. The late afternoon sun hung low, painting the dogwood trees in shades of amber. It was a normal Tuesday. A beautiful one, even. The kind of spring day that made promises about new beginnings.

Her phone buzzed in the cupholder. At the next red light, she glanced at the screen, and her stomach dropped.

The message was from Sebastian.

Gabrielle Miller has taken a turn for the worse. Parents are requesting chaplain support. Please respond if available.

She read it twice. An hour ago, that child had been sitting up in bed, squeezing her hand during prayer, talking about going home. One hour. That was all it took for everything to change.

She closed her eyes at the red light and prayed. It wasn't the prayers she recited at patients' bedsides. This one barely formed itself into words, just a plea lodged against the roof of her mouth.

Lord, be with that child. Be with her parents. And be with Brandon.

Because if Gabrielle didn't make it, she wasn't sure who it would shatter more. The family who had put their faith in God's healing, or the doctor who stopped believing that God healed at all.

The light turned green. Grace put the car in gear and turned back toward the hospital.

Chapter 5

BRANDON'S PAGER HUMMED JUST as he pulled Gabrielle Miller's lab results up on his laptop for the third time that afternoon. This was supposed to be his day off, but the word *off* had lost its meaning somewhere around hour six of searching databases for answers that didn't exist.

Sebastian's urgent code flashed on the display. This wasn't a routine update or a question about medication. This was the code that signaled it was time to get there right now.

He grabbed his keys and medical bag, sending a cascade of research notes off the coffee table as he moved. The drive to Lakeside tested every ounce of restraint he possessed. Traffic crawled along the two-lane stretch of Magnolia Boulevard, and his knuckles went tight against the wheel. Had he overlooked a result in the blood work? Had the medications interacted in a way he hadn't anticipated? His mind cycled through possibilities, sorting and discarding, building differential diagnoses from fragments of data.

But underneath the clinical calculations ran a deep-seated fear he would never have admitted out loud. It wasn't the diagnosis that terrified him. It was the thought of losing this particular child and the profound impact it would have on him.

The pediatric floor ran at a pitch he recognized from the worst nights in the ER. Nurses moved with purpose, their voices clipped and professional, stripped of the usual warmth that characterized the children's ward. The cartoon murals on the walls looked obscene against the urgency filling the corridor.

Sebastian met him at the central nursing station. His friend's face was drawn tight, and the easy humor that normally lived around his mouth had vanished.

"Her temperature spiked to 104.8 about thirty minutes ago," Sebastian said without preamble, falling into step beside him. "She's been having intermittent seizure activity and fluctuating consciousness. Her pupil responses don't match anything from her previous presentations. It's like her nervous system decided to rewrite its own rules."

"Blood work?"

"White cell count is higher than yesterday, but we still can't identify the source of an infection. Cerebrospinal fluid shows mild inflammation, but nothing that explains this level of decline." Sebastian's mouth pressed into a hard line. "Brandon, she was eating scrambled eggs and asking to go home this morning. Eight hours ago, she was a kid watching cartoons."

Eight hours. That was the span between a child talking about going home and a child whose body was shutting down for reasons no test could explain.

"What have you started?"

"IV fluids, broad-spectrum antibiotics as a precaution, and we have neurology on the way. But I wanted you here before we made any major decisions. You know this case better than anyone in this building."

Room 314 was a different world from the one he had visited that afternoon. Machines crowded the space, screens tracking vitals that told a story he didn't want to read. Gabrielle lay small and still beneath the wires and tubes, her caramel skin ashen against the white hospital sheets.

Gabrielle's parents flanked the bed. Tobias hadn't moved from his chair, his large hands clenched between his knees as though holding himself together by sheer will. Denise stood beside the bed, her fingers poised over her daughter's hair, as if caught between the fear of touching her and the fear of not doing so.

"She was eating breakfast." Denise's voice broke on the last word. "She told me she wanted to wear her purple dress when she went home."

He moved to the bedside and began his examination. Reflexes. Responsiveness. Pupil reactions. He checked each one thoroughly, driven by the belief that if he was careful enough, the answers would reveal themselves. Gabrielle's responses were sluggish, inconsistent, and entirely wrong for a child who should have been improving.

He examined each one meticulously, driven by the belief that his carefulness would lead to the answers.

"We need additional imaging," he told Sebastian. "Full neurological panel. And let's add an autoimmune workup. There's a cascade trigger we are missing."

Sebastian nodded and moved to place the orders. Brandon stayed at the bedside, adjusting Gabrielle's oxygen flow and scanning the readouts. The numbers were getting worse, not better. Her blood pressure was dropping and her oxygen saturation had begun to slide.

He didn't hear Grace enter the room. He only became aware of her when the pitch of Denise's crying changed, dropping from the sharp, panicked sound of a mother losing control to a lower, more sustained ache. He glanced over his shoulder. Grace had positioned herself beside Denise, one arm around the woman's shoulders, her body angled so that the Millers could see their daughter's face but not the growing urgency of the medical team's movements.

She didn't speak or offer promises. She was simply there, absorbing the family's terror the way a breakwater absorbs a wave.

"They're doing everything they can," Grace assured the Millers. Her voice conveyed a certainty that he was sure had been cultivated through years of experience in rooms just like this one. It wasn't a forced calmness. It was genuine and grounded. "Your daughter is in the best hands in this hospital."

For two hours, Brandon and Sebastian worked. They administered medications, adjusted protocols, and tracked Gabrielle's responses in minute intervals. The neurology consult arrived and left, offering possibilities but no certainties. The autoimmune panel would take hours to return. In the meantime, Gabrielle continued to decline in ways that defied every diagnostic pathway Brandon knew.

At six forty-seven in the evening, the cardiac alarm screamed.

Flatline.

Brandon was at Gabrielle's chest before the alarm finished its first cycle. Compressions. Rhythmic. Controlled. The count drilled into his muscle memory from a thousand code simulations. But this wasn't a simulation. This was an eight-year-old girl whose mother was weeping in the hallway. Grace had guided both parents out of the room the instant the alarm sounded.

"Epinephrine, one milligram," Brandon called.

Sebastian had the syringe ready. The code team flooded the room, bodies filling every available space as nurses, respiratory therapists, and residents took their positions. Brandon didn't look up. He counted compressions. He watched the green line. He willed it to move.

"Come on, Gabrielle." The words escaped between compressions, low and urgent. "Stay with us."

From the hallway, he heard Grace's voice. She was praying with the Millers. Not loud enough to disrupt the code, but audible through the open door. The words were indistinct, but the cadence was unmistakable, that low, deliberate rhythm of someone calling on God with the same conviction Brandon was calling on medicine.

Three minutes. The line stayed flat.

"Another round of epinephrine," Sebastian said.

Five minutes. Nothing.

Brandon's arms burned. Sweat ran down his temples. The code team had gone still around him, every face carrying the same unspoken question. He had been on the other side of that look before. He knew what it meant.

Seven minutes.

"Brandon." Sebastian's voice was low. "We need to discuss—"

"Not yet." Brandon adjusted his compression depth by a fraction. "Not yet."

Eight minutes and fourteen seconds after the alarm went silent, the green line jumped.

One beat. Irregular. Then another. And another. And then a rhythm, fragile and uneven, but unmistakably a heartbeat.

"Sinus rhythm," the nurse announced. "Weak, but holding."

Brandon stepped back from the bed. His arms shook. His scrubs were damp with sweat. The room exhaled around him as the code team transitioned from resuscitation to stabilization, adjusting drips and repositioning equipment with the coordinated speed of people who had pulled children back from the edge before.

But Gabrielle wasn't out of danger. Not by a long margin.

Her heart rate held, but it was thready and inconsistent. The seizure activity had stopped during the arrest and hadn't returned, which was a small mercy. Her temperature dropped from 104.8 to 102.1, but it should've been dropping faster with the medications they administered. And her pupils, when Brandon checked them again, responded unevenly. The left reacted to light. The right was sluggish.

"What are we looking at?" Sebastian asked, standing beside him at the foot of the bed.

Brandon shook his head. "I don't know. Based on her labs, the cardiac arrest shouldn't have happened. The partial temperature drop doesn't fit the antibiotic timeline. And the uneven pupil response..." He paused, running a hand over his jaw. "None of this follows any diagnostic model I've ever seen."

"She came back, though." Sebastian's voice was low. Not triumphant, simply observational.

"She came back," Brandon agreed. "But she's not out of the woods. Not even close." He was already shifting into the next orders, the habit of triage taking over. "We need to keep her on continuous observation, repeat the full blood panel in two hours, and get that autoimmune workup expedited."

He walked into the hallway. Grace sat with the Millers on a bench against the wall. Tobias had his face in his hands. Denise looked up at Brandon with eyes so full of desperate hope that his shoulders bowed under it.

"She's alive." Brandon chose his words with the care of a man who understood that what he said next would live in this family's memory forever. "Her heart's beating. We've stabilized her for now, but her condition is still critical. I can't tell you what caused the arrest and I can't guarantee it won't happen again."

Denise's face crumpled. "But she's alive?"

"She's alive."

Tobias lifted his head. His eyes were red, and his construction worker's hands were trembling. "Is there anything else you can do?"

"We're doing everything that medicine can do." Brandon met his eyes. "I promise you that."

It was Grace who spoke next, and she directed her words at Brandon, not the Millers. "Thank you. For not giving up on her."

He looked at her. She was sitting on that hallway bench with mascara smudged beneath her left eye and her professional composure visibly frayed at the edges. Her hands, clasped in her lap, were still trembling from the hour she had spent holding Denise Miller together. She looked exhausted. She looked human. And what she had just said was an acknowledgment that at eight minutes and fourteen seconds, most physicians would have called it.

"I wasn't ready to stop," he said.

"I know." Grace's voice was barely above a whisper. "That is exactly why I thanked you."

Later that evening, after the second set of blood work confirmed that Gabrielle's vitals were holding in their fragile equilibrium, Brandon found Grace in the staff break room. She sat at a corner table with a cup of coffee and a pen in her hand, writing in a small leather journal. Though he couldn't read it from the doorway, he could see a verse copied in neat handwriting on the open page. She looked up when he knocked on the doorframe.

"Mind if I sit?"

"Please." She closed the journal and set it aside.

He poured himself coffee from the pot on the counter. It was bitter and lukewarm. He drank half the cup in one swallow before sitting across from her. The fluorescent lights buzzed overhead. Somewhere down the hall, a phone rang and went unanswered.

Neither of them spoke for a while. Neither needed to. They had just lived through the same terrible hours, and the silence between them held a kind of understanding that words would only have interrupted.

"I've been in emergency medicine for twelve years," Brandon said at last. "I've lost more patients than I care to count." He turned the coffee cup in his hands. "But today... today I was counting seconds, Grace. I was watching that line, and I was counting. I knew the protocol says you call it after a certain point." He exhaled. "I couldn't do it."

"Why?"

"I don't know." He looked at the table as if the grain of the wood might offer the answers his training couldn't. "That's not a satisfying answer. I *always* have an answer. That's what I do. I diagnose. I explain. I identify the variable everyone else missed. But this case." He shook his head. "This case is beyond me. And I'm not accustomed to admitting that."

Grace wrapped her hands around her own cup. "When my husband died, the chaplain who came to the house was a woman named Ruth. She'd been doing military notifications for twenty years. And I remember asking her how she did it. How did she walk up to a stranger's door and destroy their lives, day after day."

Grace traced the rim of the mug, her finger following the curve slowly. "She told me that she had stopped trying to have answers a long time ago. She said that the families didn't need her answers. They needed her willingness to stand in the rubble with them."

Brandon let that sit.

"You stood in the rubble today," Grace said. "Eight minutes and fourteen seconds of it."

"I was doing my job."

Grace met his eyes, and there was no softness in her voice now. Just clarity. "No... you were doing more than your job. Your job ended at the protocol cutoff. Everything after... that was you refusing to let go of a child who wasn't yours, for reasons that had nothing to do with medicine."

He opened his mouth to argue, to offer a clinical rationale for the extended resuscitation effort, and nothing came out. Because she was right. He had stayed on that child's chest past the point of protocol, and the reason wasn't scientific. The reason was that he couldn't bear to lose another one. Not this one. Not the little girl who looked up at him from a hospital bed and told him his shoulders looked like they hurt.

"When I was in medical school," Brandon began, the words surprising him even as they left his mouth. "I believed that doctors were instruments of a larger design. That healing was a partnership between science and whatever force put the science there in the first place."

He stared at the coffee, the liquid giving nothing back. "I stopped believing that a long time ago. But today, when her heart started again at eight minutes and fourteen seconds..." He paused, something shifting behind his eyes. "For about three seconds, I wasn't sure I was right to stop."

Grace said nothing. She didn't offer an interpretation. She didn't connect the dots for him or suggest what those three seconds meant. She just sat across the table and let his words exist without rushing to fill them with theology.

He was grateful for that. More grateful than she probably knew.

"Thank you," he said. "For being there today. For the family. For the team."

"Thank you for trusting me enough to sit here and say what you just said." Her voice was tired but warm. "I know that wasn't easy."

Brandon stood, intending to leave, and then stopped. Grace had picked up her journal and opened it again. Her pen moved in small, precise strokes as she prepared notes for her visit with the Millers in the morning. She mouthed words as she wrote, rehearsing phrases under her breath, testing how they would sound in a grieving mother's ear.

A strand of hair had come loose from behind her ear and fallen across her cheek. She didn't push it back.

Brandon had been standing in the doorway longer than he realized. He took a step back, but he wasn't sure why. He cleared his throat.

"Grace."

She looked up.

"Would you want to continue this conversation sometime? Somewhere without fluorescent lighting and the smell of disinfectant?"

A beat of surprise crossed her face, there and gone. "I'd like that."

"How about Heavenly Delights? I keep hearing about it from Sebastian, who apparently considers Willow Barnes's lemon bars a food group." He paused. "Tomorrow evening? About seven?"

"I know the place well." Her mouth curved into the first real smile he had seen from her all day. "Seven works."

He walked to the parking garage through the hospital's side corridor, his footsteps echoing in the empty hallway. The evening shift had found its slower rhythm, and the building had taken on the strange, suspended quality that hospitals acquire after dark.

He was still thinking about what he had said in the break room. The admission about medical school. The three seconds of doubt. He hadn't told Sebastian those things. He hadn't told anyone. And yet, he had sat across from a woman he barely knew and offered them up like loose change, as though they cost him nothing.

They had cost him everything. And somehow that made the offering feel necessary.

As he crossed the parking lot toward his car, movement caught the edge of his vision. Near the far lamppost, a man stood watching the hospital entrance. Silver hair. A wooden cane. An unhurried posture, as though he had been standing there for hours and intended to stand there for hours more.

Brandon slowed. Mrs. Frost's description surfaced in his memory. A weathered face. A peaceful bearing. A man who knew what to say when someone needed encouragement.

He turned to get a better look, but the space beneath the lamppost was empty. Just a circle of light on asphalt and the faint hum of the lamp above it.

Brandon stood there for ten full seconds, scanning the lot. No one. Not a retreating figure nor the sound of footsteps. Just the distant hiss of tires on the highway and the muffled pulse of the hospital behind him.

He unlocked his car and sat behind the wheel without starting the engine. Forty-eight hours of broken sleep. The adrenaline crash from the code. The emotional weight of the break room conversation. His brain was apparently finding patterns in shadows. That was the logical explanation.

But as he pulled out of the parking lot and turned toward home, the image of the silver-haired man stayed with him. And so did a question that had no place in a scientist's mind.

What if it wasn't his imagination?

Chapter 6

GRACE STOOD IN FRONT of her bathroom mirror and changed her earrings for the third time.

She caught herself doing it and stopped, hands frozen at her ears, staring at her reflection with the look she normally reserved for hospital paperwork that didn't add up. She was a thirty-nine-year-old woman getting ready for coffee with a colleague. The small gold studs she had put on first were fine. The silver hoops she tried second were also fine. The fact that she was now holding a pair of amber drops that her late husband had given her for their last anniversary was the thing that was *not* fine.

She put the amber drops back in their velvet box and went with the gold studs.

A cream blouse and dark slacks would be understated and appropriate for the occasion. The outfit was appropriate for a hospital chaplain attending a casual dinner with a colleague, which is precisely what this was. It was a dinner between coworkers who happened to have shared a medical crisis and an emotionally honest conversation over terrible hospital brew less than twenty-four hours ago.

Grace picked up her phone and checked the message she sent Carmen earlier that afternoon.

Having coffee tonight with Dr. Lawson from the ER. The one I mentioned.

Carmen's reply had arrived in under thirty seconds. *The brooding one with the silver temples? The one you said was "professionally interesting"? Have fun at your NOT-date, amiga. Text me everything.*

Grace hadn't replied to that. Partly because she didn't know what to say. Partly because Carmen had an instinct for the truth that was both her best quality and her most annoying one.

She checked Gabrielle Miller's status on the hospital app before she left the house. Still critical but stable. Her temperature was holding at 100.2, down from 102.1 that morning. Sebastian's notes said the uneven pupil response had corrected itself overnight, which he called *"unusual but encouraging."* Brandon had added his own note around three forty-five that afternoon, one line of his sharp, slanting handwriting digitized into the chart system.

Will continue monitoring. No diagnosis confirmed. Etiology remains unknown.

Grace closed the app and put her phone in her purse. She had been checking Gabrielle's chart four times a day. She told herself it was pastoral concern, but she knew that part of her checked because Brandon's notes were there. Reading them had become a habit she hadn't intended to form.

Heavenly Delights Diner's pastel-colored facade glowed in the early evening light. Through the large front windows, the diner looked the way it always did. Inviting and half full of the Brookside regulars who treated the place less like a restaurant and more like an extension of their own kitchens. The scent of freshly brewed coffee, baked bread, and cinnamon reached Grace before she opened the door.

She spotted Brandon through the window before she reached the entrance. He sat in the corner booth with his back to the wall. It was the same watchful posture she had seen a dozen times in the hospital. He wore a dark blue button-down, sleeves rolled to the forearms, hair still damp from a shower. He had changed out of scrubs for this.

That detail registered in a place she wasn't ready to look at directly.

The bell above the door chimed her arrival, and Brandon looked up. Not a smile, exactly. More like the easing of a tension he hadn't known he was holding until she walked in. He stood as she approached the table. The gesture, old-fashioned and automatic, told her, without a word, exactly the kind of man he had been raised to be. She found herself smoothing the front of her blouse before she reached him, a reflex she couldn't account for.

"Grace!" Willow Barnes appeared from behind the counter, her dark brown hair twisted into its usual neat bun, a dusting of flour on her apron. Her face brightened with a welcome that had made this diner the heart of Brookside's community. "I was wondering when you would bring someone new through my door. It's been nothing but the usual crowd all week."

"Willow, this is Dr. Lawson. We work together at Lakeside." The words came out in her chaplain cadence, formal and measured, and she immediately wished she had just said his first name.

"Welcome, Dr. Lawson." Willow made every person who walked through her door feel expected. "Grace doesn't bring just anyone in here. That means you matter. Sit down and let me take care of you both."

Brandon nodded. "I've heard nothing but good things about this place. My friend Sebastian says your lemon bars are the best in the county."

Willow's face brightened at the compliment. "Sebastian's too kind. That man keeps me in business. He's always coming in for a lemon bar and cappuccino after his shifts." She gestured toward the booth. "Go on, sit down. I'll bring drinks, and Anna will take care of you."

She disappeared behind the counter, and Anna Parks arrived at the table a moment later with two menus and a fresh pot.

"Evening, Grace." Anna set the menus down. "The roasted tomato bisque is wonderful tonight, and Willow just made a fresh batch of her cinnamon scones." She poured for both of them, and the rich aroma filled the space between the booth's high-backed seats. "Take your time. I'll check back in a few minutes."

Brandon wrapped his hands around the ceramic cup and took a sip. His eyebrows lifted. "This is exceptional."

"Willow roasts the beans herself. She orders them from a farm in Colombia that her late husband James found on a mission trip years ago." Grace blew across the surface of her cup. "She's kept the relationship with that farm going ever since. Says it's her way of honoring his memory."

Brandon considered that, turning his cup between his palms. She could see him cataloging details the same way she had cataloged the rolled sleeves and the damp hair on her way in. They were two people trained by their professions to notice things.

"Tell me something," Grace said. "Tell me something that has nothing to do with the hospital."

"That's a short list."

"Try."

He leaned back in the booth. "I run. Early mornings, before the sun comes up. There's a trail that loops through Providence Park and follows the creek for about two miles before it connects with the neighborhood path. I've been running that route three or four times a week since I moved to Brookside."

"Rain or shine?"

"Rain is better. Fewer people. And the park smells different after it rains, like pine sap and wet earth. It's the only time my mind goes completely still." He paused, as though surprised he had said that much. "Your turn."

"I bake." His eyebrows rose. She couldn't blame him. "Bread, mostly. Sourdough. I have a starter that I've kept alive for almost five years. I named it."

"You named your sourdough starter?"

"Lazarus. Because every time I think it's dead, it comes back to life."

The laugh that escaped Brandon was involuntary and unguarded, a short, startled sound that brightened his entire face. Two women at the counter turned to look, as though the sound was unusual enough to warrant attention. Grace suspected it was. She doubted many people in Brookside had heard Brandon Lawson laugh in public.

"Lazarus," he repeated, shaking his head. "That might be the best thing anyone has told me in months."

He means it. And a tight place in her chest, held carefully in check since she walked in, loosened just a little.

Anna returned to take their orders. Grace chose the roasted tomato bisque and a grilled chicken panini. Brandon studied the menu with the same concentration he applied to lab results before ordering the turkey and brie sandwich and a cup of the butternut squash soup.

"Willow's soups are wonderful," Grace said after Anna left. "She changes the menu with the seasons. In the fall, she does a sweet potato bisque that people drive from two towns over to get."

"Sebastian failed to mention the soups. He only ever talks about the lemon bars."

"That's because Sebastian's a man of singular focus." Grace tore a piece of the warm cinnamon scone Willow had sent over. "He finds what he loves and stays loyal to it."

Brandon's mouth twitched. "That sounds like him."

The food arrived, and they ate. For a while, they didn't talk about faith or suffering or Gabrielle Miller or hospital politics. They talked about the things people who are beginning to know each other actually talk about.

"My father couldn't cook at all." Brandon cut into his sandwich. "He was career military. Five deployments. When he was home, he ate whatever was put in front of him and never complained. My mother worked two jobs while he was overseas, so dinner was usually whatever she could make in thirty minutes. I grew up thinking spaghetti with jarred sauce was a gourmet meal."

"And now?"

"And now I eat hospital cafeteria food and vending machine peanuts, so not much has changed." He took a spoonful of the soup and paused. "This is actually extraordinary."

"I told you."

Grace broke off another piece of scone. "My mother was the cook in our family. She made this lemon pound cake for every church potluck that people would fight over. I mean actual disagreements about who got the last slice." A small, rueful smile touched her mouth. "I've tried to replicate the recipe at least a dozen times. It never comes out the same."

"What's the secret?"

"I think the secret is that she prayed over everything she baked. And she meant it." Grace caught herself. "Sorry. I didn't mean to make it about faith."

"You didn't." His voice was matter-of-fact. "You made it about your mother. There's a difference."

That distinction mattered. She let it land and moved on.

"Tell me more about the nieces you mentioned," she said. "The ones who video call you with their glitter art."

Brandon set his fork down, and the change in his face was remarkable. The hard edges dissolved. The wary intelligence that made him so formidable in a trauma bay gave way to a warmth she hadn't seen before, open and entirely unprotected.

"My sister Bethany's girls," he stated. "Sophie is six and Mia is four. They live in Charlotte. Sophie wants to be a veterinarian, and Mia wants to be a dinosaur. Not a paleontologist. An actual dinosaur."

"Which one?"

"She hasn't decided yet. She's currently torn between a triceratops and something she calls a *rainbow raptor,* which I don't believe exists in the fossil record."

He shook his head, but there was no frustration in the gesture. Only affection. "They call me every Sunday after church. Bethany puts them on video, and they show me whatever they've made that week. Last Sunday, Sophie glued macaroni to a paper plate and told me it was my portrait."

"Was it accurate?"

"Disturbingly so."

Grace laughed, the sound mixing with the diner's ambient noise, with the low hum of conversation from the other booths, the clink of cups on saucers, and the faint sound of Willow humming in the kitchen. This was the version of Brookside she loved most. Ordinary, alive and full of people feeding each other, telling stories and pretending they weren't all holding a little more than they let on.

They had been at the table for nearly an hour when Anna came by with fresh refills. Grace realized she hadn't thought about the hospital once in the last twenty minutes. She couldn't remember the last time she had been so thoroughly pulled out of her own head by another person's company.

By his company, she amended silently. The truth of it cradled in her chest, tender and precious.

"Can I ask you something personal?" Brandon asked, turning his water glass between his palms.

"You can ask. I reserve the right not to answer."

"Fair enough." He looked at the table, his thumb pressing a slow circle against the condensation on the glass. When he spoke again, his voice was quieter, as if he were testing whether the words would fit in the space between them. "You mentioned your husband was a medic. Did you two talk about his work the way we talk about ours? The hard cases, the ones that follow you home?"

Grace considered the question. She appreciated that he had asked about Anthony as a person, not as a martyr or a theological lesson.

"We did. Anthony used to say that the worst part of being a military medic wasn't the injuries. It was the letters. He wrote letters to every family of every soldier he lost. He said that if he stopped writing them, he would stop feeling it, and the day he stopped feeling it was the day he needed to quit."

"That sounds like a man who understood the cost of the work."

"He did. And he paid it." Grace ran her thumb along the edge of her glass. "I think that's part of why I understand what I see in you, Brandon." She paused, suddenly aware that she was about to say too much, and then said it anyway. "The way you carry your patients. And the way you followed Gabrielle's case into a department that isn't even yours... Anthony would have done the same thing."

She hadn't planned to say that. Comparing Brandon to Anthony wasn't a connection she had consciously drawn before. The fact that it arrived so naturally unsettled her in a way she couldn't quite name.

Brandon held her gaze. Whatever he was thinking, he kept it behind his eyes. "Thank you for telling me about him," he said quietly. "He sounds like someone I would have respected."

"He would have liked you." The words came out before Grace could evaluate them, and she felt heat rise in her cheeks. She covered it by reaching for her water.

Brandon's phone buzzed against the table, and they both looked at it. Sebastian's name filled the screen.

He answered. Grace watched his face as he listened, reading the shifts the way she had learned to read families in crisis. Tension in the jaw. A slight release. Then a furrow between his brows, the look he wore when the data contradicted itself.

"When?" His voice was clipped now, all business. "What about the pupil response?" A pause. "And the blood work?"

He ended the call and set the phone down carefully, as though it might break. When he looked up, the earlier warmth had receded, leaving behind the watchful vigilance she remembered from the hospital.

"Gabrielle's temperature dropped to 99.1. That's nearly normal. And her latest blood work shows a marked decrease in the white cell count." He paused, and she could see him working to fit the information into a framework that would hold it. "Sebastian says the improvement curve is unlike anything the neurology team has seen."

"But she's getting better," Grace said.

"She's getting better faster than any treatment protocol should allow." Brandon's voice had taken on the clinical tone he used when he was dictating chart notes, rather than sitting in a diner booth across from a woman who could see the conflict written across his face.

"Her recovery isn't consistent with the medications we administered," he said. "The timeline doesn't match. And the neurology team is baffled by the reversal of symptoms that, twenty-four hours ago, suggested irreversible damage."

Grace waited. She didn't offer an interpretation. She didn't say the word *miracle,* though it sat on her tongue. She let the silence hold the space that his words had opened.

Across the table, Brandon's jaw flexed, as though he were chewing on words he wasn't ready to swallow. He didn't break the silence either.

"I need to go see her," Brandon finally said. He was already reaching for his wallet.

"I'll get this." Grace was already pulling cash from her purse, tucking it under the edge of her plate before he could protest. "You can argue with me about it later. Right now, we need to go." She stood and looped her purse over her shoulder. "And I'm coming with you."

"You don't have to."

"I know." She met his eyes, letting him see that she understood what he wasn't saying. "But the Millers will need someone, and you'll need to focus on the medicine without worrying about the family's emotional state." She paused. "Consider it a professional courtesy."

He looked at her. Not gratitude, exactly. Recognition. The look of a man who had been offered exactly the thing he needed, in a way that didn't require him to admit the need.

"Professional courtesy," he repeated, and she caught the warmth beneath his dry tone. He was playing along with the fiction she had offered.

"Strictly professional."

His mouth curved. Not quite a smile, but the beginning of one.

The evening air was cool against her face as they stepped onto the sidewalk. Brookside at dusk was a town that looked painted. The streetlights were coming on one by one, the dogwood trees cast long shadows across the sidewalk, and the distant sound of someone's radio carried a gospel station through an open window.

Willow caught them at the door. "You come back now." She pressed the bag into Grace's hands. "Everybody needs a place where someone's glad to see them. This is yours." She turned to Brandon. "And it can be yours too, if you let it."

Her eyes held the perceptive warmth of a woman who believed that feeding people was its own kind of ministry.

Brandon nodded. "Thank you. For the food. For..." He glanced at Grace, then back at Willow. "For the evening."

Willow's smile deepened. Her gaze flicked between them, and Grace felt herself being seen in a way that made her grateful for the dimming light.

They walked to his car, and Grace noticed that he shortened his stride to match hers without appearing to think about it. A small thing, that a man either did instinctively, or didn't do at all.

"Grace." He stopped at the driver's side door, keys in his hand. "Before we leave, I want to tell you something."

She waited.

"I had a mentor during my residency. Dr. Stephanie Whitmore. She was the best physician I've ever known, and she was a woman of deep faith." He turned his keys over in his fingers, the metal catching the streetlight. "She died of brain cancer twelve years ago. I was with her at the end."

He looked up. "I haven't talked about her with anyone except Sebastian in over a decade. But tonight, sitting in that diner, I almost told you the whole story." A pause, and she watched him decide to say the next part. "I want you to know that the fact I almost told you means something. Even if I'm not ready to say what."

She didn't rush to fill his words with comfort or interpretation. She stood on the sidewalk and let Brandon Lawson's trust land where it needed to land.

"Whenever you're ready," she said. "I'll be here."

He nodded once. Then he opened her door for her.

They drove to the hospital together, the radio off, the windows cracked, the silence between them full of things that neither was ready to name but that both, Grace suspected, were beginning to recognize.

Chapter 7

BROOKSIDE'S STREETS SLIPPED PAST beneath the sweep of Brandon's headlights. Grace sat in the passenger seat with her purse in her lap, her hands folded over it. She couldn't tell whether the knot in her stomach was worry for Gabrielle or a feeling she wasn't ready to identify.

Neither of them spoke. Fifteen minutes ago, she had been sitting in a diner booth laughing about a sourdough starter named Lazarus. Now, she was riding to the hospital with a man whose profile, lit and shadowed by passing streetlamps, she couldn't stop noticing.

She turned her head toward the window and pressed her lips together.

Brandon spoke the way he spoke about everything medical, laying out facts the way a carpenter laid out boards. "Sebastian said her temperature is nearly normal. The neurology team is calling it *'atypical rapid stabilization.'"*

"Which means what, in plain English?"

"Which means they have absolutely no idea what's happening." He pulled into the hospital parking garage. "Grace, twenty-four hours ago, that child's heart stopped for over eight minutes. With her symptom profile, a recovery this fast doesn't exist in any literature I've ever read."

He cut the engine, and the silence of the parking garage wrapped around them. Grace waited. She had learned by now that Brandon needed a beat between the clinical summary and whatever was actually on his mind.

He stared through the windshield at the concrete wall, his hands still on the steering wheel. "If the improvement holds and if the morning labs confirm what Sebastian described, then I'll have to accept that what happened in that room is beyond anything I can explain." His voice was quiet, stripped of its usual certainty. "And I'm not sure what to do with that."

She wanted to put her hand on his arm and tell him that not every question needed an answer. But Sebastian's words from the elevator came back to her, about sitting on the bench and saying nothing. She remembered her own failure at her kitchen table and the prayer that wouldn't come. She kept her hands in her lap.

"You don't have to do anything with it tonight," she said. "You just have to go upstairs and see your patient."

He looked at her. In the dim glow of the parking garage's overhead lights, the silver at his temples caught the light, and the lines around his eyes told the story of two days without proper sleep. He looked worn down and unguarded. For the first time since she had known him, she could see past the physician to the boy he must have been before medical school taught him to hide.

The realization hit her before she could brace for it.

She looked away, opened the car door and stepped out. "Come on." She kept her tone even by sheer force of habit. "Let's go see Gabrielle."

The pediatric wing at night operated in a different register than the daytime ward. The lights were dimmed to a low amber. Machines hummed at a frequency that became white noise after a few minutes. Nurses moved in rubber-soled shoes, their voices hushed. The cartoon murals along the walls took on a dreamlike quality in the softened light, their cheerfulness muted into a gentle, almost sacred calm.

Room 314 was lit from within, a warm glow spilling into the hallway. As they approached, a sound stopped Grace mid-stride.

Laughter. Clear, bright, and unmistakable.

Brandon slowed beside her. His step faltered, and she watched the effort it took him to process what he was hearing. Twenty-four hours ago, the child behind that door had been on a ventilator.

Through the doorway, Gabrielle sat propped against pillows, her dark eyes wide and animated. She was telling a story, her hands moving through the air as she described birds with silver wings that sang songs. Some of the color had returned to her face. The IV line remained in her arm. Monitors behind her tracked her vitals, which, while improved, still required watching. But she was awake. She was talking. And she was laughing.

Her father sat in the chair by the window, his large frame folded forward, his elbows on his knees, his face slack with the particular weariness of a man who had been holding himself together for days and had only just been given permission to stop. Her mother sat on the edge of the mattress, one hand resting on Gabrielle's leg as though she needed the physical contact to believe what she was seeing.

Sebastian stood near the door. He looked up as they entered. The expression on his face was one Grace hadn't seen before. It wasn't triumph or relief, but rather a kind of bewilderment, as if he had just witnessed the laws of physics gracefully step out of the room.

"I thought you'd want to see this for yourself," Sebastian said to Brandon.

Brandon moved to the bedside with the focused precision that defined him in a clinical setting. Grace watched him pick up the chart, scan it, set it down, and begin his own examination. He assessed Gabrielle with the thoroughness of a man who didn't trust good news until he had verified it with his own hands.

"Dr. Brandon!" Gabrielle's face brightened. "I feel so much better. Mama says I was really sick, but I don't remember a lot. I had the best dreams, though." She held up her hands as though framing a picture. "There were silver birds, and they sang songs, and they told me not to be scared."

In her years of chaplaincy work, she had sat with dozens of patients who described vivid dreams during serious illnesses. Most involved light or familiar faces or childhood memories. Silver birds that sang and told a frightened child not to be scared were unusual enough to make her pay closer attention.

She listened as Gabrielle told her story the way children tell stories, looping and breathless and full of wonder.

"Can you tell me how you're feeling right now, Gabrielle?" Brandon asked. The clinical tone was in place, but Grace could hear the strain underneath it, the effort of maintaining distance from an eight-year-old whose recovery defied everything he knew.

"I feel like I could run around the whole hospital!" Gabrielle grinned. "When can I go home? I want to play with my toys."

"We still need to run some more tests over the next couple of days," Brandon said. He glanced at Sebastian, who nodded confirmation. "Your body went through a lot, and we want to make sure everything is healing the way it should before we send you home."

Tobias stood and extended his hand. "Dr. Lawson. We can't thank you and the staff enough. Whatever you and your team did, it saved our daughter's life."

Grace watched Brandon take the handshake. She saw the muscle jump in his jaw, that small betraying flicker, and knew why. He and Sebastian had followed standard medical protocols. They administered routine medications and performed CPR by the book. Nothing they did explained the child sitting up in bed, talking about silver birds.

"I'm glad she's improving," Brandon said. "But I want to be honest with you. Her recovery is unusual. The medical team will continue monitoring her closely over the next forty-eight hours. We'll run additional tests to understand what happened."

"We know what happened," Denise said. The words came out low and sure, the kind of certainty that did not invite argument. "God answered our prayers."

The sentence hung in the room. Grace watched the stillness that came over Brandon, the way his breath seemed to stop and then restart, slower. He didn't argue. Didn't deflect. He held Denise Miller's gaze, and then he spoke. "I'm glad she's getting better. That's what matters most."

It wasn't an agreement. Nor was it a disagreement. It was something else entirely. It was a man standing at the edge of a cliff he had been avoiding for twelve years and choosing, for the first time, not to back away.

Brandon stepped into the hallway with Sebastian, and Grace stayed with the Millers. She could hear the two doctors through the open door, their voices pitched low enough that the family couldn't follow the conversation.

"Walk me through it again," Brandon said. "All of it."

Sebastian laid it out with clinical precision. "Her temperature began dropping around four fifteen this afternoon. By six, it was 100.2. By eight thirty, when I called you, it was 99.1. Her pupils corrected on their own with no intervention. White cell count dropped from 18,000 to 11,000 in four hours. The neurology team ran their own assessment and found no residual damage from the seizures or the cardiac arrest."

Grace could picture Brandon's face. She could see the furrow between his brows as he listened to this impossible medical recovery. "That's not possible."

"I know."

"Eight-year-old children who go into cardiac arrest and experience prolonged seizure activity don't sit up in bed twelve hours later telling stories about silver birds. That's not how the human body works."

"I know." Sebastian paused. "Brandon, I've been praying in my office before surgeries for six years, and I've never asked God for a specific outcome. I just ask for steady hands and a clear head. But last night, after you and Grace left, I sat in the chapel for twenty minutes. And I asked."

Sebastian spoke the next words as though he were sharing a confession he wasn't sure would be well received. "I asked God to save that little girl. I'm not claiming there's a connection. I'm just saying that I need to tell you that, because you're my friend, and I don't want to keep it from you."

Grace heard Brandon exhale. Not a sigh but a sound pulled from a deeper place within him. It was the sound of a man whose ordered world had just developed a fissure he couldn't patch with data.

A long silence ensued. She envisioned the two of them standing in the hallway, with Sebastian waiting patiently, while Brandon grappled to find stable ground beneath his feet.

"I don't know what to do with that, Sebastian."

"You don't have to do anything with it. I just needed you to know."

Grace spent another twenty minutes with the Millers. She helped Denise make a list of questions for the morning rounds.

She sat beside Gabrielle while the girl drew pictures of her silver birds with crayons a nurse had brought. She studied the drawings with the close attention that had defined her career.

The birds in Gabrielle's drawings had silver feathers. Every single one of them.

When the Millers finally began settling in for the night, Tobias walked Grace to the door. "Chaplain Winslow." His voice was low, thick with exhaustion and a quiet sense of peace. "I know you and the doctors are being cautious about what you call this. My wife and I believe our daughter received a miracle. We believe that God used Dr. Lawson's hands to do it, even if he doesn't see it that way yet."

She looked at Tobias. His eyes were red-rimmed and spent, but behind the fatigue was a conviction that didn't waver. She reached out and rested her hand on his forearm.

"Mr. Miller, I believe that God works through more means than any of us can track. What happened with your daughter is extraordinary, whatever name we give it."

She let her hand stay where it was. "And I want you to know that the way you and Denise held onto your faith through the worst night of your lives mattered. It mattered to Gabrielle. And it mattered to the people in that room who needed to see what trust looks like when it costs everything."

Tobias's chin trembled. He pressed his lips together and nodded. Grace recognized the look of a man who had been strong for so long that one kind sentence nearly undid him.

"Will you keep praying for her?" he asked. "And for him?"

The second question carried a different weight than the first. Grace held his gaze. "I haven't stopped."

She found Brandon in the corridor outside the break room, leaning against the wall with his arms crossed and his head tilted back against the cinderblock. His eyes were closed. He looked like a man who had run out of arguments and didn't know what to do with the silence that followed.

"Hey," she said. She leaned against the wall beside him, close enough that their shoulders nearly touched, and didn't say anything else. She spent her career learning that the first thirty seconds beside a person in pain weren't for talking. They were for arriving. For letting the other person's body register that they were no longer alone.

He opened his eyes. "Hey."

She saw the weariness in them, but also something she almost missed. A faint glow, like dawn edging over ground that had been dark for a very long time. It wasn't faith or even hope. But it was a space where those things could take root. She knew enough about that kind of soil to recognize it when she saw it.

"How are you doing?"

"I have no idea." He said it without irony or deflection. Just the plain truth of a man who had reached the edge of his vocabulary. "Sebastian just told me he prayed for Gabrielle last night."

Grace didn't want to rush past what he had just offered her, because Brandon Lawson didn't hand people his confusion. He handed them his competence. The fact he was standing in this hallway telling her he had no idea how he felt was, in its own way, an act of trust so large it took her breath.

"How did that make you feel?"

He looked at the ceiling. "Like the ground is moving and I'm the only one who doesn't know the new coordinates." He brought his gaze back to her. "Grace, I need to ask you a question, and I need you to be honest with me."

"Always."

"Do you think what happened to Gabrielle was a miracle?"

She considered the question with the seriousness it deserved. She owed him an honest answer, not a chaplain's answer. Not the tidy, theological response she could deliver in her sleep. He deserved the version of her that still wrestled with the same questions he did, even after all her years in ministry.

"I think that what happened in that room goes beyond what medicine can fully explain. I think your hands and Sebastian's knowledge were part of it. I think the medications and the CPR were part of it. And I think there may have been a force at work that neither of us has the tools to measure."

She met his eyes. "I won't tell you it was God if that's not what you're ready to hear. But I'll tell you this. I've sat with hundreds of families in the worst moments of their lives. And every now and then, I've watched something happen that the charts can't account for and the textbooks can't explain. It doesn't happen often." She paused. "But when it does, it changes the people in the room."

Her voice lowered, not quite a whisper but softened for him alone. "It's changing you right now. I can see it."

He stared at her. She could see him turning her words over the way he turned medical data, looking for flaws, testing the logic, searching for the place where her argument collapsed. And she could see the moment when he couldn't find it.

When he spoke again, his voice was lower, almost hesitant. "On the sidewalk tonight, I told you some about my mentor, Dr. Whitmore. I told you I wasn't ready to say what that meant. But sitting here, looking at you..." He paused. "I think it means I'm tired of carrying this alone. I think you're the first person in twelve years who's made me want to set it down."

The words landed in a place she had been protecting for five years. Not as a chaplain receiving a confession. As a woman hearing a man say, in the only language he had, that she mattered. That her presence had weight. That the wall he had built wasn't as solid as he believed.

And the realization that ambushed her in the parking garage, the one she tried to push aside by opening the car door and walking toward the hospital, surfaced again. Clearer this time. Harder to dismiss.

She wasn't just concerned about Brandon. She wasn't just professionally curious about his faith crisis. She wasn't just empathetic toward his grief.

She was falling for him.

And it terrified her more than any crisis she had ever walked into.

"Brandon." She kept her tone level because that was what she did. She was Grace Winslow. She held things together. That was the role she had chosen, the armor she built, the promise she made to herself five years ago in the wreckage of a life she hadn't known how to rebuild. "I'm glad you told me. And I'm not going anywhere."

He nodded. His hand rested on the wall. His fingers brushed hers as she moved past him toward the elevator. The contact lasted less than a second. Neither of them acknowledged it.

Neither of them needed to.

But Grace felt it all the way to the elevator. All the way down to the lobby. All the way to his car. She knew it in her skin before she knew it anywhere else. The way it still tingled where his fingers had been. Whatever this was, she would be feeling it for a very long time.

Brandon drove her back to Heavenly Delights to retrieve her car. The diner was dark. Grace's car sat alone in the lot, looking smaller than she remembered.

He pulled up beside it and put the car in park. The engine idled. The dashboard clock read ten forty-seven.

"Thank you," Brandon said. "For coming tonight and for sitting with the Millers. For..." He stopped, and she watched him choose his next words with care. "For not making me explain anything I'm not ready to explain."

"You're welcome." She touched the door handle, then turned back. A steady pull anchored her in place, an awareness that had been stirring all evening demanding to be voiced. "Brandon... the silver birds in Gabrielle's drawings. Have you seen anything like that before?"

His expression shifted subtly, a tension tightening around his eyes. A stillness enveloped him, the kind that takes hold when someone faces the very question they desperately hoped would remain unspoken. "Why do you ask?"

"No reason." She opened the door. "Good night."

"Good night, Grace."

She walked to her car and unlocked it, and as she reached for the handle, she saw it. Resting on her windshield, pinned beneath the wiper blade, catching the streetlight in a way that made it glow.

A single silver feather.

She picked it up. It held firm, unmistakably real. The barbs were fine and perfectly aligned, unlike any feather she had seen from a bird native to Georgia. Unlike any feather she had ever encountered. She twirled it between her fingers, aware of its weight, feeling the quiet impossibility of it settle into her palm as though it had been waiting for her.

She looked back at Brandon's car. He was watching her through the windshield. She held up the feather, and even from ten feet away, she could see his face change.

He had seen one before. She knew it the way she knew when a family was about to break, the way she knew when a prayer was being answered before the words were finished.

She tucked the feather into her purse, got into her car, and drove home through the darkened streets with her hands firm on the wheel and her mind anything but.

The parking garage. The brush of his fingers in the corridor. Gabrielle's silver birds. Sebastian's prayer. Tobias Miller's conviction. And now a feather that shouldn't exist, sitting in her purse like a question addressed to everyone and answered by no one.

When she got home, she set the feather on her kitchen table, the same table where she had sat all those days ago, unable to form a single word of prayer. She folded her hands and closed her eyes.

And this time, the words came.

Lord, I don't understand what You're doing. But I truly believe that You're the One doing it. In that hospital. In that child. In that man. And maybe, Lord, in me. Help me be brave enough to stay open to wherever this leads. Even if it scares me. Especially if it scares me. Amen.

Chapter 8

Grace pulled into the Cottonwood Faith Community Center parking lot as morning light filtered through the dogwood trees. A week had passed since the night at Heavenly Delights and the silver feather on her windshield.

Seven days of checking Gabrielle's chart, watching the numbers improve in increments that Sebastian kept calling *"medically unprecedented,"* and trying not to notice that Brandon's chart notes had started appearing with a regularity that suggested he was checking on the child at hours when no reasonable physician should be awake.

Cars filled every space. Volunteers streamed toward the building carrying folding tables, boxes of medical supplies, and hand-painted banners. The joint health fair between Lakeside Community Hospital and Brookside's local churches was the kind of collaboration this town had never attempted before. From the look of the parking lot, half of Brookside had decided to show up for it.

She spotted Brandon's car near the area reserved for hospital staff. Her hands tightened on the steering wheel.

She spent the last seven days managing the realization that arrived in that parking garage. Seven days of composure at the hospital, of measured conversations in corridors, of timing her arrivals at the nurses' station so she didn't accidentally coincide with his rounds. Seven days of telling herself that what she felt was admiration for a complicated man, and seven nights of lying in bed knowing it was more than that.

Get it together, Grace. You're a thirty-nine-year-old profession-al. Act like one.

She grabbed her volunteer badge and her tote bag and got out of the car.

"Grace!" Carmen Delgado waved from beside a bright yellow banner that read *Children's Health Zone.* She wore a volunteer T-shirt, which she had cleverly styled by knotting it at the waist. Her dark hair was pulled back into the practical ponytail she re-served for everything except church. Her ten-year-old daughter Sofia bounced beside her, drowning in a matching T-shirt that reached her knees.

"Miss Grace!" Sofia broke into a run, braids flying. "*Mami* says you're bringing the doctor who saved Gabrielle!"

"Hey, sweetie. And yes, Dr. Lawson will be here to help with the health screenings. Are you excited for today?"

"I get to take people's blood pressure! *Mami* taught me how to pump the thing without making it squeak."

Carmen arrived at a pace that suggested she had no intention of running anywhere before noon. She looked Grace up and down with her signature, unyielding once-over. "You curled your hair."

"It's humid."

"Really Grace? It's April in Georgia and it's always humid. And like I said... you curled your hair." Carmen crossed her arms, one eyebrow arched. "So, where's the brooding doctor with the silver temples?"

Grace groaned, the sound half-embarrassed, half-defensive, while a flush climbed her throat like a traitor. "Carmen."

"The one you described to me as *professionally interesting.*" Carmen's smile sharpened. "The one you went to dinner with and then rode to the hospital with and then didn't text me about until the next morning, which tells me that whatever happened was significant enough that you needed time to process it before you could talk to me." Carmen tilted her head. "Am I wrong?"

Grace opened her mouth and closed it.

"That's what I thought." The teasing drained from Carmen's face, and what replaced it was the steady, clear-eyed love that made her the best friend Grace had ever had.

"*Amiga,* you know I love you. And you know I'll support whatever this is. But I need to say one thing, and then I'll leave it alone." She held up a finger. "You've spent five years taking care of everyone except yourself. If this man makes you feel alive again... don't run from it just because it scares you. Okay?"

Grace swallowed once, hard, and managed the smallest nod. "Okay."

"Good." Carmen clapped her hands together. "Now. Where is he? I need to evaluate him in person. Text messages don't give me enough data."

She didn't have to answer because Brandon had just stepped out from the medical station set up near the community center's front entrance. He wore slacks and a hospital polo. He moved through the growing crowd with the calm confidence of a man comfortable amid organized chaos. When he saw Grace, his stride changed as he made a slight adjustment, as though she were a fixed point he had been navigating toward.

"Good morning," he said. "I was hoping you'd arrived."

"Good morning." She kept her voice even and collegial. She was aware of Carmen standing three feet behind her, observing with the intensity of a field researcher. "Brandon, this is my friend Carmen Delgado. She's the hospital social worker I've mentioned. Carmen... Dr. Brandon Lawson."

Carmen extended her hand with an expression Grace recognized as her clinical assessment face, the one that made patients confess things that they hadn't meant to share. "I've heard good things about you, Dr. Lawson. Grace tells me you're a dedicated physician."

"That's generous of her." Brandon shook Carmen's hand. "And you're Sofia's mother. She told me yesterday that she's going to be in charge of blood pressure today."

"She's been practicing on me all week. My left arm may never recover." Carmen's eyes moved between Brandon and Grace with the rapid calculation of a social worker who read family dynamics for a living. Whatever she concluded, she kept to herself. "Dr. Lawson, Sofia is going to insist on demonstrating the blood pressure cuff for you. Please humor her. She takes her volunteer work very seriously."

"I'd be honored."

Sofia materialized at Brandon's elbow. "Dr. Lawson! Do you want me to show you how the cuff works? I'm really good at it. *Mami* says I have the steadiest hands in the family."

Brandon knelt to the little girl's level. "Show me everything. I could use a refresher."

She watched him listen to Sofia's excited instructions with the same focused attention he gave to lab results. He asked her follow-up questions as though she were a colleague presenting research. Sofia was radiant. Carmen, standing beside Grace, said nothing for a full thirty seconds. Grace counted them. In her experience, Carmen's silence was the equivalent of a standing ovation.

"All right," Carmen said at last. "He's good with children, he remembers my daughter's name, and he looks at you like you're the only person in this parking lot. I approve."

"Carmen, we're colleagues." Grace reached for a stack of forms she didn't need, just to have something to do with her hands.

"Mm-hmm. And I'm the Queen of England." Carmen picked up her clipboard. "Come on. We've got families to register."

The health fair filled the community center and spilled out into the parking lot. Vision screening stations occupied the front rooms. Hearing checks and blood pressure monitoring were conducted along the main hallway. A children's activity area had been set up in the fellowship hall, complete with coloring stations and a table where volunteers distributed toothbrushes and stuffed animals.

She and Brandon worked the family intake station together for the first hour. He handled the medical screening questions while she helped families navigate the paperwork and connected anyone who seemed overwhelmed with the appropriate support services.

They fell into a rhythm that surprised her with its ease. When a mother with three children under five arrived looking frazzled and close to tears, Brandon took the eldest child to the vision station without being asked. Grace sat with the mother, one hand steady on the woman's forearm as she helped with the forms. They didn't need to coordinate. They simply moved.

When an elderly man became confused by the hearing screening instructions, she translated the medical language into plain English while Brandon adjusted the equipment with patient precision.

Halfway through the morning, Brandon left the station to get water and came back with two bottles. He set one beside Grace's elbow without saying a word. She looked at the bottle, then at him. He was already focused on the next family. She didn't know what to do with the small, inconvenient warmth that rose in her chest, so she ignored it and unscrewed the cap.

It was a simple gesture, but Grace noticed.

Twenty minutes later, she overheard Brandon explaining a blood pressure reading to a nervous grandmother. "Your numbers are a little elevated, Mrs. Patterson, but nothing that should keep you up at night. Have you been keeping up with your medication?"

She looked up from her paperwork. Mrs. Patterson. The church secretary from New Hope Baptist. She hadn't mentioned the woman's name to Brandon, and the intake form listed her as *'Claudia Patterson.'* Grace had only said *"the grandmother in the floral dress"* when she pointed her out earlier. Yet here he was, using her name as if they had been introduced. He had remembered the name from somewhere, a conversation, or a passing mention. And he used it.

The water bottle. And now the name. The evidence was beginning to accumulate.

A stir near the entrance pulled her attention. The Miller family had arrived. Gabrielle walked between her parents, holding both their hands. She wasn't skipping or bouncing with irrepressible energy. She was walking, steadily and happily, with the deliberate pace of a child whose body had been through a serious trial and was still finding its full strength. Her color was good and her eyes were bright. But she still tired more easily than an eight-year-old should. Denise kept a hand on her daughter's shoulder, as though to reassure herself that the girl was real and solid and still there.

"Dr. Brandon!" Gabrielle spotted him across the room and waved with the arm that didn't have a medical ID bracelet still clipped to its wrist. Sebastian's team released her from the hospital three days ago with instructions for weekly follow-up appointments and a list of warning signs that Denise had taped to the refrigerator door.

Brandon crossed the room to meet them. Grace watched the shift in his posture, the way his spine straightened and his stride lengthened, the physician's reflex overriding the volunteer's ease. But when he reached Gabrielle, he knelt to her level, and the formality fell away.

"How are you feeling?" he asked.

"Good! Mama still makes me rest a lot, but I can play outside now for thirty minutes at a time." Gabrielle held up her fingers to demonstrate the number. "Dr. Reid said I'm his star patient."

"I believe it." Brandon looked up at Tobias and Denise. "How is she doing at home?"

"Better every day," Tobias said. His large hands rested on his daughter's shoulders. "We still watch her like hawks, but she's eating well and sleeping through the night. The follow-up blood work on Wednesday came back clean." He paused. "We know you're still looking for answers about what happened, Dr. Lawson. And we respect that. But we also know what we believe."

Brandon held Tobias's gaze without flinching. "I'm glad she's improving. That's what matters most."

He said those exact words before, in the hospital room, in the hallway. But this time, the tone had changed. The deflection was gone. What remained was an acknowledgment that *what matters most* didn't require a diagnosis to be true.

Gabrielle tugged on Brandon's sleeve. "Can I be your helper today? I promise I'll be really careful with the equipment."

The corner of his mouth curved. "I think I could use an assistant. But you have to tell me if you get tired. Deal?"

"Deal!" Gabrielle took his hand, and Brandon walked back to the medical station with an eight-year-old girl leading him by the fingers.

Denise watched them go, then turned to Grace. "That man doesn't know what he is to our family. He thinks he was just doing his job. But we see him. We see what it costs him to care the way he does." She touched Grace's arm. "We've added him to our nightly prayers. Not just for what he did, but for whatever he's carrying."

Grace nodded, not trusting her voice.

Samantha Forrester arrived mid-morning, with her son Elijah on her hip and a diaper bag slung over one shoulder. She weaved through the crowd with remarkable efficiency, a testament to her years of experience in high-pressure environments since her very first day in the ER, though the whirlwind of motherhood was a different species entirely.

"Grace!" Samantha's grin was wide and genuine. "I was hoping I'd see you here."

"Sam, look at him." She reached for Elijah, who came willingly, his small hands patting her face with the undiscriminating affection of a baby who considered all adults equally interesting. "He's gotten so big."

"He's nine months of pure energy and opinions. Daniel says he gets it from me." Samantha shifted the diaper bag to her other shoulder and surveyed the health fair. "This is incredible. When Carmen mentioned the hospital was partnering with the churches, I had to come. This is exactly the kind of thing Brookside needs."

They found a quiet spot near the fellowship hall entrance where Elijah could chew on a teething ring and Samantha could take a breath. Grace asked about Daniel and whether Elijah was sleeping through the night. Samantha answered with the cheerful exhaustion of a new mother who had made peace with chronic sleep deprivation.

Then Samantha looked at her with the directness Grace remembered from their earliest conversations at the hospital. "Carmen said that you and Brandon have been spending time together outside of work."

"Of course she did." Grace closed her eyes. She felt Elijah's fingers curl around her thumb, a tiny grip that seemed to anchor her.

"She didn't tell me details. She just said you'd met someone who was making you ask questions you hadn't asked in a long time." Grace adjusted Elijah on her lap. She kept her eyes on the baby's face, tracing the soft curve of his cheek. "Grace, I've worked beside Brandon Lawson for years. I know how guarded he is. I know how hard he pushes himself. And I've never seen him volunteer for anything outside of the ER."

She let that observation sit. "Can I tell you something? When I first met Daniel, I was terrified. I was so scared of wanting something I didn't think I deserved." She looked across the room to where the volunteers were stacking chairs. "I'd spent years convincing myself that being alone was easier than being hurt again. And then this man shows up at Grocery Haven with a cart full of frozen dinners and a sadness he thought he was hiding... and it hit me. I knew, even before I was ready to accept it."

Grace said nothing. She simply held Elijah and listened.

"The thing nobody tells you about falling for someone after experiencing a loss, is that it doesn't erase the grief. It just makes room for something new to exist alongside it." Samantha met her eyes. The kindness there was almost too much to handle. "Anthony isn't going anywhere, Grace. Loving someone new doesn't mean you loved him any less."

She wanted to say something, to offer a response that would prove she had heard. But her voice felt distant, as if it belonged to someone else. Instead, she looked down at Elijah, who had let go of her thumb and was reaching for the teething ring again, his world condensed to what was immediately in front of him.

Near midday, Pastor Jameson Morrison stepped onto the small stage near the information booth. His tall frame and commanding presence drew the crowd's attention without effort. Twenty years of shepherding New Hope Baptist through every kind of season had given him the rare ability to command a room simply by standing still.

"Friends, can I have your attention?"

The health fair quieted. Pastor Morrison smiled, and the warmth of it reached to the back of the parking lot.

"I want to thank everyone who made today possible. The hospital staff who donated their Saturday morning. The church volunteers who coordinated supplies. And the families who trusted us with their health and their time." He paused, allowing the applause to settle. "Before we continue, I'd like to invite Pastor Scott Wilson, who was kind enough to offer this community center, to lead us in a brief prayer of thanksgiving."

Pastor Wilson stepped forward, his silver-rimmed glasses glinting in the light. Where Pastor Morrison was commanding, Pastor Wilson had a more measured presence. Both men carried the same commitment, expressed in different ways.

"Let us pray," Pastor Wilson said.

Grace bowed her head. Across the room, she saw Brandon. She watched him from behind the cover of her lowered lashes. He didn't bow his head or close his eyes. But he didn't look away, either. He stood with his hands in his pockets and his face turned toward the two pastors.

The health fair wound down in the early afternoon. Volunteers began folding tables and stacking chairs. Children chased each other through the parking lot while their parents collected paperwork and leftover pamphlets. The scent of popcorn from the children's station still hung in the air. Grace moved through the aftermath, helping where she was needed, but her gaze kept drifting across the room.

She found Brandon at the medical station, packing equipment into carrying cases. Gabrielle had returned to her parents about twenty minutes earlier, visibly tired but protesting that she was fine and didn't need to sit down.

"She lasted about three hours," Brandon said, nodding toward the Miller family's car. "That's impressive for a child who was on a ventilator ten days ago."

"She had an excellent assistant leader." Grace picked up a box of unused blood pressure cuffs and stacked it beside his carrying case. "How are you doing?"

Instead of answering right away, Brandon looked out across the community center, and Grace followed his gaze. Volunteers from both churches moved around each other with an easy rhythm that had seemed impossible a few weeks ago. The pastors stood talking with the hospital staff, not guarded or polite for appearance's sake, but open and at ease. At the craft table, children bent over their drawings while their parents reviewed health screening results with nurses who explained everything in plain, easy-to-understand language.

"This was different from what I expected," he said.

"Different how?"

"More genuine. Less like an agenda and more like..." He paused, looking at her. She watched him search for the words, watched him let himself be seen doing it. "More like people who actually care about each other."

Warmth spread through her chest. "That's because they do."

Brandon picked up the last equipment case and set it on the table. "Grace... I've been thinking about something all morning."

He turned to face her. "Would you like to take a walk with me tomorrow? Just through Providence Park. I promise... no hospital, no health fair, and no emergencies."

He stopped, and she watched the way he wrestled with the unfamiliar experience of asking for what he truly wanted, rather than what he felt obligated to seek. "Just a walk," he added.

Grace set down the blood pressure cuff she had been holding for the last two minutes without remembering when she had picked it up.

"I'd like that very much."

"Tomorrow afternoon? Around four?" he suggested, his tone hopeful.

"Four o'clock sounds great."

He nodded once, and the relief that crossed his face was subtle but unmistakable. She suspected that Brandon Lawson didn't often ask for things he wanted. The fact that he just asked her told her more than any conversation they had shared.

They finished packing in a silence that felt easy rather than empty. When Brandon carried equipment to his car, Grace watched him pause at the parking lot to wave goodbye to the Miller family. Gabrielle waved back with both hands from the back seat of her parents' car, her medical bracelet flashing in the afternoon sun.

Carmen appeared beside her, close enough to make Grace startle. "You're watching him again."

Grace kept her eyes on the parking lot a moment longer before forcing herself to look away. "I'm observing the volunteer cleanup process."

Carmen looked at the parking lot, then back at Grace. "He asked you to go somewhere, didn't he? I can tell by the way you're standing."

"How can you possibly tell by the way I'm standing?"

"Because you're standing the way you stood the morning you told me you were applying for the chaplain supervisor position. Like you're about to jump off something tall and you're not sure the net is there." Carmen squeezed her arm. "The net is there, *amiga*. You just can't see it yet."

Grace wanted to argue. She wanted to say that this was different. That Brandon wasn't a job application she could prepare for with a résumé and a list of references. But Carmen had already turned away to help a volunteer fold a table, and she was left with the truth of what her friend had seen.

She watched Brandon's car pull out of the parking lot. She thought about Samantha's words. About the room that love makes beside grief, not replacing it, not erasing it, just making space. She thought about the water bottle he had placed at her elbow without a word. About the way he remembered Mrs. Patterson's name. About an eight-year-old girl leading him through a health fair by the hand.

And she thought about the silver feather that still sat on her kitchen table, catching the morning light every day when she poured her coffee, and a question she hadn't yet answered but was no longer afraid to ask.

Chapter 9

Brandon matched Grace's easy pace as they entered Providence Park. Afternoon sunlight filtered through budding oak trees, casting patterns across the gravel path that shifted with the breeze. He had run this trail a hundred times in the dark, his feet finding the path by memory, his mind chasing whatever medical puzzle was keeping him up.

He had never walked it in daylight with another person. He had never wanted to. The park looked different at this speed. It was full of details he had been running past for years.

Grace wore a light cardigan over a simple cotton blouse. Her hair was down around her shoulders instead of pulled into the bun she wore at the hospital. The change made her look younger. Or perhaps it simply revealed her true self outside of the role she played for others.

He noticed this, and then noticed that he had noticed, felt the familiar impulse to file the observation away somewhere safe where it couldn't matter too much, and shoved his hands into his pockets.

"Aaron proposed to Meghan in that gazebo." Grace nodded toward the white octagonal structure, its posts wound with climbing vines. "It was last spring. The weather was perfect, but Aaron was still recovering from his scaffolding accident and wearing a boot on his fractured ankle."

Brandon glanced at the gazebo. He tried to picture Aaron in a boot, down on one knee, and found the image oddly comforting. "Sam told me about it. Proposing while wearing a medical boot... now that's commitment."

"Love doesn't wait for ideal circumstances." Grace stepped around a puddle left by the morning's rain. "Sometimes the best moments happen when everything else is upside down."

He filed that too, without meaning to.

They passed the gazebo and followed the path toward the pond. A breeze carried the scent of cut grass and the sweet, heavy perfume of the wisteria that draped the park's wrought-iron fences. Two joggers passed them going the other direction, and a woman with a golden retriever waved from the opposite bank.

"This is the trail you run," Grace said. "The one you told me about at dinner."

He was surprised she remembered. "Three or four times a week. Though I've never actually stopped to look at the pond. I just run past it."

"You run past the prettiest part of the park?"

"I run to clear my head, not to sightsee."

"Maybe that's the problem." Grace looked at him sideways, and the corner of her mouth lifted. "You're so busy clearing your head that you miss what's right in front of you."

He opened his mouth to argue and realized he had no argument. She was right, and the fact that she was right about more than just the pond hung in the air between them, unspoken and undeniable.

They reached a wooden bench overlooking the water and sat. Grace had left some distance between them, enough to maintain propriety, and he noticed the gap. His arm could almost brush against hers if he leaned slightly. He remained still, hyper-aware of the space separating them, just as he was of everything else about her. The proximity didn't allow for any other option.

"Can I ask you a personal question?" Grace turned toward him. "You can refuse to answer. You know I respect that."

His instinct was to say no, but he overrode it. "Go ahead."

"Yesterday, I watched you with Elijah, Sofia, and Gabrielle. You're different with children than you are with adults. The distance you keep from everyone else disappears when you're around the children. I've been wondering why."

The question was more perceptive than he expected, though by now he should stop being surprised by her intuitiveness.

"Children don't perform," he said. "They don't dress up their pain or negotiate with it. A child tells you it hurts, and they mean it hurts. There's no subtext." He watched a pair of ducks glide across the pond. "I find that easier to work with than the alternative."

"Have you ever wanted children of your own?"

The question landed in a place he normally kept locked. "I've never been married. And no, I don't have children." He knew she would let him stop there, but he didn't want to. "But I think about it sometimes. More than I used to."

He didn't say what prompted the increase in frequency. He didn't need to.

"What about you and Anthony?" he asked. "Did you talk about having a family?"

The shift in Grace's expression was quick and honest, pain that had been carried for so long it had become part of the landscape of her face.

"We wanted children. Anthony talked about teaching a daughter to fish and showing a son how to change a tire." Her voice held, but her fingers pressed into the edge of the bench. He watched her hand and resisted the urge to cover it with his own. "We had just started trying when he was deployed."

Brandon sat with that. He thought about all the promises that never got kept. He thought about the ones he had made to himself, that he had broken without meaning to. He didn't offer any empty platitudes. He just let what she had lost exist, because he had learned from watching her that sometimes the most respectful thing you could do with someone's grief was refuse to rush past it.

"I'm sorry, Grace." He said it quietly, wanting her to know that even though he didn't have the answers, he could still see what she was carrying.

"Thank you." She looked at the pond. "Some days, I think about the life we would have had. The house with the big yard. Sunday dinners. A child with his smile." Her thumb traced a circle on the bench's armrest. "And then I remind myself that grief is a terrible architect. You can't build a future on the blueprints of a life that never happened."

"Who told you that?"

"My therapist." Grace's mouth twitched. "She's very good."

Brandon laughed, short and genuine. The honesty of the admission, the fact that she had a therapist and was willing to say so, punctured the solemnity of the moment in a way that made him like her more, not less.

"Tell me about your family," Grace said. "You said that your father was a career military man."

This was the territory he usually kept fenced off. Not because it hurt in the sharp, clean way Dr. Whitmore's death hurt, but because it was tangled and difficult to name, full of loyalties and disappointments he had never learned how to explain to anyone who hadn't grown up inside them.

"My father did three tours in Iraq and two in Afghanistan. He was an Army medic." He paused, conscious that he was telling this to a woman whose husband had been the same thing.

"He came home with a Bronze Star and nightmares he never talked about. My mother worked two jobs while he was deployed. She kept the house running and kept my sister and me fed, and in school." He searched for words that felt honest without feeling disloyal. "When he was home, he was... present. That's the best way I know how to say it. He was physically present, and he loved us, but he carried things from overseas that he couldn't put down."

Grace was quiet for a moment. "Did he get help?"

"Eventually. The VA got him into a counseling program when I was in high school. And I think it helped." Brandon felt his jaw tighten before he could stop it. Some lessons settled into the body long before a man knew how to question them. "But by then, I'd already learned his approach to pain. You push through. You show up. You don't talk about the things that are breaking you. You just work harder."

He looked down at his hands, broad and steady in his lap. Hands that had stitched wounds shut, signed discharge papers, and healed failing bodies. Hands that had always known what to do when someone else was in pain. Not nearly as useful when the injury was his own.

"Medical school reinforced every one of those instincts. The culture rewards people who never stop, who absorb punishment without complaint, who sacrifice sleep and relationships and their own health for the next patient."

"And you excelled in that culture," Grace said. It wasn't a question, which somehow made it harder to answer.

"I was built for it." He turned his hands over, studying his palms as though they belonged to someone else. "My father's discipline made me a good doctor. But it also made me someone who doesn't know how to stop. Who doesn't know how to sit on a bench in a park on a Sunday afternoon and just..." His voice trailed off. He let one hand lift in a small, helpless motion toward the pond, the trees, the late afternoon light spilling gold across the water. "... and just be."

Grace's expression softened, though there was nothing pitying in it. "And yet here you are."

"Yes... here I am."

The words felt less than what he meant, but she seemed to understand anyway.

They sat without speaking for a while. The pond reflected the sky, a wash of pale blue and white clouds. On the far bank, a child tossed bread to the ducks, and the birds surged forward in a noisy, graceless scramble, making the child shriek with laughter.

Brandon watched the commotion, then the ripples widening across the water after it calmed. The tension he carried for so long began to ease, so gradually he might have missed it if Grace hadn't been sitting beside him.

The sensation was strange enough to make him wary. It felt like discovering a muscle had been clenched for years and only now realizing it could loosen. Here with Grace, he wasn't bracing for the next demand, the next crisis, or the next person who needed something from him. He was simply there, on a bench beside a woman who made silence feel less like emptiness and more like rest.

"I want to show you something."

Grace reached into her purse and withdrew a worn envelope. The edges were soft from years of handling, and the paper had the faded, fragile look of a letter that had been read and reread until the creases threatened to tear.

"Anthony's last letter arrived three days after the Army chaplain knocked on my door." Her voice carried the steadiness of a woman who learned to talk about this without breaking. "He wrote it the morning before the IED. He was preparing for a medical mission in a dangerous area, and he knew the risks."

She opened the envelope and unfolded the letter with a reverence that told Brandon everything about what he was being allowed to see. He could make out the handwriting from where he sat, neat block letters, the penmanship of a man trained to write legibly on field reports under poor conditions.

"He wrote about a lot of things. About missing me. About the men in his unit. About the food, which he said was terrible." She smiled for a moment, and the brief warmth of it made the grief underneath somehow more poignant. "But there's one part I keep coming back to."

When she began to read, her voice changed. The words carried the cadence of something long ago memorized, something that had lived inside her long before this afternoon:

I used to think God's job was to keep me safe. Now I think His job is to make my life mean something, whether that life is long or short. If I don't come home, Grace, I need you to know that I wasn't wasted here. Every life I touched, every wound I dressed, every soldier I held while they cried for their mother... all of it mattered. Don't let anyone tell you my faith failed because my body did.

Brandon couldn't speak. The words burned through every defense he had built. He was hearing the voice of a man who had looked straight at the possibility of death and used what might have been his final morning to protect his wife's faith after he was gone. He didn't know what to do with that kind of courage. He only knew it humbled him.

She refolded the letter and returned it to the envelope with the same deliberate care.

"For months after he died, I was furious. How could he trust God to protect him when God let him die? How could he write about purpose when he didn't survive to fulfill it?" She looked at him then, and there was nothing abstract in her gaze. "I think you understand that kind of anger."

"Yes." The word scraped its way out of him. "I do."

"What changed for me wasn't an answer. It was a choice. I decided that Anthony's faith wasn't wrong just because he died. His life wasn't meaningless because it was short. And the love he poured into the world didn't evaporate when his heart stopped."

She paused, and he had the sense that every word cost her something, even now. "I don't always believe that with my whole self. Some mornings, I wake up, and the doubt is so thick I can barely breathe through it. But I keep choosing it. Not because I'm certain, but because the alternative feels emptier than the doubt."

Brandon stared at the pond. The ducks had drifted into quiet clusters near the reeds. The child on the far bank had run out of bread and was now chasing a goose, which seemed inadvisable. The late sun turned the water amber.

Grace ran her thumb along the edge of the envelope. "There's a verse that carried me through the first year after he died. Habakkuk chapter 3, verses 17 and 18. Most people have never heard of Habakkuk. He was a prophet who looked around at a world falling apart and said, *Though the fig tree does not bud and there are no grapes on the vines, though the olive crop fails and the fields produce no food, though there are no sheep in the pen and no cattle in the stalls, yet I will rejoice in the Lord, I will be joyful in God my Savior.'"*

She turned the envelope over in her hands. "Everything is gone. Every harvest. Every flock. Every tangible sign that God is providing. And Habakkuk's response is *'yet'*. That one word held me together for months. Not hope. Not certainty. Just... *'yet.'"*

Brandon looked at the envelope, then at her hands wrapped carefully around it. He spent most of his life trusting what could be measured, monitored, or held still long enough to examine. The word *'yet'* sounded nothing like that. It sounded fragile. It sounded insufficient. And somehow, coming from Grace, it sounded stronger than certainty ever had.

"Thank you," he said. "For showing me that letter. I know what that couldn't have been easy."

"You showed me something too," Grace said. "In the break room, after Gabrielle's code... you told me things you hadn't told anyone in twelve years. That cost you something."

"It did."

"So... we're even."

He looked at her, and for the first time, he didn't see the calm professional or the minister who always had the right words. He saw a woman who walked through the same fire he had, who asked God the same impossible questions, and who chose to keep believing without ever pretending the answers were simple.

The fact that she was sitting beside him on this bench, offering him the most precious thing she owned without asking for a single thing in return, undid him in a way that no diagnosis ever had.

He faced death notifications, impossible cases, and the slow ruin of people he could not save. None of it had left him feeling as unguarded as this moment did. Grace Winslow was extraordinary. And he was in trouble.

They walked back along the trail as the shadows lengthened across the gravel. The park was emptying, and joggers and dog walkers gave way to the hush of early evening. Fireflies had begun to blink in the grass along the creek, small pinpricks of light that appeared and vanished like unanswered questions.

Brandon walked closer to Grace than he had on the way in. Not close enough to touch, at least not on purpose, but close enough that when the path narrowed between two oak trees, the sleeve of his shirt brushed hers. She didn't move away.

"I need to tell you something," he said as they approached the gazebo again.

She turned to him.

"When I was fresh out of medical school, every time a patient's family told me they were praying for me, it irritated me. I thought they were hedging their bets. Like maybe they didn't trust the medicine, so they were keeping God on standby in case I failed."

He shoved his hands deeper into his pockets and looked out toward the path ahead. "But yesterday, when Denise Miller told me she'd added me to their nightly prayers, I didn't feel irritated. I felt..." He stopped walking.

The word wouldn't come. Gratitude was part of it, but not all. Relief, maybe. Shame, too, for how easily he dismissed what now felt unexpectedly tender.

"I don't know the word for what I felt."

"You don't need a word for it," she said. "You just need to let it be what it is."

He looked at her for a moment, then nodded. Under any other circumstances, that answer might have frustrated him. But this didn't feel like a problem to solve. It felt more like an opening.

They started walking again.

Near the park entrance, where the gravel path met the parking lot, a glint on the low stone wall caught his eye. A feather. Silver, fine, perfectly aligned, catching the last of the evening light in a way that made it glow against the gray stone.

He stopped and Grace stopped beside him.

The feather was identical to the one Grace had found on her windshield outside Heavenly Delights. Identical to the ones Gabrielle drew in her hospital pictures. Brandon picked it up and turned it between his fingers. It was real, solid, and warm, as though it had been sitting in the sun, though this section of the wall had been in shade for the last hour.

"Brandon." Grace's voice was soft. "I found one of those on my windshield the other night. After we left the diner."

He looked at her. "I know. I saw you pick it up."

Her brows drew together slightly. "Had you seen them before that?"

He thought about the parking lot at the hospital. The figure beneath the lamppost. Mrs. Frost's description of the silver-haired man. A chill moved over his skin, though the evening was still warm.

"Yes," he answered. "I have."

They stood together in the fading light, looking at the feather. Brandon didn't try to explain it. He didn't reach for bioluminescent algae, migratory species, or atmospheric refraction. He just held the feather and let it be what it was.

After a moment, he slipped it into his shirt pocket.

"Grace." He turned to face her. "Would you have dinner with me this week? Not at the hospital or the diner. Somewhere we can sit across from each other and talk the way we talked today." He hesitated, aware that what he was asking moved past the territory of colleagues or even friends. "I'd like to get to know you better. That is, if you're willing."

Her face changed, and what he saw wasn't the chaplain's practiced composure or the minister's careful encouragement. It was the woman underneath, the one who baked sourdough bread and named things and kept her husband's last letter in her purse because love hadn't stopped mattering when sorrow arrived.

"I'd like that very much."

Pleasure spread through him, impossible to deny.

"How about The Village Eatery. Tomorrow evening? Seven?"

"Seven works."

They walked to their cars in the nearly empty lot. Brandon opened Grace's door for her, and she paused before getting in.

"Brandon. Thank you for today. For listening. For telling me about your father." She held his gaze. "And for picking up that feather instead of walking past it."

He didn't trust himself to say much, so he only nodded.

He watched her drive away, her taillights receding down the tree-lined road that led back to town. Then he sat in his car with the engine off and the silver feather resting in his palm.

He thought about her late husband's letter. About the words of a man who chose to believe his life carried meaning even if it ended before he was ready. He thought about his father, who came home with nightmares and a Bronze Star and never stopped showing up. He thought about Dr. Whitmore pressing her palms together in a hospital hallway at three in the morning.

And he thought about Grace, who had handed him the most precious thing she owned on a park bench and asked for nothing in return.

Brandon placed the feather on his dashboard, started the engine, and drove home as the last light drained from the sky. Tomorrow, he would see her again.

The thought should have made him nervous. Instead, it felt like the first unrestrained breath he had taken in years.

Chapter 10

Grace stood at her hallway mirror and made herself stop adjusting her collar. The lavender blouse brought out the green flecks in her hazel eyes, and the charcoal slacks were the right balance of polished and femininity. She had tried on two other outfits before settling on this one, which was two more outfits than she had tried on for any occasion in the last five years.

She picked up the silver feather from the kitchen table where it had been sitting since the night outside Heavenly Delights. She turned it between her fingers, feeling the solidity of it, and then set it back down. She wasn't sure why she had picked it up. Maybe it was some kind of instinct, as though touching it might clarify the evening ahead.

It didn't. She put it down and picked up her keys instead.

The Village Eatery occupied a converted Victorian house near Brookside's center. It was a restaurant that the town considered fancy without being pretentious. Edison bulbs hung from strings across the courtyard, casting pools of gold over wrought-iron tables. Inside, pressed tin ceilings and dark wood paneling created a candlelit intimacy that encouraged people to stay longer than they planned. Grace had been here twice before, both times for birthday dinners with Carmen. She had never been here with a man.

Brandon was already on his feet when she walked in. He wore a navy button-down and dark jeans. The sight of him outside of scrubs and hospital polos still caught her off guard. He looked younger in regular clothes. Less armored. When he saw her, his whole posture changed, as if he had been waiting and was relieved that the waiting was finally over.

"Grace." He pulled out her chair. "You look beautiful."

The compliment arrived without hesitation or self-consciousness, as though beauty were a fact he simply observed and reported. Grace sat down and pressed her palms flat against the linen tablecloth until the flush across her collarbones had a chance to settle.

"Thank you. You clean up well yourself."

"I own exactly three shirts that aren't hospital-issued. This is the best of the three." He sat across from her. The small table brought their knees close enough that she was aware of the proximity without either of them touching. "I hope this place is all right. I found it a few months ago when I needed somewhere to think."

"It's lovely." She looked around the room. White candles flickered on each table. A low murmur of conversation filled the space, intimate enough to feel private but present enough to feel alive. "I've only been here for birthdays. This is different."

"Different how?"

She met his eyes. "Different because I'm nervous, and I don't get nervous."

His mouth curved. "That makes two of us."

A server appeared with menus and took their drink orders. Water for Grace, coffee for Brandon. The server, a young woman with a pleasant manner, listed the evening specials and left them to decide.

She opened her menu, grateful for the few seconds of cover it provided. Twenty-four hours ago, she had been sitting on a park bench listening to Brandon describe his childhood faith and watching him hold Anthony's letter in his hands. The intimacy of yesterday's conversation built a bridge between them that didn't yet have a name. Sitting across from him in a restaurant with candles and cloth napkins felt like an acknowledgment that they both knew what this was becoming.

"How was the ER today?" she asked.

"We had three cardiac events, two car accidents, and one case of suspected food poisoning that turned out to be a panic attack." Brandon's mouth twitched. "Dr. Martinez reminded me, for the second time this week, that emergency medicine is about treating the person, not just the symptoms."

"Allegra Martinez is a wise woman."

"She's the best ER director I've worked with. She sees patients as whole people." He paused. "She also mentioned that your chaplaincy work has made an incredible difference in how families process difficult news. Coming from Dr. Martinez, that's high praise."

Grace set down her menu. The plastic surface felt cool against her palms. She hadn't realized anyone in the ER was tracking the impact of her work. "I didn't know it was on anyone's radar."

"Well... it's on mine." Brandon said it simply, without any embellishment. This was how he said most things that mattered. She thought of the water bottle at the health fair. She remembered him recalling Mrs. Patterson's name. Now, he noticed her. It was a pattern too consistent to dismiss and too personal to ignore.

When the server returned, she ordered the herb-crusted salmon with roasted vegetables and Brandon chose the grilled chicken with wild rice. They handed back their menus, and the barrier between them was gone.

"I have a question," she said. "But it has nothing to do with faith or the hospital or Gabrielle or any of the things we usually talk about."

"I'm intrigued."

"What is the last book you read that was not a medical journal?"

Brandon looked at her as though the question had arrived from a direction he wasn't expecting. "That's a harder question than you might think."

"Take your time."

He leaned back in his chair. "There's a bookstore on Fourth Street. Hearthside Reads. The owner, Mr. Finch, wears a cardigan regardless of the season and has opinions about everything. I wandered in about a year ago because I was early for a dentist appointment and had nothing to do. I left with a copy of a novel about a man who builds a boat in his backyard and sails it to an island where nobody knows him."

"What was it about?"

"On the surface, it was about a man who needed to get away from everything. But underneath..." He turned his coffee cup between his palms. "Underneath, it was about a man who didn't know how to ask for help, so he built a boat instead."

She watched his face as he talked. His expression changed. The precision was still there, but layered over it was an enthusiasm she had only caught in glimpses before. The kind of unguarded interest that surfaced when a person forgot to be guarded.

"Did you like it?"

"I sat in the parking lot of the dental office and finished it. I was forty minutes late for my cleaning."

Grace laughed, delighted by the image of Brandon choosing a novel over punctuality. "Brandon Lawson, late for an appointment. I didn't think that was possible."

"Mr. Finch would be pleased to know he ruined my punctuality record." Brandon's eyes crinkled at the corners. "What about you? What are you reading?"

"I'm on a Henri Nouwen kick at the moment. But for non-theology reading, I just finished a novel about a woman who inherits a crumbling bakery in a small town and has to decide whether to sell it or learn to run it." She shrugged. "I have a weakness for stories about women who choose the hard thing."

"Of course you do."

The food arrived, and they ate. Brandon cut into his chicken with the same deliberate attention he applied to everything. Grace noticed that he tasted each element separately before combining them. It was such a small thing, and yet it felt revealing. Even here, over a simple meal, he paid attention to details most people would miss. For reasons she couldn't have explained without sounding foolish, she found it endearing

"This is excellent," he said.

"The Village Eatery doesn't get enough credit. Everyone goes to Heavenly Delights, which is wonderful, but this place has its own thing."

A hint of curiosity moved across his face. "What is its thing?"

"Quiet competence." Grace looked at him over the rim of her water glass. "It doesn't announce itself. It just does the work well and trusts that people will notice."

Brandon held her gaze. "I know someone like that."

Grace looked down at her salmon and took a very deliberate bite, more to fill her mouth than because she was hungry. There were too many possible responses, and all of them felt more revealing than she was prepared to be.

They were halfway through their entrees when Brandon set his fork down and looked at her in a way that told her the next sentence wouldn't be about food, books, or the restaurant's ambiance.

"Grace, can I ask you something that I've been thinking about since yesterday?"

"Of course."

"At the park, you told me that you keep choosing faith. Not because you're certain, but because the alternative is emptier than the doubt." He turned his water glass between his fingers.

"I've been turning that over in my head all day. And what I keep coming back to isn't the theology. It's the fact that you and Anthony had completely different outcomes and completely different relationships with faith. But you both arrived at the same conclusion. He chose to believe his life mattered, even if it ended. And you chose to believe his death mattered, even though it broke you."

Grace set down her fork.

"The thing that keeps me up at night isn't whether God exists," Brandon said. "I've been asking that question for twelve years, and I'm no closer to an answer. The thing that keeps me up is whether it's possible to live with that question and still build a life that matters. A career... and a relationship." The word *"relationship"* sat between them like a confession neither had expected.

Her heart gave one hard, unsteady beat.

"I think it is," she said, keeping her voice gentler than the feeling inside her. "But I think it requires a willingness to live with uncertainty that most people find uncomfortable."

He gave a small breath of what might have been frustration or reluctant amusement. "I'm a scientist. I'm trained to eliminate uncertainty."

She couldn't help it. "And how's that working out for you?"

The question landed, and for one suspended moment, she wondered if she had been too direct. Brandon stared at her, and then he laughed. A real laugh that seemed to come from the center of his chest and surprised him as much as it surprised her.

"Not well," he admitted.

"Then maybe the experiment needs a new variable."

"Is that what you are? A new variable?"

"I'm a hospital chaplain who bakes sourdough bread and names things. I'll leave the variable classification to the scientist."

Brandon shook his head, and the look on his face was one she hadn't seen before. It was a look a man only wears when he's stopped trying to control what his face reveals. "You are something else, Grace Winslow."

She felt herself soften under the words, even as she tried to keep her tone light. "I'll take that as a compliment."

"It was meant as one."

A familiar voice pulled her attention toward the restaurant entrance. The Forresters had just walked in. Samantha's hand was tucked through the crook of her husband's arm. Daniel wore the slightly dazed look of a new father who had been released from the house for the first time in weeks.

"Grace!" Samantha spotted them and grinned. "Dr. Lawson. What a nice surprise."

Brandon stood to greet them. "Sam, Daniel. Good to see you both. Date night?"

"Our first since Elijah was born." Daniel's voice carried the mix of relief and guilt Grace recognized in every new parent she had ever counseled. "My sister Miranda and her husband Noah practically pushed us out the door. I think Mandy wanted Elijah all to herself."

"That sounds like Mandy." Grace smiled. "How's Elijah doing?"

"He's still a bundle of pure energy." Samantha laughed. "He has opinions about everything, especially food. Daniel's convinced he gets it from me."

"Because he does," Daniel said.

Brandon pulled out a chair for Samantha's coat, a gesture so automatic that Grace doubted he was aware of it. Samantha noticed, though. Her eyes moved between Brandon and Grace with the quick assessment of a nurse trained to read situations. The knowing look she gave Grace was subtle enough that Brandon missed it entirely.

"Thanks, but we'll let you two enjoy your evening," Samantha said. "You deserve a night out."

Grace nodded her silent thanks. "So do you." Samantha held her gaze for a beat. The tenderness in her expression said everything her words didn't. "Enjoy your dinner."

As the couple moved to their own table, Grace caught Daniel pulling out Samantha's chair, the same way Brandon had pulled out hers. Two different men shaped by different histories, yet marked by the same kind of quiet courtesy. The kind that rose without show or self-consciousness and stood when a woman entered the room. They had been raised to mean what they said and trust their words to stand on their own.

Brandon watched them settle into their table. A look passed over his face. Wistfulness, perhaps. Or longing so new he had not learned to hide it yet. He looked like a man watching a marriage with deep roots and wondering whether that kind of partnership might still be possible for him.

"They're good together," he remarked.

"They are." Grace picked up her fork, then set it back down. "They've also been through more than most people know. Sam lost both her parents when she was young. Daniel lost his first wife to a brain aneurysm. They didn't come to each other whole. They came to each other honest."

He absorbed this. "Honest," he repeated, as though testing the word.

"It's underrated as a foundation." Grace met his eyes. "Most people think love starts with attraction or compatibility. I think it starts with the willingness to let someone see the parts of you that you've worked the hardest to hide."

She didn't look away. Neither did he. The candle between them flickered, throwing light and shadow across his face. She was aware that she had just described exactly what had been unfolding between them for the last few weeks. Piece by piece. Truth by truth.

They ordered dessert. Brandon chose the chocolate torte. She chose the lemon tart because it reminded her of Willow's lemon bars, and because she wasn't ready for the evening to end. They split both desserts, trading plates back and forth across the table with the easy coordination that felt both innocent and intimate.

Brandon was in the middle of telling her about his sister Bethany's latest attempt to set him up with a colleague from her husband's bank when his pager cut through the sentence.

He looked at the display, and Grace saw the change happen almost instantly. The man who had been laughing about his sister's matchmaking attempts vanished. In his place sat Dr. Brandon Lawson, emergency physician, already mentally moving through triage priorities, possible impact, and patient urgency before he had read the full message.

"There was a multi-vehicle accident on the interstate. Pediatric casualties. They need me in now."

He was on his feet, pulling bills from his wallet and dropping them on the table with hands that had already gone steady. Grace felt the familiar shift in herself as well. The quick gathering of focus. The yielding of personal plans to someone else's emergency.

She stood. "I'm coming with you."

Brandon looked at her. "Grace, it's your night off. You don't have to."

"Those families will arrive at that hospital terrified and alone. They'll need someone before they need medicine." She picked up her purse. "I'm coming."

He didn't argue. He nodded once, and the gratitude in his expression was layered with a recognition she had seen building all evening. He looked like a man who spent his entire career walking into emergencies alone and had just realized he didn't have to.

They left the restaurant, their steps falling into the same rhythm they had found at the health fair, the park, and the hospital corridors. As they reached the parking lot, he turned to her.

"Grace. Thank you," Brandon said. "For tonight. For all of it."

His voice was low, and the urgency of the pager competed with an unfinished tenderness in his eyes that he didn't have time to say.

"I'll see you there," he said.

"Drive safe." Grace unlocked her car and watched him pull out of the lot ahead of her, his headlights slicing through the evening darkness. Then she followed, one hand tight on the steering wheel, whispering a prayer as she drove.

Lord, be with the families coming to the hospital tonight. Be with the children. And be with the doctors and nurses fighting for them, especially the one who's still learning that he doesn't have to fight alone. Amen.

Chapter 11

Brandon stripped off his gloves. The snap of the latex was barely audible over the ringing in his ears. His hands were steady. They were always steady. That was the cruelest part of emergency medicine. The hands kept working long after the rest of a person who wanted to stop.

Six hours. Six hours of every technique he knew, every medication in the protocol, every intervention he could justify, and a few he couldn't. The multi-vehicle accident on Interstate 185 delivered nine patients to Lakeside's emergency department in the space of forty minutes. Three of them were dead before midnight.

But Emma Robinson's death was the one that would follow him home.

The six-year-old arrived with injuries the triage team classified as non-survivable. Brandon didn't accept that classification. He stabilized her in the ER, fought the internal bleeding, and held her vitals together with interventions that bordered on desperation.

When Sebastian arrived to transport her to pediatric surgery, Brandon handed her off with a feeling he recognized, in retrospect, as hope. Not clinical optimism, but a hope that belonged in churches, not operating rooms.

Sebastian's call came at one forty-seven in the morning.

"We lost her, Brandon." Sebastian's voice had gone hollow, the way a surgeon's voice goes when he's done everything right, and it hadn't made a difference. "Her body couldn't recover from the trauma. I'm sorry."

Brandon had been sitting in the corridor outside the surgical suite, still in his stained scrubs, when Grace found him. She had spent the last four hours with Emma's parents, sitting in the family consultation room, holding their hands, and saying the things chaplains say when there's nothing left to say.

When she saw Brandon, she didn't speak. She sat down beside him in the hallway and stayed there until Sebastian came through the doors.

Then she went back to the family. Brandon watched her walk into that room, knowing what she was about to tell them. Knowing that the words would break those parents apart. Knowing that she would sit with the wreckage because that was what she did.

He watched the surgical suite doors swing closed, and the hallway fell silent.

He should have gone home. He had only come in because he was on call. His car sat in the parking garage, and the drive to his apartment was fifteen minutes of familiar roads his muscle memory could navigate while the rest of him shut down.

Instead, he walked through the hospital's side exit and crossed the street toward Providence Park.

The park was officially closed. A low chain barrier stretched across the entrance, more suggestion than prohibition. He ducked beneath it and kept walking. The gravel crunched under his shoes, and the sound was the loudest thing in the world. Streetlamps threw pools of gold light between the oaks, and the May air carried a chill that had no business being this sharp in Georgia during the spring.

He reached the pond and dropped onto the bench where he and Grace had sat two days ago. It had been forty-eight hours since he held her late husband's letter and listened to a dead man's faith speak louder than twelve years of his own doubt. Forty-eight hours since he picked up a silver feather, put it in his pocket, and drove home, wondering whether the universe was trying to tell him what he spent twelve years refusing to hear.

Now a child was dead, and the universe had not a thing to say about it.

Emma's chart replayed in his mind. Every choice. Every dosage. Every minute he believed the next intervention would be the one that turned the tide. Logic told him her injuries were incompatible with life. Logic told him that truth from the moment the ambulance doors opened. But logic was useless against the memory of her small fingers gripping his hand, or the sound her mother made when Sebastian walked into the consultation room.

He pressed the heels of his hands against his eyes. He was forty-three years old. He should have been past the point where a single case could dismantle him. But a child's death had a way of making all the years of training and all the carefully constructed defenses feel like paper walls in a hurricane.

He dropped his hands and stared at the water. The pond reflected the moon in broken fragments, scattered by a breeze that smelled like rain.

"What's the point? I mean... what's the point of any of it?" he said aloud, to no one.

"Rough night?"

Brandon's head came up. A man was approaching along the path, moving with the slow, deliberate pace of someone whose body had learned patience by necessity. He leaned on a carved wooden cane, and his silver hair caught the lamplight like a signal fire. His face was deeply lined, etched by decades of weather and expression. Despite the hour, he carried himself with the unhurried calm of a man who was exactly where he intended to be.

Under any other circumstances, Brandon would've been startled. It was after three in the morning, and he was in a closed public park. But weariness stripped away his usual vigilance. The stranger's presence felt less like an intrusion and more like an arrival.

"Something like that." Brandon gestured to the space beside him on the bench. "You're up early."

"Or late, depending on how you look at it." The man settled onto the bench with careful, deliberate movements and propped his cane against the armrest. A silver cross hung from a thin chain around his neck. His hands, resting on his knees, were gnarled and calloused. "I'm Liam."

"Brandon." The handshake was brief. Liam's grip was surprisingly firm, and his skin was warm despite the chill in the air.

Liam's gaze drifted toward the hospital, its lights visible through the trees. "Medical work can be heavy. Especially on nights like this."

The muscles along Brandon's neck stiffened. "How'd you know I work at the hospital?"

"The scrubs." Liam nodded toward Brandon's rumpled top. "And the way you're sitting. Like a man with a load he can't put down." His eyes, sharp and clear despite the deep creases surrounding them, held no judgment, only recognition. "I've known a few healers over the years."

A fraction of the pressure behind Brandon's ribs eased. He didn't know why. He didn't know this man. But the words came out anyway, pulled by a need that overrode every instinct telling him to be cautious.

"We lost a child tonight. Six years old. She was in a car with her grandmother when a drunk driver hit them on the interstate." The words came out flat, stripped of inflection, the way they did when the grief outgrew language. "Her grandmother died on impact. But the little girl held on for hours. We tried everything."

Liam nodded. His face carried a sorrow that looked old and familiar, the kind that comes from sitting with loss so many times that it's become a companion rather than a stranger. "You fought for her."

"I failed her."

"Is that what you believe?"

"She's dead." Brandon's voice cracked on the word. He pressed his palms against his thighs to still the tremor in his hands. "What else would I call it?"

Liam was quiet for a while. His fingers tapped a slow rhythm against his cane. Brandon heard the distant sound of a train passing through the far side of town, its whistle thinned by distance into a note that was almost musical.

"Do you think preventing death is the only measure of a doctor's success?" Liam asked.

"That's literally the definition of the job."

Liam tilted his head. "Is it? What about the child's parents? They spent hours watching you and the other doctors and nurses fight for their daughter. They saw a man refuse to give up on a little girl who wasn't his own. Do you think that counted for nothing?"

"She's still dead."

Liam spoke without hurry, without apology. "Yes... and they'll carry that for the rest of their lives. But they'll never have to wonder whether anyone cared enough to fight for her. That isn't a small thing, Brandon. For a grieving parent, that is the difference between a world that makes no sense and a world that still has people willing to stand between a child and the dark... even when they know they may lose."

A night heron landed near the water's edge with a quiet splash. Brandon watched the ripples spread across the reflected moon, each one reaching farther than the one before.

"I had a mentor once." His words came out rough at the edges. "A physician. She believed that doctors were instruments of healing, not the source of it. She said every surgery was a kind of partnership between the surgeon's hands and whatever put the surgeon there."

"What happened to her?"

"Cancer. Brain cancer. She was thirty-four." He swallowed against the ache that rose without warning. "She never stopped believing, not even at the end. Not even when the treatments failed, and the prayers went unanswered, and her body turned against her. She died with more faith than I've ever had in my entire life."

Liam studied him. "And you've been angry about that ever since."

It wasn't a question. Brandon looked at the old man and felt the accuracy of the observation settle into the center of his chest, into the place where he had been carrying his anger for twelve years like shrapnel he couldn't cut out.

"I've been angry at a God I'm not even sure exists," he responded. "And that may be the most useless kind of anger there is."

Liam's mouth curved into a small, knowing expression. "Or the most honest. You wouldn't be this angry at someone you'd stopped believing in entirely."

Brandon opened his mouth to argue, but found he couldn't. The old man had just put his finger on the truth that Brandon spent years avoiding. His anger at God wasn't proof of disbelief. It was proof of a relationship that had never fully died, no matter how hard he tried to smother it.

"She used to say that bearing witness is its own kind of medicine," Brandon said. He wasn't sure why he kept talking. But the words felt necessary, like setting a bone that had healed wrong and needed to be rebroken before it could mend properly. "I never understood what she meant until tonight."

"What did you understand tonight?"

Brandon looked at the hospital through the trees. The ER's lights glowed red against the retreating darkness. He could see the shape of the building he walked in and out of a thousand times. But this time, he saw it not as the place where he had fought and lost, but as the place where he had stayed.

"That I couldn't save Emma. But I was there. And my friend Grace was there. And the nurses were there. And every single person in that hospital treated that child's life as though it mattered, even when we knew the outcome. Even when the numbers told us to stop."

He pressed two fingers against his mouth for a moment, then let his hand fall. "Maybe that's what my mentor meant..."

Liam's face broke into a smile that changed the entire landscape of his weathered features. The lines around his eyes deepened, and the lamplight caught the silver at his temples. For a disorienting moment, he looked like a man who had heard exactly what he had been waiting to hear.

"Now you're getting somewhere," he said.

They sat together for a while longer. The sky had begun to lighten at the eastern edge, the first gray suggestion of dawn pressing against the darkness. The night heron took flight from the pond's edge, its wings beating slow and heavy over the water.

"I still don't understand why children have to suffer," Brandon said. "Or why some people live and others don't."

Liam looked toward the hospital. "Maybe understanding isn't the point. Maybe showing up is."

Brandon rose from the bench, staring out into the night. His body ached with a bone-deep tiredness that sleep alone couldn't touch. Across the park, through the trees, the hospital's lights pulsed against the coming dawn.

"I should go," he said. "I need to try to get some rest before my next shift."

"Rest well." Liam's voice carried a depth of kindness that shouldn't have been possible from a stranger. "Healers need their strength."

Brandon turned to say goodbye, but the bench was empty.

He blinked. He looked up the path in both directions. The gravel was undisturbed. The lamplight illuminated deserted walkways in every direction. There was no retreating figure, no sound of footsteps, no tap of a wooden cane on stone.

On the weathered wood of the bench, exactly where Liam had been sitting, lay a single silver feather.

Brandon picked it up. It wasn't hot, or pulsing, or supernatural in any way that his senses could dramatize. It was just warm, the way a living thing is warm, in a place where no living thing had been for the last several seconds.

He turned it between his fingers. It was identical to the one he found on the stone wall at the park entrance two days ago. Identical to the one Grace had found on her windshield. Fine barbs. Perfect alignment. A silver sheen that caught every available particle of light.

His scientific mind offered its usual objections. Sleep deprivation. Emotional distress. Confirmation bias. Pattern recognition in a brain desperate for meaning. All were reasonable explanations. All were perfectly adequate.

None of them accounted for the empty bench. None of them explained a man who arrived without sound, departed without a trace, and left behind a feather that shouldn't exist.

A verse from the Book of Psalms surfaced from the same buried place that produced *Jesus wept* on the night Frederick Brooks died. Childhood Sunday school. His mother's voice reciting it in the kitchen while she packed his lunch.

Where can I go from your Spirit? Where can I flee from your presence? If I go up to the heavens, you are there. If I make my bed in the depths, you are there.

He had spent twelve years fleeing, and a man with a wooden cane had just sat down beside him in the dark as though distance were irrelevant.

He slipped the feather into his shirt pocket, beside his hospital ID badge, and stood looking at the place where Liam had been.

"I don't know who you are or what you are," he said to the vacant bench. "But thank you."

Movement caught his eye near the park entrance. A figure crossing the street from the hospital parking lot, moving with purpose through the early morning haze. Grace. Her chaplain badge caught the streetlight as she scanned the pathways. A door opened inside his chest that he had forgotten was there. There was now an opening, one that happens when a person you've been trying *not* to need appears at the exact moment you need them most.

She had spent hours holding a family together through the worst night of their lives. And now, she had come looking for *him*.

Their eyes met across the dew-covered grass. She stopped at the park entrance, one hand on the chain barrier. Brandon stood at the bench with the feather in his pocket and the first suggestion of dawn at his back.

Neither of them spoke. The distance between them held everything that happened tonight. Emma's small hand. Sebastian's phone call. The Robinsons' grief. Liam's unhurried voice. The bench where a stranger sat and vanished. And underneath all of it, the growing, undeniable, terrifying recognition that the woman standing at the entrance to this park had become the person he most wanted to see at the end of the worst night of his life.

Brandon walked toward her. His legs were heavy with the night's toll, and his scrubs were stiff with dried sweat. His eyes burned from hours of fluorescent light and tears he hadn't allowed himself to shed. But he walked toward her because she was there. She had come, and that was enough.

Chapter 12

Grace hadn't planned what she would say when she found him. She spent the last four hours sitting with the Robinson family while their world ended in slow, unbearable pieces. When Brandon disappeared from the hospital corridor after Sebastian's phone call, she knew where he would go. He would go to the place where he ran, because Brandon Lawson processed grief the same way he processed everything else. In motion. Alone. As far from comfort as he could get.

She crossed the street from the hospital parking lot and found him walking toward her from the direction of the pond. His scrubs were dark with sweat. In the gray light of early dawn, his face was stripped of every defense she had ever seen him wear. He looked like he had come to the end of his reserves and didn't know what came next.

When he reached her, neither of them spoke. The chain barrier of the park entrance hung between them. The first birds of morning had begun their calls in the trees overhead, indifferent to what happened in the hospital that night.

"You came," he said. His voice was raw, stripped down to its barest register. "You should be home. You should be sleeping."

She was overcome by the tenderness in the reprimand. "So should you."

He looked at her. Whatever he saw in her face made the last of his composure fall away. He let out a slow exhale that seemed to empty him of everything he had been holding for the last six hours. His shoulders dropped. His hands, which had been clenched at his sides, opened as if he no longer had the strength to keep them closed.

"It's not safe for you to be out here at this hour," he said. Even now, the instinct to protect overrode everything else. "Let me walk you to your car."

"I'm parked across the street."

They crossed together. Brandon positioned himself between her and the road without appearing to think about it. Grace noticed it the way she noticed all the small things he did. The shortened stride to match hers. The chair pulled out at dinner. The quiet vigilance that seemed stitched into him so deeply, he probably no longer knew it was there.

Her car sat beneath a streetlight, alone in the hospital's visitor lot. The air carried a chill that had no business existing this close to summer. She pulled her cardigan tighter.

"I keep thinking about her parents," Brandon said. His voice was rough, as though the words were being pulled over gravel.

"You were there, Grace. You saw their faces when Sebastian came through those doors." His gaze went past her, to a point she couldn't perceive. "How do you tell people that every single thing we did still wasn't enough?"

She leaned against the driver's side door. The metal pressed cold through her blouse. "You tell them their daughter was loved and fought for until the very end. That's what happened tonight. Every person in that hospital treated Emma's life as though it mattered."

"It wasn't enough."

"No... it wasn't." She didn't soften it. She didn't add a qualifier. She let the truth stand because he needed someone who wouldn't flinch from it.

He turned toward her, and the distance between them was suddenly very small. She could see the exhaustion in the lines around his eyes, the dried salt of sweat at his hairline, the slight tremor in his hands that she knew came from hours of sustained adrenaline followed by the crash. He smelled like antiseptic, hospital soap, and coffee that had gone cold hours ago.

"Grace." His voice had dropped to barely a whisper. "When Emma died, and everything fell apart tonight, the first person I wanted to talk to was you. Not Sebastian. Not anyone else. Just you."

The confession landed in her hands, in her throat, in the backs of her knees. Not in her chest where romance novels put things. But in the places where her body registered what it meant to be chosen by a man who didn't choose easily.

"I know we come from different places," he said. "You have your faith. I have my questions. But I can't stop thinking about you. And I'm tired of pretending that what I feel is professional respect or collegial admiration or whatever other word I've been using to keep this at a distance."

He raised his hand and stopped. His fingers hovered near her face, and she could see them trembling. This was the tremor of a man asking permission without words.

She didn't move away.

His thumb traced the line of her cheekbone, and his fingers rested against the curve of her jaw. His hand was calloused and warm and slightly unsteady. The tenderness of the touch undid her sealed-shut grief in the space of a single breath.

"Grace," he said again, and her name in his mouth sounded different than it had ever sounded. Heavier. More deliberate, as though he were speaking it for the first time.

She closed the distance.

The kiss wasn't what she expected. It wasn't the sweep of orchestral music or the rush of blood she remembered from her early days of dating when everything was new and electric. It was entirely its own. It was the rough scratch of a jaw that hadn't been shaved in twenty hours. It was the faint bitterness of cold hospital coffee on his lips. It was the slight catch of his breath when her mouth met his, as though he had been bracing for her rejection and didn't know what to do with being met with fervor instead.

His free hand came to rest on her waist, tentative, as though she were precious and he knew it. Her own hands found the front of his scrub top, her fingers curling into the fabric. She felt his heart hammering beneath the thin cotton. The rhythm was fast and uneven. Knowing that this controlled, disciplined man's heart was racing because of her sent a current through her entire body, entirely physical, entirely specific to him.

When his fingers threaded into her hair, a sound escaped her that she hadn't made in years. A small, helpless intake of breath that came from a place beneath her composure, beneath the chaplain's poise, beneath the armor she wore for everyone else. She was just a woman being kissed by a man who was shaking. That vulnerability, his, not hers, was what undid her.

She kissed him back. And not with the restraint of a widow testing the waters. She kissed him the way she wanted to since they were in the parking garage. Since the corridor outside Gabrielle's room. Since the moment on the park bench when he held her late husband's letter in his hands and looked at her as though she had entrusted him with a gift he didn't know he had been yearning for.

And then she stopped.

She pulled back just enough to break the contact and feel the cold air rush into the space between their mouths. Her forehead rested against his. Her breath came in uneven bursts that fogged in the morning chill.

"I can't." The words scraped out of her. They tasted wrong. Her body still leaned toward him, still reached for the warmth she had just stepped away from. "I'm sorry, Brandon. I can't do this."

His hands immediately fell away. She could see the effort it took, the conscious unfurling of his fingers, the deliberate step backward. He didn't look angry. He looked confused, and underneath the confusion, afraid.

"Did I misread this?"

Grace pressed her palms flat against the car door behind her, bracing against the metal's cold solidity. "No... you didn't misread anything. That's the problem."

She could still feel the impression of his mouth on hers. She could still smell the coffee and the hospital soap. Her body was a traitor, still humming with the contact, still wanting to close the distance again.

"I don't know how to do this." The honesty cost her more than the kiss had. "I've spent years building a life around service. My work, my ministry, my faith... all of it is built on the idea that I'm fully available to other people. And standing here with you, all I want is... is to be unavailable. To everyone except you. And that scares me."

Brandon leaned against the car beside her. The few inches between their shoulders felt like a canyon. "You're allowed to want things for yourself, Grace."

She looked at him. "Am I?" she asked.

The question wasn't rhetorical. She needed him to understand. "Since Anthony died, every time I've wanted anything for myself, it's felt like a betrayal. I feel like I'm betraying his memory, my calling, and... and the woman I promised God I'd become." Her voice cracked. "What if the reason I'm so good at taking care of everyone else is because it keeps me from having to figure out who I am without a role to play?"

The question hung in the predawn air. She heard it leave her mouth and recognized it as the truest thing she had said in months. Truer than the prayer at the kitchen table. Truer than the confession to Pastor Wilson.

This was the fear underneath all the other fears, the one she had been circling since the parking garage, since the corridor, and since the first night in the supply closet when Brandon Lawson made her laugh, and she realized she missed the sound of her own laughter.

He was quiet. She watched him take in her words the way he did everything, systematically, turning each piece over, looking for the variable that would unlock the equation.

At last, he spoke. "The woman standing in front of me right now... scared and honest and showing up at four in the morning for a man she barely knows... that isn't a role, Grace. That is *exactly* who you are."

She blinked, and a tear escaped. Just one. She brushed it away with the back of her hand.

"I need time," she said. "I need to think. And I need to pray before I say anything I'm not ready to stand behind."

He straightened. "I understand," he replied. She could see him rebuilding the composure that the kiss had dismantled, brick by deliberate brick. "I meant what I said, Grace. My feelings for you are real. Whatever you decide, that won't change."

She opened her car door and situated herself behind the wheel. "Thank you... for tonight. Thanks for trusting me and... and for being the kind of man who walks a woman to her car at four in the morning, even when he can barely stand."

Grace pulled out of the parking lot, and in her rearview mirror, Brandon stood beneath the streetlight watching her taillights until she turned the corner. She gripped the steering wheel with both hands and didn't cry. Not yet. That would come later, at home, in the shower, where no one could see the chaplain come apart.

The lunch crowd at Heavenly Delights had thinned by the time Grace pushed through the door. She managed a few hours of restless sleep, a shower, and three attempts at prayer that produced nothing except the growing certainty that she needed to talk to Carmen.

Willow looked up from behind the counter. Her dark brown hair was escaping its bun after a morning of work, and flour dusted her apron.

"Grace. Perfect timing. I just pulled a batch of lemon scones from the oven." She paused, studying Grace's face with the intuition that made her the person half of Brookside confided in. "You look like you need one."

"I need several." Grace scanned the diner. "Is Carmen here?"

"Back corner booth." Willow reached for a coffee pot. "I'll bring you both fresh cups. Go sit down."

She wove through the remaining lunch tables to the corner booth where Carmen sat with a stack of case files and her reading glasses perched on her nose. She looked up as Grace slid into the opposite seat. Grace watched Carmen's assessment kick in. There was a quick scan of her face, a keen observation of the shadows lingering under her eyes, and the conclusion that was most likely forming before Grace could utter a word.

"The hospital was terrible last night," Grace said. "We lost a six-year-old. Emma Robinson. Drunk driver on the interstate."

Carmen's hand was across the table before Grace finished the sentence, closing hard over hers. For one fragile second, Grace thought she might cry right there in the booth.

"What happened?" Carmen asked.

"Her grandmother died on impact. Emma held on for hours. Sebastian took her to surgery, and Brandon and I stayed at the hospital. I sat with her parents through the whole thing. When Sebastian came out..." Grace stopped and swallowed. "It never gets easier. Especially with children."

"Of course it doesn't." Carmen's voice was firm and grounding. "You say what you always say. That it's terrible and unfair and that you're not going anywhere. And that's enough. It's always been enough."

Grace picked at the edge of a napkin. "I know. And that's what I did. But it's what happened afterward that has me sitting in your booth looking like this."

Willow arrived with coffee and a plate of warm lemon scones. She set them down with a kind look and returned to the kitchen without asking questions. Grace wrapped her hands around the mug.

"I kissed Brandon this morning."

Carmen's coffee mug stopped halfway to her lips. She set it down, a soft click of ceramic against wood. "Where?"

"At Providence Park. Around four-thirty this morning."

Carmen closed her eyes and opened them. "Four-thirty th is... alright, Grace. Start from the beginning, and don't leave anything out."

She told her. The accident. The hours in the ER. Emma's death. Finding Brandon at the park. Walking to the car. His confession that she was the first person he wanted after the worst night of his career. His hand on her face. The kiss. The pulling away.

Carmen listened without interrupting, which was unusual for her and therefore a measure of how seriously she was taking this. She didn't reach for her coffee. She didn't break off a piece of scone. She just watched Grace's face.

"You pulled away," Carmen clarified when Grace finished.

"Yes."

"Why?"

Grace let out a breath that did nothing to ease the pressure in her chest. The answer had been circling inside her for hours now, wearing grooves through every thought.

"Because I don't know who I am outside of being the person who takes care of everyone else." The sentence came out cleaner than it had at four o'clock this morning, polished by a morning of anguished replaying. "And I'm scared that wanting someone this much will make me a person I don't recognize."

Carmen removed her reading glasses and set them on the table. "Grace, I need to tell you a truth. And I need you to hear it as me being your friend, and not as me being your colleague."

Carmen's voice was direct but not unkind. "You're using your ministry as a bunker. You've been doing it ever since Anthony died, and everyone who loves you has been too polite to say it. You haven't been fully available to other people because you love serving... you've been making yourself available because it means you never have to be fully available to *yourself*."

The words landed like a diagnosis. Accurate. Clinical. Devastating.

"Carmen..."

"Wait, I'm not finished." Carmen held up a finger. "Did loving Anthony affect your ability to be a good chaplain?"

"No." Grace didn't even second-guess the answer.

"Did being married make you less committed to serving others?"

"No, but that was different. Anthony and I shared the same..." She stopped herself too late, the old refrain rising up like a reflex.

"You and he shared the same faith... I know. You've said that. But let me ask you something." Carmen leaned forward. "After the health fair, Sofia asked me why you and the doctor with the sad eyes look at each other like you're living in a movie."

A smile cracked through Grace's fatigue before she could stop it. "Sofia said that?"

"She's ten. She picks up on everything adults think they're hiding." Carmen picked up her coffee again. "Here's what I see. I see a man who's spent his entire career fighting for other people. He doesn't know how to let anyone fight for him. And I see a woman who's spent the last five years convincing herself that needing someone is the same as failing at her calling. You're both wrong. And you're both so stubborn that it's going to take a miracle to make you admit it."

Grace's fingers tightened around her mug. "A miracle already happened. I kissed him."

"You kissed him and then ran away. That doesn't count." Carmen broke off a piece of scone, the crust flaking under her fingers. "What counts is what you do next."

Grace stared at the table. Outside the diner window, afternoon traffic moved in its usual unhurried rhythm. People went about their ordinary lives with their ordinary problems. She envied them.

"He told me his feelings are real," Grace said.

"And yours?"

"Mine are too." She looked at Carmen. "That's what terrifies me. Because if this fails, I don't just lose a colleague or a friend. I lose the person who's made me feel like there might be a version of me who's allowed to want a life for herself."

The sharpness in Carmen's face receded. Underneath it was the woman raising a daughter alone, navigating her own losses and her own questions about what she deserved.

"*Amiga.* That version of Grace has always been there. She's just been buried under years of excellent excuses." She reached across the table and squeezed Grace's hand. "Talk to him. Not as a chaplain with a speech about boundaries and professional guidelines.

Talk to him as the woman who kissed him at four in the morning and meant it."

Grace sat with that. She drank her coffee and ate a lemon scone that tasted like Willow had baked forgiveness into the batter. She let Carmen's words do what they needed to do, which was take apart, with the unflinching love only a best friend can wield, every defense Grace had built between herself and the possibility of being happy.

"What if his questions about faith shake mine?" Grace asked. It was the last wall standing, and she needed Carmen to address it.

"Then your faith gets shaken, and you find out what's left standing after the shaking stops." Carmen's eyes were steady. "Any belief that can't survive a good question was never worth holding onto in the first place."

Grace exhaled, long, slow, and shaky. A tightness she had been carrying since four-thirty that morning, or maybe since Anthony's funeral, or maybe since the first night in the supply closet when a skeptical doctor accepted a cup of coffee from a stranger and said thank you as though he meant it, finally let go.

"Okay." Grace said it again, just to feel the shape of it. "Okay."

Carmen's eyebrow arched. "Okay... what?"

"Okay, I'm going to talk to him." Saying it out loud made it real in a way the thought hadn't.

Carmen's face broke into a grin. "*Gracias a Dios.* I was running out of ways to say the same thing."

Grace laughed. The sound surprised her. It was the first real laugh she had produced since the kiss. It felt like proof that the woman underneath the chaplain was still breathing.

"Thank you," she said. "For not letting me talk myself out of this."

"That's what I'm here for." Carmen picked up her case files and tapped them into a neat stack. "Now go home and get some *actual* sleep. And when you're ready, call that man and tell him what you want."

Grace stood and hugged her friend, holding on for an extra beat. Carmen patted her back with the firm, no-nonsense affection that defined everything she did.

"One more thing," Carmen said as Grace pulled away.

Grace paused. "What?"

"If you hurt that man, I'll have words with you. He has enough people in his life who disappoint him. Don't be another one."

The warning was delivered with a half-smile, but Grace heard the seriousness underneath it. Carmen wasn't only protecting Grace. She was protecting Brandon, too. That told Grace everything she needed to know about how clearly her friend saw both of them.

"I won't," she promised.

"Good." Carmen sat back down and put her reading glasses on. "Now leave. I've got eleven case files, Sofia has a soccer game at five, and I still need to figure out what to feed that child for dinner."

Grace walked to her car in the afternoon sun. The light was golden and forgiving, the kind of late spring light that made the oak-lined streets look like they belonged in a painting. She sat behind the wheel and didn't start the engine. Instead, she folded her hands in her lap and closed her eyes.

Lord, I'm scared. I'm scared of wanting something that might not work. I'm scared of being wrong about him. I'm scared of being right about him. But I'm more scared of spending the rest of my life hiding behind good work to avoid the risk of being known. Help me be brave. Not chaplain-brave. Not ministry-brave. Just brave. The regular kind. The kind it takes to love somebody when you've already lost everything once. Amen.

She opened her eyes. She started the car. And she drove home through Brookside's quiet streets, already composing in her head the words she would say to Brandon Lawson when she was ready to say them.

Chapter 13

"YOU LOOK AWFUL." SEBASTIAN slid into the chair across from Brandon with two steaming coffee cups. "And I mean that with all the loyalty of a friend who's seen you at your worst."

Brandon accepted the cup. The hospital cafeteria hummed around them with the usual morning noise, the clink of silverware, the chatter of residents between rounds, and the persistent smell of burnt coffee and eggs that had been sitting under heat lamps for too long. Their corner table, marred by years of medical students carving their initials into the laminate, offered enough distance from the nearest occupied table for a conversation that Brandon wasn't sure he was ready to have.

"I kissed Grace."

Sebastian's coffee cup paused halfway to his mouth. He set it down. "When?"

"After Emma Robinson died. At four-thirty in the morning in the hospital parking lot." Brandon wrapped his hands around his cup. "She came looking for me at Providence Park. We walked to her car, and then I kissed her."

Sebastian was quiet for a moment, and Brandon was grateful for that. Another person might have filled the silence with questions, opinions, or some version of congratulations. Sebastian just sat with it, the same way he sat with bad lab results or unexpected complications, processing before speaking.

"How did she respond?"

"She kissed me back." Brandon stared at the table. "And then she pulled away. She said she couldn't do it. She said she didn't know how to want anything for herself without feeling like she was betraying her calling."

"That sounds like Grace."

"It does." Brandon looked up. "She asked for time. To think and pray. I told her I understood."

"Do you?"

"Not even a little." Brandon let out a breath and stared past Sebastian toward the beverage station, where an intern was trying and failing to get the orange juice machine to cooperate.

"I haven't felt this way about anyone in years. And the one person who makes me want to stop running from everything I've been avoiding is the one person whose entire life is built on the faith I can't bring myself to accept."

Sebastian leaned back in his chair. The cafeteria noise filled the pause. Someone dropped a tray near the beverage station, and the crash drew a few glances but no real attention. In a hospital, people were accustomed to loud noises at inconvenient moments.

"Can I tell you something about Sloane?" Sebastian asked.

Brandon looked at him. In six years of friendship, Sebastian had mentioned his wife in passing a hundred times but had rarely talked about their relationship in any depth.

"When I met her, I was the skeptic. Not about God exactly, but about organized faith. I grew up going to church because my parents expected it, not because I believed it. I went to medical school thinking I'd leave all of that behind."

He turned his coffee cup between his palms. "Then I met this woman at a campus fellowship meeting who talked about prayer the way I talked about surgical technique. She talked as if it were a skill that required practice and discipline. And instead of being impressed, I spent three months arguing with her about every theological inconsistency I could find."

Brandon could picture it. Sebastian, relentless and razor sharp, coming at a woman like Sloane with the full force of his intellect and probably mistaking resistance for clarity.

"What changed?" Brandon asked.

"She stopped arguing back." Sebastian smiled at the memory. "She invited me to volunteer at a free clinic she was helping to run. She was finishing her medical degree and a minor in social work at the same time. She said treating a body without understanding the life attached to it was only half the job."

He paused, and Brandon could hear the respect in the silence that followed. "I watched her coordinate care for families who had nothing. I watched her hold a mother's hand while that mother's son was getting a breathing treatment, and I watched her pray over that child without an ounce of performance in it. And I realized that her faith wasn't a theory she was defending. It was the thing that made her get out of bed every morning and go fight for people the system had forgotten."

Brandon thought of Grace. "That sounds familiar."

"It should." Sebastian met his eyes. "Brandon, I didn't marry Sloane because she answered my theological questions. I married her because the way she lived her life made me want to be a better version of myself. The faith came later. Slowly. In pieces. And honestly, there are still mornings when I scrub in for surgery, and I don't know whether the prayer I say before the first incision is habit or conviction. But I say it anyway, because the man I became through loving her is someone worth being."

Brandon stared at his coffee. The parallel was obvious. Sebastian wasn't a man who dealt in subtlety. But the story landed differently than any of the faith conversations Brandon had endured over the past few weeks. It felt like a confession offered from one man to another. More than that, it felt like a love story. And somehow that made it harder to dismiss.

"There's more." Brandon reached into his shirt pocket and withdrew the silver feather. He set it on the table between their coffee cups.

Sebastian looked at it, but he didn't touch it. "Where did you get that?"

"A man at Providence Park. The night Emma died." Brandon heard how strange it sounded and kept going anyway. "Silver hair.

Wooden cane. He sat on the bench beside me and talked to me for twenty minutes about loss and purpose and bearing witness."

Even now, Brandon could hear the man's voice with unsettling clarity, calm and steady, as if the words had found some deeper place to lodge.

"Then I turned around to say goodbye, and the bench was empty. No footsteps. No sound. Just this feather where he'd been sitting."

Sebastian looked at the feather, and then he looked at Brandon. His expression had shifted, the easy collegiality giving way to something more focused. "A silver-haired man with a wooden cane?"

The question put Brandon on alert. "You know someone who fits that description?"

"No. But you just described a figure that sounds remarkably similar to a man my daughter Rachel told me about."

Brandon felt his grip tighten around the coffee cup.

"She said she saw an old man with a cane watching the hospital from the parking lot one evening when Sloane was picking me up after a late shift. She said he smiled at her, and then, he wasn't there anymore." Sebastian paused. The cafeteria noise seemed to recede, or perhaps Brandon was just no longer hearing it. "I told her she was imagining things, but now... I'm not so sure."

Brandon frowned, mulling over the memories. "The description matches perfectly. Not to mention Gabrielle's silver birds in her drawings and the feather Grace found on her windshield." He picked up the feather, turning it between his fingers. "I don't know what it all means, but I'm done pretending it means nothing."

Sebastian nodded slowly. A long exhale escaped him. "That might be the most honest thing you've said in twelve years."

Brandon's phone vibrated with a text before he could respond. He glanced at the display and pushed back his chair.

Patient refusing treatment in the ER. Requesting spiritual support instead of medical intervention.

"Mind if I come?" Sebastian stood with him. "Families in crisis sometimes benefit from more than one perspective."

Brandon gave a short nod. Right now, he was glad for the company.

They reached the emergency department in three minutes. Brandon's stride ate up the linoleum, his shoes squeaking slightly where the floor had been recently mopped.

Samantha met them at the nurses' station. Her eyes looked tight in the way pediatric cases always made them look. Brandon knew that expression well. In a hospital, children changed the feel of an entire floor.

"Room three," she said, getting straight to the point. "Sixteen-year-old girl. Acute appendicitis. She has significant right lower quadrant pain, elevated white count, and a low-grade fever that's climbing. Her mother brought her in about an hour ago and consented to the initial exam. But the father arrived twenty minutes later, and he shut everything down. He's refusing consent for the CT scan, and he's refusing surgical evaluation. The family belongs to a congregation that believes medical intervention can obstruct God's direct healing."

Brandon kept his voice low, aware of how little privacy an emergency room really offered. Curtains, exhaustion, and basic courtesy were often the only things holding people's worst moments together.

"Why did the mother bring her in if they believe that?"

Samantha lowered her voice as well. "I talked to the mother while the father was parking. She told me their daughter had been in pain since yesterday evening, and it kept getting worse through the night. The mother got scared and brought her in while the father was at his early morning shift at the warehouse. When he arrived and found out where they were, he was upset. He feels the mother acted without consulting him and without consulting their pastor."

The dynamic made sense to him now. The mother's fear for her child had overridden the family's convictions, but the father felt blindsided. This wasn't a unified theological stance against medicine. It was a family in conflict, and the daughter was caught in the middle.

"How much time do we have?" he asked.

"If it's appendicitis, and everything points that way, we're looking at hours, not days. The risk of rupture increases significantly with every hour of delay." Samantha's mouth pressed into a hard line. "She's in real pain, Brandon."

He pushed open the door to room three. The girl lay curled on the gurney, her face ashen and slick with sweat. Her hands gripped the side rail, and her breathing came in shallow, ragged pulls.

Her mother sat beside her, one hand on the girl's forehead, her face torn between the terror of a parent watching her child suffer and the guilt of having defied her husband's authority.

The father stood at the foot of the bed. He was a thick-shouldered man in his forties, still wearing his work boots. His hands were clasped in front of him in a posture Brandon recognized instantly as prayer, but there was something else in it too. The man looked like he was trying to hold himself steady against a force already bigger than he was.

"Mr. and Mrs. Harmon. I'm Dr. Lawson, and this is Dr. Reid." Brandon kept his voice level. "I understand there are some concerns about your daughter's treatment. Can we talk about what's happening and what your family needs?"

The father raised his head. His eyes were red, and his jaw was set. Brandon realized with a start that the man wasn't angry. He was terrified.

"We believe God heals, Doctor." Mr. Harmon's voice was hoarse and scraped raw. "We've seen it in our congregation. People laid hands on, prayed over, and then healed. Our pastor teaches that relying on medicine shows a lack of faith in God's power."

"I brought her because she was screaming." Mrs. Harmon's voice broke on the last word, splintering. "She was screaming, and I couldn't just sit there and pray while my baby was screaming."

Brandon looked at the girl. According to the chart, her name was Rebekah. She was sixteen and weighed about a hundred and twenty pounds. Her vital signs were deteriorating in the way that appendicitis vitals deteriorated when the clock was running out. He could see the pulse fluttering too fast at her throat.

"Mr. Harmon, I respect your faith." Brandon said it and he meant it. The fact that he meant it surprised him almost as much as it would have surprised the Brandon of just a few weeks ago. "I understand that your beliefs are deeply important to you and to your family. I'm not here to argue with what you believe. But I need to tell you, as honestly as I can, what I see when I look at your daughter."

He sat down. Not at the computer. Not behind a chart. He pulled a chair to the foot of the bed and sat at the father's level, close enough that the conversation felt private even in the small room.

"Rebekah's symptoms are consistent with acute appendicitis. That means a small organ in her abdomen is inflamed. Based on her pain and her bloodwork, I'm very concerned that it's close to rupturing. If the appendix ruptures, the infection spreads throughout her abdominal cavity. That condition is called peritonitis, and it can be fatal."

Mrs. Harmon pressed her fist against her mouth.

"The standard treatment is a CT scan to confirm the diagnosis, followed by surgery to remove the appendix. The surgery is one of the most common procedures performed in this country. The recovery is typically quick, and the risk is low."

Brandon paused. "I'm asking you to let us run the CT scan. Not the surgery. Just the scan. That way, we can know exactly what we're dealing with. Can we start there?"

Mr. Harmon looked at his daughter. Rebekah's eyes were closed, and her breathing had become more labored in the last two minutes. His hands, still clasped, tightened until his knuckles blanched. Brandon could see the war playing out across his face, the love and the fear and the faith all tangled together.

"Just the scan," he conceded.

Brandon nodded at Samantha, who moved to prepare the orders. Sebastian stepped closer to the family, his white coat brushing against the gurney.

"Mr. Harmon, while the team prepares the scan, would it help if we contacted the hospital chaplain? She can pray with your family right here, right now, while the medical team does its work. Your faith and your daughter's care don't have to be in conflict."

The father's posture shifted, like a man finding a door he hadn't known was there. "A chaplain? One who would pray with us?"

"Her name is Grace Winslow. She's someone I trust deeply." Sebastian glanced at Brandon. "She has a gift for meeting people wherever they are, without judgment."

Mr. Harmon nodded. His wife reached for his hand, and he took it.

Brandon stepped into the hallway and paged Grace. She arrived in four minutes, her badge clipped to her cardigan, her hair in its professional bun. Their eyes met. The parking lot, the kiss, and the pulling away lived between them like something neither had fully set down. But they set it aside with the unspoken agreement of two professionals who had a child to help.

"What do we need?" Grace asked.

Brandon gave her the short version. Grace listened and asked two clarifying questions about the family's denomination. Then she walked into the room.

Through the open door, Brandon watched her introduce herself to the Harmons. She didn't sit behind authority. She pulled a chair to the mother's side, the same way he had pulled a chair to the father's, and asked the family to tell her about their faith.

She listened and didn't interrupt. When Mr. Harmon described miracles he had witnessed in his church, Grace nodded without challenge. When Mrs. Harmon described the terror of hearing her daughter scream, Grace placed her hand on the woman's arm and held it there.

Then she spoke. "Would you allow me to pray with you while the doctors take care of Rebekah? We can ask God to guide their hands and to be present in this room. Your prayers and their medicine can work together. One doesn't have to replace the other."

Mr. Harmon's face crumpled. Not with defeat, but with the relief of a man who had been given permission to be both faithful and afraid.

They prayed together, all four of them, Grace and the parents and Rebekah, who opened her eyes long enough to whisper *"Amen"* before another wave of pain closed them again.

The CT scan confirmed acute appendicitis with early signs of perforation. Grace stayed with the family while Sebastian presented the results and explained the surgical necessity. Mr. Harmon, who had been holding his wife's hand throughout the entire scan, looked at the images on the screen, looked at his daughter, and gave his consent.

"Please take care of my girl." His voice was rough. "And please let the chaplain stay."

"She isn't going anywhere," Brandon stated.

Grace remained with the Harmons through the surgery, through the waiting, through the moment when Sebastian emerged and told them Rebekah was going to be fine. She held Mrs. Harmon while the woman wept with relief, and she shook Mr. Harmon's hand when he thanked her for understanding what his family needed.

In the corridor afterward, Brandon stood beside Grace. The adrenaline of the case was still ebbing. The fluorescent lights buzzed overhead in the particular frequency that only hospital corridors produce.

"You were remarkable in there." His voice came out lower than he intended.

"Mr. Harmon told me what you did," Grace said. "He told me you pulled up a chair and sat at his level and talked to him like a person, not a problem. Two weeks ago, you would have argued the science and demanded the consent."

She was right. Two weeks ago, he would have been furious at the delay. He would have seen the father's faith as an obstacle to overcome, not a fear to address. He would have escalated to hospital administration and legal counsel before he ever sat down in a chair.

"Something's changed," he said.

"Yes." Grace looked at him. "Something has."

She didn't say more. She didn't need to. They both knew what had changed, and they both knew they weren't ready to name it in a hospital hallway.

Chapter 14

That afternoon, Grace met Brandon outside the pediatric consultation room. The Miller family had arrived for Gabrielle's two-week follow-up appointment. Gabrielle had apparently been telling every nurse on the floor that she needed to speak with Dr. Brandon and Miss Grace.

"Any idea what this is about?" Brandon asked as they approached the door.

"The nurse who called me said Gabrielle's been having vivid dreams and wants to share them with both of us." Grace adjusted the strap of her bag. "That's all I know."

They entered the consultation room. Gabrielle sat in a chair between her parents, legs swinging because her feet didn't reach the floor. She looked markedly better than the last time Grace had seen her at the health fair, but she wasn't yet the picture of full health.

There were still faint shadows under her dark eyes, but her color was good. When she saw them walk through the door, her face split into the kind of grin a child wears when she has been guarding a secret and finally gets to tell it.

"Dr. Brandon! Miss Grace!" She sat up straighter, her small hands gripping the edge of the chair. "I've been waiting for you."

Brandon knelt beside her chair, bringing himself to her eye level. "I hear you've got news for us."

Gabrielle nodded with exaggerated seriousness. "I keep having dreams about the man with the silver hair. The one I told you about before, with the birds."

Grace glanced at Tobias and Denise. Tobias gave a small nod, indicating they had already heard what Gabrielle was about to share and had decided to let her tell it in her own words. Denise's hand rested on her daughter's back.

"He's very nice," Gabrielle continued. "He has a cane, and he smells like the church does on Christmas morning. Like the candles." She tilted her head. "He told me some things, and he said I should tell you."

Grace kept her voice even and pastoral. "What did he say?"

Gabrielle looked at Brandon with the frank directness of a child who hadn't yet learned to cushion difficult truths.

"He said you lost somebody you loved a long time ago. A teacher. And he said that losing her made you very sad, and the sadness turned into something hard, like a rock you carry around." She paused, as though making sure the words were exactly right. "He said the rock is too heavy, and you should put it down."

Grace watched Brandon's face. He didn't move. His hands were still at his sides, his breathing even. But a single muscle worked in his jaw, the only visible sign that an eight-year-old had just described, with devastating accuracy, the sorrow he had carried for the past twelve years.

Gabrielle had no way of knowing about Dr. Whitmore. She had no context for Brandon's faith crisis or the specific shape of his loss. And yet she just laid it bare in the plain, unvarnished language of a child reporting what she had seen in a dream.

"He said something else." Gabrielle turned to Grace, and the shift in her attention felt like a spotlight swinging over. "He said you're brave, Miss Grace. But he said being brave for other people isn't the same as being brave for yourself. He said you know the difference, and it's time for you to choose."

The words landed in the space below the professional composure to where the real Grace lived. She pressed her lips together and blinked twice, a response rising in her that she had no words for.

"Was there anything else?" Brandon's voice stayed level and controlled, but Grace could hear the effort it cost him.

Gabrielle thought about it, her forehead scrunching. "He said that the feathers are gifts. And that you should stop trying to figure out where they come from and just be glad they're there." She grinned suddenly, the solemnity breaking like sunlight through clouds. "I like the feathers. In my dreams, the birds drop them when they sing. They're really pretty."

Tobias cleared his throat. "We don't fully understand the dreams," he said. "But our daughter's been insistent about sharing this with both of you. We felt it was important to honor that."

"We're grateful you did," Grace said.

They spent a few more minutes with the family, reviewing Gabrielle's progress. Grace listened, nodded, asked the appropriate questions, but Gabrielle's words kept circling back through her thoughts. *It's time for you to choose.*

Sebastian's latest notes indicated continued improvement across all indicators, with another round of bloodwork scheduled for the following week. The neurology team officially closed their consultation, noting only: *Unexplained spontaneous resolution. No further intervention is recommended.*

When the Millers left, Grace followed Brandon into the hallway. He leaned back against the wall and closed his eyes.

"An eight-year-old girl who has no knowledge of my history, no access to my personal life, and no reason to know anything about my mentor's death, just told me to put down the rock I've been carrying for twelve years."

He opened his eyes and looked at her. "And she told you to stop being brave for everyone else and start being brave for yourself."

Grace leaned against the opposite wall. The corridor was empty. Afternoon light slanted through a window at the end of the hall, casting a long rectangle of gold across the linoleum between their feet.

"I don't have an explanation for any of this," she stated.

"Neither do I." Brandon straightened. "But I told Sebastian this morning that I'm done pretending it means nothing... and I meant it."

He looked at her. The expression on his face was nothing like the guarded, clinical mask she had grown accustomed to. It was open.

Unfinished. The face of a man standing at the edge of a threshold he hadn't yet decided to cross.

"Grace, when you're ready to talk about us... about what happened, I'll be here."

"I know you will." She pushed off the wall, her palms pressing briefly against the cool surface. "And I'm getting closer to ready than I was this morning."

She walked toward the elevator. He didn't follow. She could feel his gaze on her back the whole way. When she reached the doors and glanced over her shoulder, he was still standing exactly where she had left him, shoulders relaxed in a way she couldn't remember seeing before.

Chapter 15

G ΓΡΑΣΕ PARKED OUTSIDE COTTONWOOD Faith Community Center as the first bruise-colored clouds gathered above the dogwood trees. The weather had been brewing all week, the air heavy and electric in the way that every Georgian recognized as a warning of an impending storm.

Four days had passed since she told Carmen she was going to talk to Brandon. Four days since she drove home, composing words in her head. She hadn't yet said any of them. It wasn't because she wasn't ready. The hospital had swallowed every spare minute with Gabrielle's follow-up appointments, the Harmon family's emergency surgery, and the relentless pulse of spring in the ER. Every time she saw Brandon in the corridors, the words she rehearsed seemed to evaporate, losing their substance.

She needed more than courage. She needed spiritual anchoring.

Pastor Wilson's office was unchanged. Afternoon light poured through tall windows, illuminating the cracked theology spines and the small wooden cross on his desk. He looked up as she entered, his reading glasses slipping down his nose.

"Grace. I was hoping you'd come by. Please, sit down."

She sank into the leather armchair, and for a moment, she didn't speak. She didn't need to. Pastor Wilson had known her long enough to recognize the posture of a woman carrying too many things at once.

"You already talked to Carmen," he began. "And you already know what you need to do about Brandon. So that isn't why you're here."

Grace almost smiled. "No."

"Then why?"

She let out a breath and looked down at her hands. "Because I'm about to walk into a crisis, and I need to hear something true before I do."

Her fingers tightened together. "I've spent the last two weeks watching Brandon sit with terrified families and treat them like people instead of problems. I've watched him soften in places I don't think he knew were there. And I keep telling myself that what I'm seeing is faith, that it's God at work in his life. But honestly, part of me wonders if I'm only seeing what I want to see. Maybe he's not changing in any spiritual sense. Maybe he's simply becoming a better doctor, and I'm the one attaching meaning to it because I need there to be meaning."

Pastor Wilson removed his glasses and cleaned them with the edge of his handkerchief. The gesture was so familiar that it grounded her more than any words could have.

"Grace, do you remember Galatians chapter 6, verse 2?"

She nodded. "*'Carry each other's burdens, and in this way you will fulfill the law of Christ.'*"

"That verse doesn't say carry everyone's burdens by yourself." His words carried the quiet firmness she had come to depend on. "It says carry each other's burdens. Mutually. Together."

He set his glasses back on his nose, and the lenses caught the afternoon light for a moment. "Perhaps what you're seeing in Brandon isn't projection. Perhaps it's recognition. You see him becoming someone willing to share a load that he's been carrying alone. And that unsettles you, because you've been carrying yours alone, too."

The words landed cleanly, with the kind of precision that only came from someone who loved her enough to tell the truth without softening it into something easier.

Before she could respond, Pastor Wilson's phone buzzed. He glanced at the screen, and the lines around his mouth deepened.

"Emergency weather alerts," he said. His voice had changed, carrying an edge she rarely heard.

He turned his computer screen toward her as a banner scrolled across the top of the page. Grace leaned forward, her hands gripping the arms of the leather chair.

The National Weather Service is tracking a severe storm system. Multiple supercell thunderstorms with rotation. EF-3 or higher tornadoes are possible. Brookside is in the projected path. They're saying it could arrive as early as Friday evening.

The air left her lungs as she read the screen. Spring storms were a part of life in Georgia, something you learned to watch and wait out. But the language on the screen was different from the usual warnings people half-ignored while they checked porch furniture and lit candles just in case.

EF-3 or higher. Projected path.

The words registered in her body before they fully registered in her mind. "I need to get to the hospital," she said, already reaching for her phone.

"I'll mobilize the churches." He was already reaching for his phone. "Cottonwood and New Hope can serve as emergency shelters. And Grace... whatever this storm brings, we'll face it together. That's what the body of Christ is for. I'll have volunteers ready by tomorrow morning."

Relief moved through her so quickly that it almost felt like weakness. Almost. "Thank you, Pastor."

"Grace." He waited until she looked at him. "Whatever happens this weekend. You're not carrying it alone. Remember that."

She called Carmen from the parking lot, the engine still running, her eyes on the darkening sky.

"I was about to call you," Carmen said. She had already shifted into professional mode, her cadence clipped and efficient. "The hospital is going to full alert. Dr. Martinez has activated mass casualty protocols. Are you seeing these weather reports?"

"I just saw them at Pastor Wilson's." Grace's gaze kept pulling back to the sky, to that unsettling greenish light seeping through the cloud base. "How quickly do we need to mobilize?"

"We need to start right now", Carmen responded. "We'll need spiritual support teams on standby. And we'll need a plan for staff families. Parents can't focus on saving lives if they're worried about their children during a tornado." Carmen paused, and Grace heard her exhale hard. "I'm already calling the church childcare coordinators. Can you handle the chaplain mobilization?"

"I'll have additional chaplains at the hospital by morning. Pastors Morrison and Wilson are already organizing shelter volunteers."

"Good. I'll see you at the emergency meeting in forty-five minutes."

Grace ended the call and pulled out of the parking lot. The sky to the west had taken on the greenish cast that meant business. She drove toward Lakeside with both hands on the wheel and a prayer running through her mind that was less formal and more desperate than anything she would have admitted in a professional setting.

Lord, protect this town. Protect these people. And help me be useful when it matters most.

She pressed the accelerator a little harder and watched the sky.

Chapter 16

THE HOSPITAL CONFERENCE ROOM was standing room only. Grace slipped into a chair near the back and found Brandon immediately. He sat beside Dr. Martinez and the ER team, his posture locked in the rigid stillness she had come to recognize as his crisis mode. Their eyes met across the room.

Only for a moment.

Two seconds, maybe less. Long enough for recognition. Long enough for the ache between them to flare and settle again. Long enough to acknowledge what hadn't yet been said and what would have to wait. Then the moment was gone, and Grace felt the same silent agreement pass between them that she felt in her own chest.

Right now, the town came first.

Janet Crawford, the hospital administrator, opened the meeting. "We're facing an unprecedented weather emergency. Multiple tornado watches are active across our region, with the possibility of EF-3 or stronger storms striking Brookside directly."

She introduced a meteorologist from the local National Weather Service office, who appeared on the conference room screen. Josiah Hamilton's expression left no room for optimism.

"This storm system has all the markers of a major outbreak," he said. "We're tracking multiple supercells with dangerous rotation. Atmospheric conditions are, frankly, textbook for violent, long-track tornadoes. Prepare for sustained winds that could exceed one hundred and fifty miles per hour."

The room took that in without a sound. No one shifted. No one coughed.

Dr. Martinez stood. Her voice cut through the stillness with the authority of someone who had commanded trauma bays through worse nights than this.

"Mass casualty protocols are active as of this meeting. The ER will serve as the primary triage center. Every department should prepare for overflow trauma patients and for possible structural damage to the hospital itself."

She looked at Grace. "Chaplain Winslow. We'll need full-scale spiritual support. Not only for families, but for our own staff. People are going to be working under conditions that test every limit they have."

Grace straightened in her seat. "I'm coordinating with local churches. We'll have additional chaplains positioned throughout the hospital within hours. Pastors Morrison and Wilson are mobilizing volunteers for community shelters as well."

Carmen spoke from the other side of the room. "And I'm organizing emergency childcare for hospital staff families through the church networks. We'll establish safe zones so parents on shift can focus on patient care."

Brandon addressed Ms. Crawford. "What about evacuation procedures if the hospital itself takes a direct hit? Do we have protocols for moving critical patients?"

"We're developing contingency plans," Ms. Crawford replied. "But our priority is keeping this facility operational. If the tornado hits Brookside, Lakeside may be the only functioning medical facility within thirty miles."

The meeting ran for another hour. Supply logistics. Communication protocols in the event of power failure. Backup generator capacity. Staff rotation schedules to ensure continuous coverage through at least seventy-two hours. Grace took notes, her pen moving steadily while her mind ran ahead to the families who would need her when the worst arrived.

When the meeting broke up, the room emptied fast, everyone already moving toward the next task. Grace caught Brandon in the corridor. He was walking fast, already making mental calculations about supply readiness. She had to lengthen her stride to keep up.

"We've got a long night ahead," she said.

"And a potentially devastating weekend," he replied. The responsibility sat heavy in every word, making his voice sound lower and more worn than usual. "This storm is going to test every system we have. Mass casualties. Infrastructure damage. Days without normal support."

She kept pace beside him, feeling the urgency gather around them like pressure before rain. "I know. That's why I want to talk to you about the chaplain deployment. I'm planning to position spiritual care teams throughout the hospital. Not just in the family waiting areas, but in the staff break rooms and near the surgical suites. The people working this crisis will need support as much as the families do."

They reached the elevator. Brandon pressed the button and stood beside her. For a moment, they waited in silence, close enough for Grace to feel the tension coming off him in waves. When the doors opened and they stepped inside, the small enclosed space changed everything. The noise of the corridor vanished. The fluorescent light felt too bright. The quiet between them turned sharp and intimate all at once.

"Let me make sure I'm hearing you correctly... you want to station prayer teams alongside the medical staff during a mass casualty event?" Brandon's tone was almost incredulous, as though the suggestion had caught him completely off guard. The easy collegial professionalism was gone. What replaced it was edged in resistance.

"I want to station chaplains alongside the medical staff," she said evenly. "People who are trained to support families in crisis and to help staff process what they're experiencing. Prayer is part of what they do, but it's not all of what they do."

"Grace, when this storm hits, my priority is keeping as many people alive as possible. Medical intervention. Evidence-based treatment. Rational decision-making. That's what determines who survives."

He turned to face her, standing close enough that lowering his voice was all the privacy they had. "I've seen what happens when people waste critical minutes seeking spiritual comfort instead of consenting to the treatment that could save their child's life."

The reference to the Harmon family was unmistakable and Grace felt the sting of it.

"You were in that room, Brandon. You saw what happened when we worked together. The family consented. Their daughter is alive. Prayer and medicine worked side by side."

"Yes, but what about the forty minutes of delay that could have cost that girl her life?" His words were clipped, tight. "Forty minutes of a sixteen-year-old in agony while her father debated whether God needed to heal her before the surgeon could."

Grace took a deep breath. "You sat down in a chair and talked to that man like a human being. That's what made the difference. It wasn't the debate. And it wasn't your medical credential. It was your willingness to connect with him on his level." She held his gaze, refusing to let him look away from the impact of his actions. "That's exactly what chaplains do, and that's what I'm proposing we do on a larger scale during this crisis."

Brandon frowned, the lines of his face tight. "Hope can be a dangerous thing, Grace." His face had hardened, locked into the clinical mask he wore when he was protecting himself. "When people are facing death, every minute spent on comfort that doesn't produce a positive medical outcome is a minute that could have been spent trying to save a life."

She didn't flinch. "And every person who collapses under the burden of what they've seen because nobody bothered to check on them becomes one more casualty you can't treat with a scalpel."

The elevator doors opened on Grace's floor. She stepped out and turned back. Brandon stood inside, his face a map of conflict, frustration, and fear. And underneath, the faint outline of a man who was beginning to hear what she was actually saying.

"I'm not asking you to believe in prayer, Brandon," she said quietly. "I'm asking you to believe in the people who pray. There's a difference." She held his gaze for one beat. "Think about it."

The doors closed between them.

Grace found Carmen in the family services office, three phones going at once, and a laptop open to an emergency shelter co-ordination spreadsheet. Carmen looked up, read Grace's face in approximately one second, and understood enough to ask the right question.

"What happened?"

Grace sank into the chair beside Carmen's desk. "Brandon and I just had our first real argument. It was about the chaplain deployment during the storm. He thinks prayer teams will interfere with medical decision-making."

Carmen set down one of the phones, the receiver clicking softly against the base. "And what did you say?"

"I told him I wasn't asking him to believe in prayer. I was asking him to believe in the people who pray."

Carmen considered this. "That's a good line. Was he convinced?"

A tired breath slipped out of Grace before she could stop it. "The elevator doors closed before I could tell."

Carmen picked up the phone again. "Grace, that man has watched you sit with families through the worst nights of their lives. He isn't fighting your ministry. He's fighting the part of himself that wants to trust it."

She looked at Grace over the top of the phone. "Give him room. He'll come around. Right now, we've got a tornado to prepare for."

She nodded. Carmen was right. The personal stuff would have to wait. Brookside was about to be tested in ways none of them had experienced. The families they served would need every ounce of her compassion, training, and faith.

She pulled out her phone and began calling the chaplains on her contact list, scrolling through names she had known for years. There would be time later to sort through the bruise Brandon had left on her heart.

For now, there was only the storm.

Chapter 17

Brandon pushed through the emergency department doors into a sky that looked as if it were deciding whether to tear itself apart. The clouds to the west had taken on the greenish-black tint that every person who grew up in the South learned to fear, and the air carried a pressure that made his teeth ache.

Fifteen hours on shift. Four cardiac events, a compound fracture, two cases of severe dehydration from a nursing home whose air conditioning had failed, and an hour-long emergency planning meeting that ended with a directive. *Mass casualty protocols are now active.*

His body operated on fumes and the residual caffeine from six cups of hospital coffee that tasted like someone had brewed it from asphalt.

Through the glass doors of the chaplain's office, he saw Grace. She was on the phone, her brow furrowed, her free hand jotting notes on a clipboard. Speaking into the receiver with focused determination, it was clear she was coordinating deployments. Brandon realized she was mobilizing chaplains, organizing spiritual care teams, and building the support infrastructure that would hold families together when the tornado tore everything else apart.

She looked up, and their eyes met through the glass.

The elevator argument stood between them like a physical barrier. He could still hear his own voice, clipped and hard, telling her that prayer was a distraction, that hope was dangerous, that every minute spent on comfort was a minute stolen from saving lives. He could still see her face when she stepped out of the elevator, the hurt she hadn't tried to hide, and the line she delivered before the doors closed.

I'm not asking you to believe in prayer. I'm asking you to believe in the people who pray.

The apology he owed her would have to wait. Right now, the sky was telling everyone in Brookside to go home, lock their doors, and pray. Brandon could manage the first two.

His apartment was exactly as he left it that morning. The place looked like a model unit, staged to suggest that a person lived there without providing any actual evidence of a life being lived.

Fresh jeans and a flannel shirt replaced the scrubs, but the change of clothes did nothing for the replay running in his head. Every word from the elevator. Every expression on Grace's face. Every argument he made that he now recognized as fear dressed up in a lab coat.

The argument hadn't been about prayer teams. It had been about control. About the terrifying possibility that a crisis was coming and he wouldn't be able to manage every variable. Prayer represented the one variable he could never account for. The one that defied measurement, resisted protocol, and operated on a frequency his instruments couldn't detect. And instead of admitting that the inability to control it frightened him, he attacked the woman who represented it.

He microwaved leftover Chinese food from the fridge and stood at the kitchen window eating it out of the container. He watched his neighbors drag patio furniture off balconies and into their apartments before the wind could send it through a window. The Frosts worked together, Mitchell moving slowly because of his heart condition while Vivienne directed operations with the authority of a woman who managed a household through half a century of Georgia weather.

Brandon watched them and thought about what it took to build a life with someone. Fifty years of storms. Fifty years of medical scares, disagreements, and the daily, unglamorous work of choosing the same person again and again. Mitchell and Vivienne had done that. Daniel and Samantha were doing it. Sebastian and Sloane had done it. Every couple he knew who made it work had done it by weathering disagreements that felt, in the moment, like they could end everything.

Brandon set the food container on the counter and picked up the silver feather from where it rested beside the coffee maker. It was warm, the way it was always warm. He stopped trying to explain the temperature. It was simply a property of the feather, like weight was a property of lead and softness was a property of cotton. The feather held heat. That was all.

He turned it between his fingers as he thought about Liam. About a man who appeared on a park bench at three in the morning and said the exact things that a broken doctor needed to hear. And then vanished without a trace. About Gabrielle's dreams, and the silver birds, and an eight-year-old girl telling him to put down a rock he'd been carrying for twelve years.

About Grace, who hadn't asked him to abandon his training. Who hadn't asked him to pray, believe, or convert. Who only asked him to leave room for what he couldn't measure. And he treated that invitation like an assault on everything he stood for.

The television was muted. The screen filled with red and purple weather graphics, which meant the National Weather Service had run out of measured language and was simply telling people to take shelter. Brandon watched the storm cells converge on the map. The radar signatures rotated with the slow, deliberate menace of a system locked onto its target.

Brookside sat directly in the projected path.

He unmuted the television long enough to hear the meteorologist say *"life-threatening," "seek shelter immediately,"* and *"this isn't a drill."* He muted it again. He had heard enough. Tomorrow, the ER would be a war zone. He would walk into it the way he always did. With his training, his hands, and whatever reserves of endurance his body could produce.

But this time, Grace would be there too. Working in the same building, under the same threat, holding the same families together while the storm tried to pull them apart. And he had spent their last exchange telling her that her work was a dangerous distraction.

The couch accepted him. The apartment was dark except for the television's shifting light. Wind whistled through the gaps around the windows, a high, thin sound that grew louder as the minutes passed.

He thought about the Harmon family. The father's terror. The mother's guilt. The sixteen-year-old girl curled on the gurney, her face contorted in pain. He remembered sitting in that chair at the foot of the bed, talking to Mr. Harmon as a man, not a problem. He remembered Grace arriving and praying with the family while the CT scan ran. He remembered the father's face crumpling with relief when he was told he didn't have to choose between his faith and his daughter's care.

That had worked. Medicine and faith, side by side, each doing what it was designed to do. No conflict. No competition. Just two different instruments aimed at the same goal.

And then, twelve hours later, he stood in an elevator and told Grace that her instruments were useless.

The hypocrisy of it burned.

He closed his eyes, remembering the parking lot, the early morning kiss, and her words that had stayed with him every night since.

What if the reason I'm so good at taking care of everyone else is because it keeps me from having to figure out who I am without a role to play?

That question made sense to him now in a way it hadn't at four in the morning, because he was the same. He didn't know who he was when he wasn't saving lives. The hospital wasn't just where he worked. It was where he hid. The same way Grace hid behind her ministry, he hid behind his medicine. Both of them built their hiding places so well that they had forgotten they were hiding at all.

Carmen apparently told Grace she was using her ministry as a bunker. Brandon didn't know Carmen well, but based on what Grace shared, the woman had a gift for naming things others tiptoed around.

And if Grace's ministry was a bunker, then Brandon's skepticism was a moat. A wide, deep, well-fortified moat that kept everyone at a safe distance. Where their prayers and their hope and their inconvenient belief in things he couldn't measure would never reach him.

Grace had swum across that moat. She had shown up at the park that morning and kissed him back. She was the first person to make it to the other side in twelve years. And what had he done? Raised the drawbridge.

Thunder crashed directly overhead, close enough to rattle the windows. Brandon opened his eyes. The storm was no longer approaching. It was here. The leading edge of the system had arrived, and the worst was still hours away.

His phone showed three messages. Sebastian texted a brief update on Gabrielle's latest bloodwork, which showed continued improvement. Dr. Martinez sent the finalized staff rotation schedule for the next seventy-two hours. And there was a group message from the nursing staff confirming that all stations were prepped and supplies were inventoried.

No message from Grace.

He didn't expect one. He hadn't earned one.

Sleep was the rational choice. His shift started at five in the morning, and his body needed every hour of rest it could get before the storm's casualties began arriving. But his mind wouldn't settle. It kept circling the same questions he spent twelve years asking, but simpler ones. Harder ones.

Did he push Grace away because he believed prayer was dangerous? Or because he was afraid that she was right, and the world he had built to keep faith at a distance wasn't as solid as he needed it to be?

Was his skepticism a principled position? Or was it the last defense of a man who was terrified of hoping again and having it taken from him?

He lay down and stared at the ceiling. The wind howled. Rain began to hit the windows, fat, heavy drops that sounded like gravel thrown against glass. Somewhere across town, Grace was probably at the hospital, making sure her chaplains were positioned and her teams were ready. She would be the last person to leave and the first person to arrive, because that was who she was. She would walk into the storm because people needed her.

And he had spent their last conversation telling her that what she brought into those rooms didn't matter.

Sleep didn't come. By three-thirty, he gave up trying. Fresh scrubs, a bag with a change of clothes and a toothbrush, and the dark drive to the hospital through streets that were already beginning to flood. The wind bent the trees into arcs and debris skittered across the pavement in the headlights.

The hospital parking lot was half full. Staff had been arriving in waves since midnight. The emergency department's lights blazed against the predawn darkness. Sirens sounded in the distance, earlier than anyone had predicted.

He sat in his car for thirty seconds. The silver feather rested on the dashboard where he had placed it after the Providence Park walk with Grace. The rain streaked across the windshield in patterns that looked random, but probably weren't. Nothing in the last three weeks had been random. Gabrielle's illness. Liam's appearance. Grace showing up at the supply closet with coffee at midnight. The feathers. All of it woven together by a thread he couldn't see but could no longer pretend wasn't there.

He picked up the feather and slipped it into his shirt pocket, over his heart.

Then he got out of the car and walked toward the hospital entrance. The wind tore at his jacket. The rain hit his face. The sirens grew louder. And somewhere inside that building, Grace Winslow was already doing the work that he had called a distraction, holding people together while the world fell apart.

He owed her an apology. He owed her more than that. But the apology would come first, and it would come as soon as the storm gave them both a moment to breathe.

Brandon pushed through the hospital doors, and the controlled chaos of a building bracing for catastrophe swallowed him whole.

Chapter 18

Grace knelt on the chapel floor. The stone pressed into her knees. Six hours had passed since the tornado sirens split the predawn dark. Six hours since the EF-4 tornado ripped through Brookside, turning streets she had driven for years into landscapes she no longer recognized.

She should have been praying. That was why she was here, in the one quiet room the hospital still had, on her knees with her Bible open on the pew beside her. But the words wouldn't come because the woman who always had the right words for everyone else had finally run out of them for herself.

Pastor Morrison and Pastor Wilson had positioned chaplains throughout the hospital following the protocols she had developed during the planning meetings that now felt like they had happened in another lifetime. The system was working. Her teams were deployed. Families were being supported. Everything she crafted was functioning exactly as designed.

And here she was, kneeling on a chapel floor, unable to pray, with the elevator argument lodged between her ribs like a splinter she couldn't reach.

Thunder crashed overhead. The meteorologists warned about a second wave, and the sky outside the chapel's high windows confirmed it. The morning light had taken on the sickly yellow tint that meant the atmosphere was loading itself for another strike.

She closed her Bible and stood. Her body was stiff from hours of kneeling, walking, and standing beside gurneys and sitting in consultation rooms. The chapel's meditation bells chimed from the draft coming through a window the storm had cracked overnight.

It was time to go back to work.

The emergency department had been running at surge capacity since four in the morning. Grace pushed through the double doors into what had become, in the space of six hours, a field hospital. Every bay was occupied. Stretchers lined the corridors. Staff moved between patients with the grim efficiency of people who had stopped counting the hours and were operating on adrenaline, training, and whatever reserves of compassion they had left.

Carmen intercepted her near the nurses' station, phone in one hand and clipboard in the other. Sweat plastered her dark hair to her forehead, and the ponytail she had pulled it into hours ago had long since surrendered any claim to neatness. But her eyes were sharp.

"The childcare situation is handled," Carmen said, pitching her words to carry over the corridor noise without shouting. "Staff families are safe at three different church locations. Elijah and Sofia are at New Hope Baptist with some of the other children. Daniel worked with Principal Watkins to set up Greater Pines High School as another shelter. Meghan and a few other teachers are already there helping."

Grace exhaled. The knot in her shoulders loosened by one degree. "Supply concerns?"

"Medical supplies were ordered from Atlanta, but the damaged roads are blocking deliveries. We're working with what we have, which isn't enough. Dr. Martinez says it'll hold through tonight if the second wave doesn't generate the casualty volume they're predicting." Carmen lowered her clipboard and looked at her more closely. "How are you holding up?"

Grace almost laughed at the question, not because it was funny, but because it felt impossible to answer honestly in the middle of a corridor that smelled like antiseptic, sweat, and storm-soaked clothing.

"I'm here," she said. "That's the best I can offer right now."

Carmen studied her for half a second, then nodded. "That's enough. Go. Trauma bay three needs you. Jessica said a family is en route with multiple injuries, and they're asking for a chaplain."

She moved toward the trauma unit. Brandon stood near the entrance, directing his team. His scrubs were streaked with things she didn't want to identify. His face carried the lines of a man who had been running on nothing but discipline for six consecutive hours.

But his commands cut through the chaos with the calm precision that made nurses and residents follow him without hesitation.

She passed within three feet of him. One second. Maybe less. In that second, the elevator argument, their kiss, and every conversation they shared since the supply closet compressed into a single look that said what neither of them had time to say out loud.

Then the trauma bay doors burst open, and everything else fell away.

Paramedics rushed through with radios crackling, voices overlapping as they called out details about a family whose farmhouse had taken a direct hit. The first stretcher held a man in his forties, conscious but pale. His left side was wrapped in field dressings that were already soaked through. His eyes found Grace the moment the stretcher cleared the doorway.

"Chaplain." The lead paramedic nodded toward the patient. "He's been asking for spiritual support since we loaded him. Abdominal trauma, possible internal injuries. He wants to pray before surgery."

Grace positioned herself beside the stretcher while Brandon and the trauma team converged from the other side. She could hear him issuing orders. He moved with the fierce concentration that always seemed to sharpen him in crisis, as if everything unnecessary had been burned away and only purpose remained.

"Sir, I'm Grace, one of the hospital chaplains." She took the man's uninjured hand. "What's your name?"

"Wilbur." The single word looked painful to produce. His chest rose and fell in shallow pulls. "Wilbur Danes."

"Wilbur, tell me what you need."

"My family." Each word sounded weaker than the one before it. "My wife, Sarah. My daughters, Lily and Abigail. They were in the storm cellar when the house came down. Are they here? Are they alive?"

Grace looked up and caught Jessica's eye across the bay, then mouthed the question. Jessica checked the intake board, held up three fingers, then gave Grace a quick thumbs up.

Three family members had been admitted. All alive.

She turned back to him, holding on a little tighter. "Your wife and daughters are here. They're being treated. All three are alive."

The sound he made was the broken release of a man who had been holding himself together by sheer force since the world split open around him. Tears ran from the corners of his eyes into his hair, tracking through the dust still clinging to his face. His grip on Grace's hand tightened until her knuckles ached.

"Thank you, God," he whispered. "Thank you."

"Would you like me to pray with you?" Grace asked.

"Please."

She bowed her head. The prayer she offered was short and specific. Strength for the surgical team. Healing for his body. Comfort for Sarah and the girls. Peace that would outlast the fear. She spoke the words into the narrow space between the man's stretcher and the monitors beeping above him. She meant every one of them with a conviction that surprised her given the emptiness she felt in the chapel thirty minutes ago.

Somewhere behind her, between patients and shouted orders, she felt Brandon's attention. It was the unmistakable awareness of being watched by someone who mattered. Not with skepticism now. Not with challenge. Only a stillness that suggested he was seeing her in a way he hadn't expected. A man watching a woman do the work he had once dismissed, and finding himself quiet in the presence of it.

The hours that followed were the longest of her career. She moved between families the way water moves through a cracked dam. Finding the gaps. Filling them. And then, moving on.

A woman whose husband of sixty-two years was in surgery with a crushed chest. A young mother whose three-year-old had been cut by exploding kitchen glass. An elderly man from a nursing home that no longer existed, sitting in a wheelchair in the hallway with a blanket around his shoulders, with no idea where he would sleep that night.

She sat with each one. She offered no easy answers and made no attempt to explain why a tornado tore through a town full of people who loved and served one another. She simply stayed, sat in the wreckage of their lives, and refused to leave them alone in it.

The hospital's power failed twice. Each time, the backup generators kicked in hard enough to make the floor seem to tremble beneath her shoes. The lights flickered. Monitors blinked and reset. During the second outage, the entire emergency department went dark for ten long seconds, and in that span, everyone operated in complete darkness.

The generators finally caught and the lights returned. Work resumed with the same ruthless momentum, as though the interruption had been nothing but a dream.

Through all of it, she was always aware of Brandon. Not as the man who had kissed her in a parking lot before dawn. Not as the unfinished ache she kept setting aside because the town needed more from her than that. She saw him simply as a colleague giving everything he had to keep people alive.

She saw the way his face locked down when he called a time of death. She saw the brief slump of his shoulders before he straightened and moved to the next bed. She saw him working with an intensity that would cost him later, physically and emotionally, and she recognized the cost because she was paying the same one.

It was nearly four in the afternoon when Carmen found her in the family consultation room. She had just finished sitting with a family whose teenage daughter had been airlifted to Children's Healthcare of Atlanta. Carmen stood in the doorway, the color drained from her face.

"You need to see the news."

They hurried to the waiting area, where a television mounted high on the wall was broadcasting continuous emergency coverage. Aerial footage showed a Brookside that Grace barely recognized. The afternoon wave of tornadoes had struck while the hospital was consumed with the morning's casualties. The damage was catastrophic. Neighborhoods that survived the first storm were leveled. The elementary school was a pile of wreckage. Several churches had been hit.

The camera angle shifted, and Grace stopped breathing.

Cottonwood Faith Community Center. The building where she worshipped. Where Pastor Wilson's office held the leather armchair she had sat in a hundred times. Where the theology books lined shelves older than she was. The bell tower lay broken across the parking lot. The sanctuary walls had collapsed inward, reduced to a heap of splintered wood and shattered glass.

Gone. All of it.

Grace pressed her hand against the wall to keep herself upright. That building wasn't just a church. It was the place where she had knelt after Anthony's death and asked God whether there was anything left of her worth saving. It was where Pastor Wilson told her that denying her heart wasn't the same as holiness. It was where she prayed before every chaplain deployment, every difficult conversation, every moment when her faith buckled beneath what the work demanded of her.

Carmen's hand gripped her arm. "There's more. The chaplain's wing here at the hospital took structural damage when the first tornado sideswiped the east wall this morning. They sealed it off. I was so focused on the ER that I didn't think to tell you sooner."

Grace turned to her, already afraid of the answer. "The chapel?"

"I don't know." Carmen's voice softened. "I just know the wing is blocked off."

They walked together to the restricted area. Yellow caution tape crossed the corridor entrance. Grace ducked beneath it without thinking. Carmen followed.

Ceiling tiles and drywall fragments littered the hallway. Water dripped from exposed pipes. Emergency lights cast long, uneven shadows across a floor thick with plaster dust and broken glass.

The chapel doors hung crooked on their hinges. Grace pushed one open.

The altar lay smashed. The stained-glass window that had thrown colored light across her knees that morning was a carpet of glittering shards on the floor. The meditation area where she knelt in prayer was buried under chunks of ceiling tile and twisted metal from a collapsed roof section. Water pooled in the depressions between the debris, and the emergency lights gave the ruin the look of a place that had been bombed.

Grace stood in the doorway and stared. She didn't move into the room. She didn't pick through the rubble to see if anything was salvageable. She just stood there while everything the day had taken from her arrived at once.

Her church. Gone. Her chapel. Gone. The two places where her faith lived in physical form. The rooms where she went to be restored when the work of restoring others depleted her. Both had been destroyed in the span of twelve hours.

"Grace." The word came from behind her, low and steady. Julian Dawson stood in the damaged hallway, his face calm despite the chaos. The retired firefighter had arrived hours ago to help with emergency response coordination, and the dust on his jacket said he had been working in the restricted areas since.

"I'm so sorry about the chapel." He stood beside her in the doorway, looking at the destruction. Julian knew about loss. His wife had died of cancer three years earlier, and Grace had sat with him through the worst of it. He repaid that debt a hundred times over by volunteering at almost every hospital and church event since.

"It was more than a room." The words came out smaller than she meant them to, fragile against the wreckage in front of her.

"I know it was." Julian looked at her. "When Caroline died, I thought that my being in the house would kill me. Every room still had her in it. Her reading chair. Her tea set. The garden she planted. I came close to selling the place."

He paused. "But one morning I woke up, and I realized that Caroline wasn't in the house anymore. She was in me. In the way I talked to people. And in the way I couldn't stop volunteering, even when my body told me to sit down." He nodded toward the ruined chapel. "The rooms matter, Grace. I won't lie about that. But whatever happened in those rooms... that lives in you. No tornado can touch that."

Grace pressed her lips together. She wouldn't cry. Not yet. There were too many families who needed her for her to cry.

Footsteps sounded in the corridor. Brandon appeared from the direction of the main hospital. His hair was damp with sweat. His scrubs were wrinkled and streaked with the long evidence of a brutal shift. His face carried the hollowed-out look of a man who had been fighting all day and losing more than he was winning.

"Grace." Exhaustion and urgency fought for control of his tone. "I need you to know the current situation. We've lost four patients since this morning. Our blood supply is critically low, and the resupply convoy from Atlanta is stuck on damaged roads."

He stopped, and she could see the next words gathering in him before he said them. Whatever he was about to tell her, it hurt.

Before he could speak, Carmen stepped forward from the hallway. She had followed Grace from the chapel and had been checking her phone, her face tightening with each new update. Now, she lifted her eyes to Grace's, and the resolve in them intensified her dread.

"Wilbur Danes didn't survive surgery." Her tone was even, the way it always was when she delivered the worst news. "Two of his daughters are stable. But the youngest, Abigail, has injuries beyond our capacity here. We're arranging transport, but nothing is flying in this weather, and the ground routes are compromised."

Grace took in the news the way she had taken in everything since the initial weather announcements. One piece at a time. Each blow heavier than the last. She thought about Wilbur's hand crushing hers. And his broken gratitude in his voice when she told him his wife and daughters were alive.

He had died believing his family was safe. He died with a prayer on his lips and a chaplain holding his hand.

Brandon had called that a distraction. But standing in the ruins of her chapel, with Wilbur's face in her memory and his youngest daughter's life suspended somewhere between need and impossibility, Grace couldn't summon the energy to argue about it anymore.

She looked at Brandon. She looked at the destroyed chapel behind her. She looked at Julian, who stood quietly in the hallway with the patience of a man who understood that some moments couldn't be fixed, only witnessed

"I need a moment," she said, and the last word cracked in half.

She didn't try to stop it. She turned and strode toward the hospital's main entrance, moving past the nurses' station and the intake desk, past families huddled in plastic chairs with blankets around their shoulders and the same stunned expression she could feel on her own face.

The automatic doors slid open. Rain fell in sheets across the parking lot. Emergency vehicles crowded every available space, their lights streaking the wet pavement in red and blue pulses that, from a distance, looked like a heartbeat.

She stood at the threshold and peered through the rain. The town she loved was almost unrecognizable. Trees lay across the roads like broken bones. Power lines sagged over intersections like fallen jump ropes. The roof of a house sat in the hospital parking lot, deposited there by a wind that had no respect for the lives built beneath it.

Behind her, the hospital pressed on. Brandon was still fighting. Carmen was still coordinating. Her chaplains were still moving from room to room, holding frightened families together. The system she had built was functioning without her. She wasn't sure whether that was a testament to its strength or evidence that she had finally been broken beyond what her training could repair.

Grace leaned her forehead against the cool glass of the hospital doors. The rain streaked the pane in front of her, and the parking lot lights blurred into an impressionist painting of a disaster.

"Lord." Her whispered breath fogged the glass. "I don't know how to help them find their way when I'm this lost. I don't know how to help anyone else when I can't even help myself."

She stayed there, forehead against the glass, and waited for an answer that didn't come. The silence on the other side of her prayer felt not like the silence of God listening, but like the silence of an empty space.

Chapter 19

"Dr. Lawson, you're needed in trauma one." Jessica's call cut through the ER noise. Brandon tied off the last suture on an elderly woman's forehead laceration and stripped off his gloves. Jessica's auburn hair had abandoned its clip entirely, and the shadows under her eyes looked like bruises.

He headed toward the trauma bay without speaking. There wasn't anything left to say. Eighteen hours of unbroken crisis had compressed time into a single, continuous present tense. Patients arrived. Brandon treated them. Some lived. Some didn't. The ratio was getting worse.

The patient in trauma one was a man in his fifties with crushed ribs and internal bleeding after a garage wall caved in. Brandon's hands moved through the protocols. Medication. Pressure. Stabilization. His mind registered what the monitors were telling. The damage was too extensive, the bleeding too diffuse. This man's body had already made a decision that medicine couldn't override.

Thirty-seven minutes later, at seven twenty-three in the morning, the monitors went flat.

He stood beside the bed. This was his eighth loss since the tornado. He pulled off the bloodstained gloves, dropped them in the biohazard bin, and walked out of the trauma bay without a backward glance. Hanna, who had been assisting, watched him go with an expression that combined compassion and concern in equal measure. She had been a nurse long enough to recognize the look on a doctor's face when the accumulation had reached a threshold.

Through the glass partition of the break room, Brandon saw Grace.

She sat at the small table with her head in her hands. Used cups surrounded her... four, five, maybe six of them. Each one signified a family she had sat with, a hand she had held, and a prayer she had spoken into the ear of someone whose world was ending.

Her shoulders weren't trembling, and that was what got to him. They were completely still, resembling someone who had exhausted everything. And now, she was sitting in the wreckage waiting for any of it to return.

She had been in this hospital since before the first sirens. Three days. Brandon knew because he had been present for those same three days, and every time he looked up from a patient, she was somewhere in his peripheral vision.

She was in the corridors, the family consultation rooms, and beside gurneys. She had been in the hallway outside the surgical suite, holding a mother's hand while Sebastian operated on her son.

She was everywhere. He had gotten used to finding her at the brink of every calamity. She never wavered. Never complained. And right now, one look at her told him her body had reached its limit, whether she was willing to admit it or not.

Brandon pushed open the break room door. The smell of stale coffee permeated the small space. Grace lifted her head. Her eyes were red-rimmed and glassy. The poise she had maintained for the past seventy-two hours was gone. She looked at him the way he had seen patients look at him in the final hours, grasping for a handhold and finding none.

"You need to go home," he stated.

"The families—"

"Will survive without you for a few hours." The words came out harder than he intended. He sat down across from her. "Grace, look at yourself. When's the last time you slept?"

"When's the last time *you* slept?" she asked.

He didn't answer because the answer was the same as hers, and they both knew it.

What transpired next didn't feel planned so much as inevitable. Brandon had been compressing his misery into smaller and smaller compartments, sealing each one shut because there hadn't been time for anything else. Now, one of those compartments gave way, followed by another. He felt the explosion before he heard it in his own voice.

It started with Mrs. Fletcher.

"Do you know what happened at two o'clock this morning?" He spoke low and controlled, but the control was the tenuous kind, the kind a person exhibits right before they stop trying. "Mrs. Fletcher's husband was in respiratory failure. He needed to be intubated. The respiratory team was ready. But his wife spent two hours at his bedside, praying for a miracle. She refused to sign the consent for the ventilator, because she was convinced that God was going to heal him if she just prayed hard enough."

Grace's hands tightened around her cup.

"He died, Grace. He died at four-fifteen because by the time she finally signed the paperwork, his oxygen levels had dropped so far that his organs were shutting down." The crack in his words was audible, a fissure in the dam he was attempting to uphold. "Two hours. Two hours of a man drowning in his own lungs while his wife knelt beside his bed and whispered to a God who didn't answer."

"She was scared," Grace said. The words barely carried across the table, spoken by a woman who didn't have the energy for volume. "She was watching her husband die, and prayer was all she had left."

"No Grace... she had medicine. She had a respiratory team standing ten feet away." Brandon leaned forward. "And what did you tell her? What did you say when she asked you whether God would save him?"

Grace's face went ashen. "I told her I couldn't promise her that. I told her that the medical team was there to help, and that prayer and medicine could work together."

"But you prayed with her," he insisted, seizing onto that detail like it was proof of wrongdoing.

"Yes. I prayed with her. Because she asked me to."

"And while you were praying, he was suffocating." Even as the words left his mouth, part of him knew he was distorting the truth into something crueler than it had been. He knew she had tried to help. But his frustration sought a target more than it sought accuracy. "You sat beside that woman and helped her feel peaceful about a decision that was killing her husband."

"That isn't what happened." The first sign of strength she had shown in three days pierced through her exhaustion. Her voice didn't rise, but it intensified, focusing on him with a clarity that should have signaled a warning. "I urged her to consent. I told her that medicine was one of the ways God works. She wasn't ready to accept it. She needed time."

"She needed someone to tell her the truth." Brandon stood. The chair scraped against the linoleum, and the sound was loud enough to turn a head or two in the hallway beyond the glass. "She needed someone to say, *'Sign the form. Let the doctors do their job. Your husband is dying, and prayer isn't going to change that.'*"

Grace stood too. She swayed slightly, weariness visible in every line of her body, but she locked eyes with him. "Is that who you want me to be? Someone who tells a terrified woman that her prayers are worthless while her husband is dying in the bed beside her?"

"I want you to stop pretending that what you do in those rooms affects the outcome," he almost shouted.

The words came faster now, louder. Some part of Brandon, the part that was still rational, the part that kissed this woman in a parking lot, held her hand on a park bench, and confided that she was the first person he wanted to talk to at the end of the worst night of his life... that part was screaming at him to stop.

But the other part, the part that had watched eight people die in three days, the part that still bore Dr. Whitmore's death in the center of his chest like a wound that refused to close... that part couldn't stop.

"You sit with families and hold their hands and whisper prayers, and they leave those rooms believing that their loved ones have a chance. And then I have to walk into those same rooms and tell them the truth. That their child is dead. That their husband didn't survive surgery. That the God they were praying to didn't show up."

His last word fractured, ugly, and jagged, the sound of him breaking apart in front of the one person who had made him believe he didn't need to hold himself together.

"Do you have any idea what that does to me? I'm the one who has to deliver the news that your prayers didn't work. I'm the one who watches the hope drain out of their faces. And every single time, I think about my mentor, who believed exactly the way you believe. She prayed exactly the way you pray, and she died anyway! In agony... at thirty-four years old!"

The break room was silent. Through the glass partition, Brandon could see staff members in the hallway who had stopped moving. Samantha stood at the nurses' station with a chart in her hand and an expression of stunned disbelief on her face. Further down the corridor, Sebastian walked toward them, his face grim.

Grace pressed both palms flat against the wall behind her. Tears streamed down her cheeks. Her lips moved, and what came out was barely audible.

"All these years, I thought what I did made a difference."

The words were neither a challenge nor a defense. They were the sound of a woman whose foundation had just been demolished by the person she trusted most. And Brandon, hearing them, felt the devastation of what he had done crash down on him with a force that no medical training had prepared him for.

"It didn't," he replied. "Not the way medicine matters. Not the way *real* healing does." The lie tasted like poison in his mouth even as he said it, because he *knew* it was a lie.

He had watched her hold Wilbur Danes's hand in the trauma bay. He had seen the relief on his face when she told him his family was alive. He heard her pray with the Millers and the Harmons and countless others who emerged from those rooms transformed by what they received from her. He knew it wasn't true. But he said it anyway.

Grace pushed past him, her arm grazing his as she went. The brief contact resonated throughout his entire being. Then she was gone, her footsteps fading down the corridor. The break room was barren except for him, the scattered cups, and the silence that followed a detonation.

Sebastian appeared in the doorway. He stood there with his hands in the pockets of his white coat and regarded Brandon the way a surgeon appraises imaging results that confirm the worst.

"You just ruined the best thing that's come into your life." Sebastian's voice was low and measured, which was worse than if he had shouted. "And you did it in front of every nurse, resident, and family member on this floor."

Brandon stared at the table. The cups. The crumpled tissues. The remnants of a woman who devoted three days to caring for other people in a room Brandon had just turned into the setting of her worst moment.

"I know," he replied. His voice was a stranger's.

"Do you?" Sebastian didn't move from the doorway. "Because from where I was standing, it looks as if you're ashamed of needing someone, and so you destroyed it before it could be taken away from you."

Brandon's hands shook. He pressed them flat against the table, the way he pressed them against patients' chests during compressions, as though applying enough pressure could undo what he had just done.

"I lied to her, Sebastian." The admission barely escaped his lips. "I told her what she does... I told her that what she does doesn't matter. I knew it was a lie when I said it."

"Then you already know what you need to do." Sebastian turned and walked back toward the surgical wing. He paused once, half-turned. "But I wouldn't wait too long. Some things, once broken, don't always mend the way we want them to."

Hours passed. Brandon lost two more patients. He delivered the news to their families with the mechanical precision of a man functioning solely on training because everything personal had been cauterized. He checked vitals, adjusted medications, ordered imaging, and dictated charts. He did the work because the work was all he had left.

At some point after nightfall, he ended up back in the break room. He didn't remember choosing to go there. The cups from the morning were still on the table. No one had cleaned them up. He poured himself coffee from the pot on the counter and sat in the chair where Grace had been sitting when he walked in and destroyed everything.

The fluorescent lights hummed. The door was closed. Through the glass, the corridor had finally hushed to the weary rhythm of a hospital running at surge capacity for three days, and was just beginning to slow.

He gripped the cup and fixated on nothing. He thought about the man with the crushed ribs. He thought about Mrs. Fletcher's husband. He thought about Wilbur Danes, who died believing his family was safe because Grace told him they were alive.

And then, he thought about Grace's face when he shattered her spirit.

When he looked up, Liam was sitting across from him.

Two steaming cups rested on the scarred table, though Brandon hadn't heard anyone enter the room. The door was still closed. The silver-haired man sat with his wooden cane leaning against the chair and his hands cradling one of the cups. His weathered face carried the same expression of serene attentiveness Brandon remembered from the park bench.

The silver cross at his throat caught the fluorescent light.

Brandon stared. His analytical mind, the part that diagnosed, calculated, and demanded evidence, grasped the impossibility of what he was seeing. A man had materialized in a locked break room during a hospital crisis. There were no footsteps. No door opening. No explanation.

He was too tired and too broken to be afraid.

"How did you manage to get in here?" The question came out cracked and hollow.

Liam took a leisurely sip, as though locked doors and security protocols were details that didn't apply to him. "Sometimes doors open when they need to."

He set the cup down and looked at Brandon with eyes that held a depth of knowing that surpassed anything a stranger should possess.

"The real question isn't how I got in. The question is why you're sitting here alone while the woman you love is somewhere in this hospital, hurting, because of words you didn't mean."

The woman you love.

The phrase landed like a diagnosis he had been refusing to read. Not attraction. Not professional respect. Not the start of a possibility. Love. The simple, unembellished word that he had been running from since the night in the supply closet when Grace Winslow handed him a cup of coffee and made him laugh.

He loved her. And he eviscerated her in front of all their colleagues.

"I ruined everything," Brandon said.

Liam regarded him with an expression that conveyed neither judgment nor pity. Just patience. The patience of a man who had all the time in the world and intended to use it.

"Tell me," Liam urged.

Chapter 20

Brandon told him.

Not the sanitized version. Not the detached summary. He told Liam about the three days. About the patients who died despite everything he knew how to do. About Mrs. Fletcher's husband suffocating while his wife prayed. About Wilbur Danes, a farmer whose house collapsed on his family, who died believing they were safe because Grace told him they were. About standing in the break room, looking at a woman who had given everything she had, and choosing that moment to cut her open with words.

"I told her that what she does doesn't matter." The unadulterated truth came out stripped of everything except itself. Saying it aloud made something inside him recoil.

"I watched her face when I said it. And even as I was saying it, I knew." His voice roughened. "I knew it was a lie. That's the part I can't get past. Not just that I hurt her... that I knew. I knew and said it anyway."

He looked down at the table. His hands, flat against the surface, were very still. "I've seen what happens in those rooms when she's there. I've seen families walk in shattered and then walk out changed. Whatever that change is, however it works, whether it's God, hope, or just the presence of another human being who refuses to leave... it's real. And I looked into her eyes and told her it wasn't."

Liam listened without interrupting. His hands rested on his coffee cup, and his face reflected the patience of one who had heard confessions before, understanding that the most important part wasn't the words, but the silence that followed them.

"Why?" Liam asked. One word. Nothing more.

He stared at the table. Grace's cups were still there. Proof of everything she had sacrificed. "Because I'm afraid."

"Afraid of what?"

Brandon swallowed. His throat felt raw. "I'm afraid of needing her too much." The admission came from somewhere below speech, below pride, below the disciplined, controlled part of himself that had kept him functioning for years. Below everything he had erected since Dr. Whitmore's death.

"If I let myself need Grace... if I let myself love her, then I'm back in the same place I was twelve years ago. Believing. Hoping. And if I lose it again..." He stopped. His hands had started shaking, and he curled them into fists against his thighs, as if that might stop it. "I don't know how to survive that a second time."

"So you tried to destroy it yourself," Liam suggested. "Before it could be taken from you."

Brandon closed his eyes for a moment. There it was. Stripped down to its ugliest shape. "Yes."

"And how's that working?"

Brandon almost laughed. The sound that came out was closer to a cough, hollow and wrecked. "It's the worst thing I've ever done."

Liam remained still for a long beat. Then he leaned forward, and the atmosphere in the room changed. "Brandon, do you know why Jesus wept at the tomb of Lazarus?"

The question was unexpected. For a second, he was back in a church basement classroom, staring at felt board figures and paper cups of juice, hearing stories he spent years pretending had left no mark on him. He didn't like how quickly this one came back.

"I always assumed it was because His friend was dead."

Liam's voice softened. "But Jesus already knew that He was going to raise Lazarus," the older man replied. "He already knew the outcome. So why weep?"

Brandon had no answer. Or maybe he had too many.

"Perhaps because grief is holy," Liam offered. "Perhaps because love aches even when hope is certain. And perhaps because tears don't mean you've stopped believing. Sometimes they mean you believe so deeply that the pain of the world breaks your heart open."

He paused before continuing. "That's what Grace does, Brandon. She sits beside people whose hearts are breaking, and she lets hers break alongside them. She doesn't fix them. She doesn't guarantee outcomes she can't fulfill. She stays. And sometimes staying is the holiest thing a person can do."

Brandon thought about Wilbur's hand gripping Grace's in the trauma bay. The relief on his face when she told him his family was alive. The prayer she whispered over his stretcher while Brandon worked to stop the bleeding. Wilbur died in surgery three hours later, but he hadn't died alone. He hadn't died without hope. And the difference between dying alone, and dying with someone beside you, was the difference Grace made in every room she entered.

"I need to find her," Brandon said.

"You do." Liam stood and picked up his cane. "But first, hear me. An apology that comes from guilt won't be sufficient. She needs to hear that you see her. Not the chaplain or her ministry, but her. The woman who's as frightened of loving you as you are of loving her."

Brandon looked up. "How do you know she's frightened?"

A small smile touched Liam's mouth. "Because courage and fear aren't opposites. They're companions. Every brave thing a person undertakes is done alongside the terror of doing it. Grace walks into those rooms afraid. She prays over dying patients... and she's afraid. She kissed you in that parking lot... and she was afraid. Fear isn't failure. The failure is in allowing the fear to decide for you."

Brandon stood. His body ached, but his internal fog had lifted, like a window being washed after years of grime. He could see through it again. Not perfectly. Not with the certainty his scientific mind demanded. But clearly enough to know what he needed to do.

"Will I see you again?" he asked.

Liam's expression bore the warmth of someone bidding farewell to a person they expected would be alright. "Yes... whenever you need to."

Brandon blinked, and the chair across from him was deserted. The cane had vanished. The second coffee cup sat on the table, still warm, still steaming, with no hand to hold it. On the scarred laminate, beside the cup, lay a silver feather. Warm. Real. Inexplicable.

He picked it up. He placed it in his shirt pocket with the other one, over his heart, where two impossible feathers now rested against the fabric of his scrubs like a weight that was also, somehow, a lightening.

He pushed through the break room door and walked into the corridor.

Chapter 21

Grace didn't recall leaving the break room. She remembered Brandon's face. She remembered her arm brushing against his as she pushed past him, and then the corridor was a blur of light and indistinct faces.

Her feet carried her through the hospital on an instinct older than her training. She ducked under the yellow caution tape and picked her way through the debris-scattered corridor of the damaged wing, heading toward the only place left that made sense, even if it was destroyed.

The chapel doors hung crooked on their hinges. She pushed one open and stepped inside.

The destruction was worse than she had seen earlier that day. A second round of structural settling had dropped additional ceiling tiles. Water from the damaged roof pooled across the floor, turning the plaster dust into a gray sludge that clung to her shoes. The emergency lights cast long, erratic shadows. One intact pew sat in the middle of the wreckage like an island.

She perched on it, drawing her knees to her chest, wrapping her arms around them, trying to make herself as small as she could.

What if he was right?

The thought lodged itself in the only quiet space her mind had left. What if she had spent years offering families a comfort she couldn't prove, calling it sufficient? The ruined chapel mocked the question. If God protected sacred spaces, why was she sitting in rubble? If prayer worked the way she told families it worked, why had ten people died in this hospital since Friday, while chaplains prayed in every corridor?

For the first time in her career, she had no answer and had no idea how to pretend otherwise.

Careful footsteps echoed in the hallway. Carmen appeared in the doorway, picking her way through the wreckage with the tenacity of a woman determined not to let structural damage stand between her and her best friend.

"I figured I'd find you here." Carmen crossed the room, glass crunching under her shoes, and sat on the pew beside Grace. She didn't ask if Grace was all right. The question would have been insulting.

They sat together for a full minute without speaking. The emergency lights flickered once and held. Somewhere beyond the damaged wing, the hospital's ventilation system hummed, a reminder that the building was still standing, even if parts of it weren't.

"He was completely out of line." Carmen kept her tone even, but Grace heard the anger underneath it, the protective fury of a friend witnessing someone she loved being publicly humiliated.

"Was he?" The rawness in Grace's own words surprised her. "Maybe he said what everyone's been too kind to say. Maybe all I've ever given people is a warm hand and a prayer that changes nothing."

Carmen turned on the pew to face her. "Grace... I need you to look at me."

Grace lifted her eyes. Even that took effort. Holding Carmen's gaze felt harder than it should have, as if shame itself had weight.

"What have you been doing for the last three days?"

Grace frowned. "What?"

"Answer the question. What have you actually been doing since Friday night when the storm hit?"

Grace stared at her. Then, an answer began to rise within her. A list formed from someplace deeper than her mind, as if her body had been keeping its own record all along.

"I sat with families and held their hands. I prayed with patients. I organized meal deliveries, temporary housing referrals, contacted next of kin, and walked families through the process of consenting to surgeries their children needed. I found a translator for the Hernandez family at two in the morning. I helped Mrs. Patterson locate her sister, who'd been moved to a shelter in the next county. I sat next to a man in the trauma bay and told him his wife and daughters were alive while the doctors worked to save his life."

By the time she finished, her throat throbbed. She could visualize each moment. None of it felt insignificant as she spoke. None of it felt empty either, which only made Brandon's words hurt more.

"And was any of that real?" Carmen's voice was quiet but insistent.

"Of course it was real."

"Did those families know they weren't alone because you were there?"

"Yes."

"Did that man die knowing his family was safe?"

Grace's throat closed. "Yes."

Carmen held her gaze. "Then I need you to listen very carefully." She spoke with the same directness she used with families when comfort alone wasn't enough, and what was needed instead was the truth they could lean on.

"Brandon is an exceptional physician who's been awake for three days watching people die. He's carrying more pain than he knows what to do with. He directed that pain at you because you got too close to the part of him that's still capable of feeling. He didn't attack your ministry because it's worthless. He attacked it because it scares him."

Carmen drew in a slow breath.

"What you do forces him to face the one thing he still can't bring himself to accept... he can't accept that some things are beyond his control, and that staying present in the face of that is important. It heals in a different way, but it still matters."

Grace pressed her palms against her eyes. The pressure only made everything burn hotter.

"He isn't fighting you, Grace," Carmen said, more gently now. "He's fighting the part of himself that watched you pray and wanted to believe it made a difference. He's lashing out because losing control is the thing he fears most."

Carmen's expression softened, but her voice didn't. "His words tell you more about his fears than they do about your calling."

Grace dropped her hands. "That doesn't make them hurt less."

The anger in Carmen's tone receded, and compassion took its place. "No, it doesn't. But you need to decide. Not tonight, while you're sitting here with glass in your shoes and all of this on your shoulders. But soon. You need to decide whether you're going to let a wounded man's worst moment define what you're worth."

The chapel was silent, except for the drip of water from the damaged roof and the distant, perpetual hum of the hospital beyond the caution tape.

"Carmen." The name came out barely above a whisper. "I love him."

Carmen's expression didn't change. "I know."

"Not the way I thought... not cautiously or in the way that I envisioned. I'm completely in love with him, and it happened while I wasn't looking. I can't undo it, and... and I don't want to."

Carmen wrapped her arm around Grace's shoulders. "I know that too."

Grace stared at the shattered stained glass strewn across the floor, the fractured color capturing what little light remained.

"With Anthony, love felt safe. We shared the same faith and wanted the same things. I knew who I was supposed to be." She swallowed hard. "With Brandon... I don't know who I'm supposed to be. He challenges every certainty I've ever had. And instead of shying away from that, I want to go deeper into it. That scares me more than anything he said in that break room."

"Good." Carmen's arm tightened. "That shows you're finally being honest with yourself."

Grace turned to look at her. "What do I do now?"

"You stop trying to be invincible. Let yourself love a man who's afraid of being loved. And you trust that God is big enough to hold two scared people who are trying to figure this out."

Carmen released her and stood. "But right now, you grieve. You sit in this ruined chapel, and you grieve what was lost. The patients, the buildings, and the version of yourself that thought she had to be perfect to be worth loving."

Her voice gentled even further. "Let it go, Grace. All of it. And see what's still standing when the dust settles."

Grace looked around the destroyed chapel. The altar was gone. The stained glass was gone. The meditation corner where she knelt in prayer a thousand times was buried under debris. Everything she had used to anchor her faith in a physical space was destroyed.

But she was still here. Carmen was still here. The families she served were still being cared for. And somewhere in this hospital, a man she loved was working through his own wreckage. He was learning slowly, painfully, and against every instinct in his being, that needing someone wasn't the same thing as losing them.

"Carmen." She wiped her face with both hands. "When this is over and I can think straight, I need to talk to him."

"I know you do." Carmen helped her stand. "And he needs to talk to you. But tonight, you both need to survive the rest of this storm. The talking can happen when you're both standing on solid ground."

They picked their way through the debris toward the chapel doors. Grace paused at the threshold and looked back one more time at the wreckage. The room that housed her faith for years was gone. Yet faith itself still existed. Smaller, but present, like a candle in a room without walls, burning because the flame didn't need a room to thrive.

As they stepped into the corridor, footsteps resonated from the direction of the main hospital. Pastor Wilson emerged from the shadows, his face streaked with tears, his silver-rimmed glasses askew on his nose. His sleeve was torn, and his shoes were caked with mud.

"Grace," he said, relief and exhaustion breaking through every syllable. "Thank God, I found you. We need to talk."

Chapter 22

GRACE TURNED AT THE sound of her name. The man step-ping through the damaged doorway bore little resemblance to the composed spiritual leader she relied on for years.

The storm had impacted him in ways that went beyond just how he looked, though his appearance was shocking enough. But it was the tears cutting through the grime on his cheeks that told Grace a man she thought unshakable had been shaken to his foundation.

"Pastor Wilson." She moved toward him, her chaplain's instincts overriding her own tiredness. The impulse to care for someone else's pain came first... it always came first. "I saw the news about Cottonwood Faith. I'm so sorry."

He halted a few feet away and removed his glasses, cleaning them with shaky hands. The familiar motion that grounded her in a dozen conversations over the years now looked like a man attempting to hold himself together through muscle memory alone.

"I've just come from the site," he said. "Seeing it on television didn't prepare me for standing in the middle of it."

Grace pictured what he must have encountered. The bell tower that stood over Brookside's skyline for sixty years, broken across the parking lot. Sanctuary walls flattened. Pews where generations had worshipped, married, mourned, and celebrated, reduced to splinters and twisted metal. The building where he devoted thirty years of his ministry, obliterated in the time it took a tornado to travel a city block.

Carmen kept her hand on Grace's shoulder. "Were there any injuries? Was anyone in the building?"

"By the grace of God, no." Pastor Wilson moved carefully through the debris and sat on the intact section of the pew beside them.

"Earlier today, during the emergency planning, I had the strangest feeling. A pressure I couldn't explain kept urging me to change the shelter assignments. I'd already announced that Cottonwood Faith would serve as a primary shelter, but something made me feel I couldn't stop there. I called Principal Watkins and asked if we could redirect families to Greater Pines High School instead."

He paused and looked down at his hands. "I can't explain it. It wasn't a voice or a vision. It was just an insistence I felt I couldn't ignore."

The chapel was silent except for distant sounds from the corridors.

"If I hadn't listened to that prompting, dozens of families would have been in the sanctuary when the tornado struck," he said. "The building took a direct hit. Everyone inside would have perished."

Grace stared at her pastor. God had prompted Pastor Wilson to relocate the families. God had spared them. And then God let the building be destroyed anyway.

The logic of it would have infuriated Brandon. Protect the people but flatten the sanctuary. Preserve lives but devastate the place where those lives gathered to worship. Sitting in the wreckage of this chapel, Grace wasn't entirely sure what argument she could make against his view of the world. The mathematics of mercy and ruin refused to balance.

"I sat in that rubble for an hour," Pastor Wilson said. He had shifted into a tone that indicated he was no longer addressing them as a minister but as a fellow human being. "I sat on what was left of the altar step, and I looked at what was left of a building I've served in since before you were born, Grace. And I couldn't find God anywhere."

Grace stilled. She had brought this man every kind of fear over the years. Doubts she was too ashamed to say aloud anywhere else. Questions she thought might expose the vulnerabilities within her faith.

He had always been the one with the answer, or at least with the calm conviction that an answer could be found. Hearing uncertainty creep into his voice felt akin to witnessing the last standing wall in a storm finally collapse.

"You've always been so sure," she whispered. "If you're questioning God's presence, what hope is there for the rest of us?"

Pastor Wilson looked at her, and his eyes held a transparency she hadn't seen in them before. She was seeing the naked uncertainty of a man who had just lost the visible center of his life's work and was searching the wreckage for his faith.

"I've questioned God's goodness three times in thirty years of ministry," he said. "When my daughter nearly died from leukemia at seven years old. When the Hendricks boy was killed by a drunk driver on his way home from youth group." He drew in a breath that sounded unsteady. "And now... tonight. Each time, I was convinced I was finished serving Him."

"But you didn't stop," Grace said.

"No. I didn't stop." He leaned forward and began sifting through the debris at their feet. His fingers moved through shattered stained glass, plaster fragments, and sodden hymnbook pages until they closed around a single shard of cobalt blue. He held it up to the emergency light, and the fragment caught the beam and threw a small, concentrated splash of color across the dust-covered floor.

"Do you know what I realized while I sat in the rubble of our church this afternoon?" He rotated the shard between his fingers. "I realized that every time I've questioned God's goodness, I was asking the wrong questions."

Grace waited. Carmen sat beside her, still and attentive.

"I kept asking why," Pastor Wilson continued. "Why doesn't God protect the innocent? Why does He allow the faithful to suffer? Why does He let children die and churches fall?"

He held the shard higher, letting the blue light dance across the broken walls. "But those questions assume that God owes us a life untouched by pain... that if we believe correctly, we'll be safe and carefree."

He turned the shard between his fingers. "Paul wrote from a place of genuine suffering. He had been beaten, shipwrecked, and imprisoned. In Second Corinthians, chapter 4, verses 8 and 9, he said, *'We are hard pressed on every side, but not crushed. Perplexed, but not in despair. Persecuted, but not abandoned. Struck down, but not destroyed.'*"

Pastor Wilson surveyed the rubble around them. "Hard pressed. Perplexed. Struck down. That's where we find ourselves tonight. But the verse doesn't end with the damage. It ends with what survives."

He wasn't preaching or delivering a sermon. He was a man who had sat in the wreckage of his own beliefs and discovered, underneath it, a foundation he hadn't known was there.

"The better questions are these. How do we love without guarantees? How do we choose hope when everything around us screams to give up?" He looked at Grace. "What if faith isn't about having God all figured out? What if it's about choosing to trust Him in the middle of the mystery?"

The words landed like the blue light from the stained-glass fragment, small, concentrated, and aimed at the exact spot that needed illumination. Grace felt them settle into her hollowed space, almost as if they were saying this was where the healing could begin.

"You've been doing that for years, Grace," Carmen said, with the cadence of a friend who knew when to speak and when to let another's words do the heavy lifting. "You support families during their darkest moments. Not because you have all the answers... but because you're willing to stand with them in the not-knowing."

Grace glanced at the shard in Pastor Wilson's hand. She observed the emergency lights casting their uneven glow across a room that had once harbored her certainties and now contained only rubble and the people who loved her.

"Pastor Wilson," she said. "Will you pray with us?"

He nodded. Carmen took Grace's hand on one side, and Pastor Wilson took her hand on the other. His grip was calloused and warm, and his fingers quivered. Grace realized that for the first time in their relationship, she was holding him up as much as he was holding her.

Pastor Wilson bowed his head. "Lord, we sit in the ruins of what we thought was solid. We confess that we've wanted guarantees. We've wanted to see the whole road before we took the first step."

His words gathered strength, filling the broken chapel the way light invades a room when the walls are gone, leaving nothing to keep it out.

"But Your Word tells us that Your grace is sufficient, and that Your power is made perfect in weakness. Help us trust that love doesn't require a building to be real. Help us trust that faith doesn't require certainty to be true. And be with every person in this hospital tonight, who's carrying more than they were made to carry. Give them strength, Lord. Not the strength to be invincible. Just the strength to keep showing up. Amen."

"Amen," Grace murmured.

"Amen," Carmen echoed.

They sat together for a moment, hands still linked. Through the demolished chapel windows, Grace could see the faint suggestion of dawn beginning to lighten the eastern sky. The storm was passing and moving on, leaving behind the damage, debris, and the task of putting things back together.

Grace released their hands and stood. Her legs were unsteady, but a decision had solidified in her center during the prayer. A small, private, irreversible choice that didn't require anyone's approval.

"I need to find Brandon," she stated.

Pastor Wilson regarded her over the top of his crooked glasses. "That doesn't sound like a woman seeking permission."

A faint, tired smile touched her mouth. She brushed the plaster dust from her slacks.

"I'm done hiding. I'm done trying to protect myself from the possibility that loving someone could change who I am." She looked at her pastor. "Because it already has. And the woman it's made me is someone I'd rather be."

Carmen stood beside her. "Then go."

"I will. But not while I look like I've been living in a construction zone." The smile came a little easier this time. "Give me five minutes."

"You've got three," Carmen replied. "That man's been suffering long enough."

Before Grace could move toward the chapel doors, footsteps echoed from the corridor beyond the damaged doorway.

Brandon appeared in the broken frame of the chapel entrance.

He looked worse than she had ever seen him. His eyes were hollow from exhaustion and red rimmed with something deeper than fatigue. Regret was written all over him, not in some fleeting manner, but in the heavy, structural way damage settled into a building after a storm.

In his right hand, he held a silver feather.

He stood there staring at her. And she looked back at him. Neither of them spoke.

Carmen and Pastor Wilson exchanged a glance. "Carmen," he said. "I think we should give them some privacy."

Carmen crossed the room to Grace and squeezed her shoulder. The look she gave her was wrapped in affection. Then she turned to Brandon, delivering a steadfast and unyielding warning with her gaze.

"Be careful with her," she said, making it clear it wasn't just a suggestion.

Brandon met Carmen's eyes. "I intend to."

Carmen and Pastor Wilson picked their way through the debris toward the corridor. Their footsteps faded, and the ruined chapel held only the two of them. The broken glass. The fallen beams. The single undamaged pew. And the silence that arises when two people reach the same destination by way of the longest night of their lives.

Brandon took one step into the chapel, then another, still holding the silver feather.

"Grace." Her name came out rough, as if it had scraped against everything in him on the way out. "I knew I'd find you here."

He took another step. Close enough now that she could see the tremor in his hand where it held the feather. Close enough to see that his eyes were red-rimmed, not just from fatigue but from tears she suspected Brandon hadn't allowed himself to shed in front of another person in years.

"Please," he said. "Can we talk? I know I have no right to ask. But there are things I need to say, and if I don't say them now, I'm afraid I'll lose the courage."

Grace looked at him as he asked for a conversation he didn't deserve. He was a man standing in the wreckage with regret on his face, fear in his voice, and honesty stripped so bare it almost hurt to witness.

She sat down on the pew and made room beside her.

"Sit down, Brandon," she said. "I'm listening."

Chapter 23

Brandon sat on the pew beside Grace. The space between them was no wider than a hymnal, but it felt like the width of a canyon.

The ruined chapel held them in its broken arms. Nothing in this room had been spared. Everything that once felt solid had been broken open, and Brandon couldn't miss the mercy in that. At least the room looked the way he felt.

He looked at his hands. The same hands that performed CPR on eight patients in three days. The same hands that sutured wounds, adjusted ventilators, and held pressure over bleeding that wouldn't stop.

The same hands that cupped Grace's face in a parking lot and kissed her like a man who had finally stopped lying to himself. And the same hands that hung useless at his sides while he stood in a break room and told her that her life's work was a lie.

He didn't know where to begin. Every version of the apology he composed on the walk through the damaged corridor felt inadequate. Words were Grace's territory. She used them to steady frightened people and build shelter where there was none. He had used his to level her.

"I don't know how to say what I need to say," he admitted. The raw honesty in his own words surprised him, stripped of the clinical expertise he wore in the ER. "I've been rehearsing it in my head since I left the break room, and every version sounds like an excuse."

Grace sat beside him with her hands in her lap. She didn't look at him. She looked at the debris on the floor and at the place where the altar had once stood. She was letting him speak without rescuing him from what he had to say. He understood the distinction because she had taught it to him without ever meaning to. Comfort made room for pain. Truth required a person to face it.

"Then don't make excuses," she said quietly. "Just tell me the truth."

His breath shuddered on the way out.

"I told you that what you do doesn't matter. I said it to your face in a room with glass walls while half the staff watched." He didn't soften it. He laid it on the floor between them like a surgical instrument, precise and unadorned. "I said it when I was so angry after losing so many patients. I felt so empty I... I needed somewhere to put it. And you were there."

Grace said nothing. Her stillness made it harder, not easier. There was no interruption to hide behind. No quick sympathy to soften the edges.

"But that isn't the whole truth." His hands pressed flat against his thighs, trying to steady himself.

"The whole truth is that I was afraid. I watched you pray with Wilbur in the trauma bay. I watched his face change when you told him his family was alive." Brandon swallowed, but the ache in his throat held. "And then he died three hours later in surgery."

His voice caught on the last word.

"He died believing his family was safe because you told him they were. He died with peace instead of terror, and that mattered. God help me, Grace, it mattered more in that moment than anything I did with a scalpel or a suture."

The chapel seemed to go even quieter around them.

"And I hated that I knew it."

He turned his hands over and stared at them, as if he might find an answer in the lines of his own skin.

"I hated that there was something happening in that room that I couldn't chart, or force into a set of numbers that I could live with. I hated that you walked in carrying something I've spent twelve years training myself not to believe in, and I watched it change people. I watched it happen right in front of me. And I knew it was real even while I was trying to deny it."

He finally looked at her.

"So I attacked it. I attacked the thing in you that unnerved me, because that's what I do when I don't understand something. I reduce it. I cut it apart. I tell myself it isn't real before it gets the chance to undo everything I've built my life on."

Grace's chin lifted. Her eyes were wet, but she wasn't crying. She was listening with the same focus she gave every family she sat with, the kind that said she heard every word and wasn't going anywhere, but she also wasn't going to spare him from the weight of what he had done.

"You didn't just attack my work," she said, each word placed with deliberate care. "You attacked it in front of Sam... in front of Jessica and Hanna. In front of the residents and the families who were sitting in that hallway. You took the thing that I've given my life to, and you called it a lie in front of every person who has ever trusted me to sit with them in their worst moment."

He closed his eyes.

"I've spent seventy-two hours holding people together," she continued. "I've sat with mothers whose children died. I've prayed with men who lost their wives. I've organized meal deliveries and housing referrals. I found a translator at two in the morning. I contacted next of kin for families who didn't even know their loved ones were in the hospital. I've done all of that on hardly any sleep and nothing but coffee and the belief that what I do matters."

The last sentence dropped to nearly a whisper. "And you stood in that break room and told me that it doesn't."

"I know." The words came out stripped bare. No defense. No explanation. Just the ugly fact of it.

"You need to hear this, Brandon." Grace turned on the pew to face him, and her expression held no anger, only transparency.

That was worse. Anger would have given him something to push against. This gave him nowhere to hide.

"I can forgive the words. I understand where they came from. I understand that you were tired and grieving and that your fear turned into cruelty. Carmen and Pastor Wilson tried to explain it to me. But I don't need an explanation."

She held his gaze. "What I need to know is whether you meant it. Not whether you meant to say it. I need to know that if underneath all of what we've all been going through... do you actually believe that what I do in those rooms is worthless?"

The question went straight to the one thing that mattered, and it didn't allow for evasion or qualification.

Brandon opened his eyes and looked at her.

"No," he said. "I don't believe that. I've *never* believed that. Not since the first night you brought me coffee in a supply closet and sat with me without trying to fix anything."

The thickness in his throat made each word an effort. "I lied to you, Grace. And the worst part is, I knew I was lying while I said it. I watched Wilbur die, believing that his family was safe, and I knew that the peace on his face was something I couldn't have given him. I've watched you sit with families and give them something that no medication or surgery can give. And I looked into your eyes and told you it didn't count because I was too afraid to admit what it meant."

Grace didn't move. "What does it mean?"

"It means that healing is bigger than I thought it was." The words came slowly, as though he were dragging them from a place that had been sealed shut for a long time.

"It means that what you do in those rooms is as real as what I do in the ER. It means that Mrs. Fletcher's husband, even though the delay cost him, and even though I was right about the medical timeline... he wasn't failed because his wife prayed. She prayed because she was terrified, and you were the person who helped her find the courage to let him go."

He swallowed hard. "It means I was wrong. Not about everything... but about the thing that matters the most."

Grace sat with his words for a long time. Brandon didn't rush her. He had already taken enough from her. He would not take her silence too.

"I need you to hear me too," she said at last. "What you said in that break room didn't just hurt me... it shook something fundamental in me. I've been sitting in this chapel asking myself whether you were right. Whether I've been offering families a comfort I can't prove. I've been asking myself whether my prayers change anything or if they're just words I say when there isn't anything else to give."

The damage of it spread through him all over again. Not just that he had hurt her, but that he had reached all the way down into the place where she stood before God. He was so sorry he had caused her to question that as well.

"And I don't have an answer," Grace said. "I've been a chaplain for years. After tonight, I genuinely don't know whether what I do changes anything. I believe it does. I choose to believe it does. But I can't prove it, and... and you were right about that. I can't point to a lab result and say, here, look, this prayer moved this number. That isn't how it works."

"Grace—"

"Please, Brandon... let me finish." The words were firm but not hostile. She was drawing a line, and he let her. He hadn't earned the right to interrupt.

"What I can prove is that families who have someone sitting beside them during the worst hours of their lives process that experience differently than families who are left alone. What I can prove is that staff members who have access to spiritual support during prolonged crisis events show lower rates of burnout and compassion fatigue. What I can prove is that a man named Tobias Miller told me his daughter's doctor seemed like he was carrying a burden too heavy for one person. And that man and his wife have been praying for you every night since, because they saw in you someone worth praying for."

She looked at him.

"I can't prove that God exists. I can't prove that prayer heals. But I can prove that showing up matters. And I've been showing up and... and I'm tired. And the man I'm in love with told me it was worthless. But I'm still here."

The last two words seemed to break apart in her mouth, and for the first time since he sat down, she let the tears fall. "I'm still here, Brandon. Sitting in rubble... with you. Because that is what I do. I stay."

Something in his chest gave way.

The man I'm in love with.

She had said it plainly, with tears on her face and wreckage all around them, and Brandon could hardly take in the fact of it. Not because he doubted her, but because some part of him still couldn't believe he had been loved this way at all, much less after what he had done.

And still here. Still with him. Still choosing not to leave.

Brandon reached into his shirt pocket and withdrew the silver feather. He set it on the pew between them. Grace's eyes widened, and the guarded steadiness in her face gave way to one of surprise.

"Where did you get that?" she asked.

"It came from a man I can hardly explain." The words came out quiet, almost reverent. "He showed up at Providence Park the night Emma died. He has silver hair and walks with a wooden cane. He sat next to me on a bench, asking questions that made me reevaluate everything I thought I knew about healing. And when I turned to say goodbye, the bench was empty. This feather was the only thing left behind where he'd been sitting."

Grace reached into her bag and withdrew her own feather. She placed it on the pew beside his. The two feathers rested side by side, identical and warm, catching what little light the emergency fixtures emanated.

"I found mine on my windshield on the night we went to the hospital after dinner at Heavenly Delights," Grace said.

"I know. I watched you pick it up."

They looked at the feathers. For once, Brandon didn't feel the need to explain what couldn't be explained. He didn't want to pin it down or reduce it to something manageable. Whatever this was, it didn't need his permission to remain mysterious. Beside him, Grace made no attempt to interpret it either. She sat with him in the strangeness of it, which felt, somehow, like its own kind of grace.

"He came to me again tonight," Brandon said. "In the break room... after the fight. He was sitting across from me as if he'd always been there. He told me to find you. He told me that an apology rooted in guilt wouldn't cut it... that you needed to hear that I see you." Brandon looked at her. "Not the chaplain, and not the ministry. Just... you."

Grace's eyes searched his face. "And do you?"

He let out a breath. "I see a woman who trusted me with her flaws. I see a woman who named her sourdough starter Lazarus because it keeps coming back to life. I see a woman who carries her husband's last letter in her purse every day and handed it to me on a park bench because she believed it would help me cope with my own grief."

His voice roughened, his throat tight with everything he had been holding back. "I see the woman who kissed me at four in the morning and pulled away because she was more honest about what it meant than I was. And I see someone who's spent days in this hospital giving everything she has to people she may never see again, and who's sitting in a destroyed chapel with a man who tore her apart... and she's still here."

She wiped her face with both hands.

"I love you, Grace."

He said it without dressing it up. No qualification. No careful framing. Just the truth, bare and irreversible, in a chapel full of broken glass.

"I love the way you challenge everything I think I know. I love the way you stay when everyone else leaves. I love that you're afraid of this and you're here anyway."

Grace looked at him for a long time. Somewhere in the hospital beyond the caution tape, a phone rang and went unanswered. In the silence that followed, Brandon could hear his own heartbeat, loud and unsteady, waiting for her response.

"I love you too," she said. "And I'm furious with you. And I forgive you. All three of those things are true at the same time, and I'm not going to pretend they're not."

Brandon almost laughed. The sound that came out was wrecked and grateful and somewhere in the vicinity of joy. "I can work with that."

"You'd better." Her mouth twitched. Not quite a smile, but close enough that hope moved through him with no regard for his permission.

"Because I meant what I said, Brandon. I'm done hiding. And I'm done pretending that loving you is a threat to my calling when it's actually the bravest thing I've done since I walked into this hospital and chose to sit with people in their darkest rooms."

He raised his hand. The same tremor from the parking lot. The same careful approach, as though asking permission with his fingers before his mouth could form the question. He hesitated for a fraction of a second, close enough to feel the warmth radiating from her skin, close enough that his knuckles almost brushed her hair.

Grace didn't move away. When his hand touched her jaw, the contact shook him more than he expected. Her skin was warm, softer than he remembered. She turned her face into his touch, and the gesture was so small and so complete that it said everything the last hour of conversation had been building toward.

He kissed her.

Not the desperate, parking-lot kiss of a man frightened that what he found would vanish before he could hold it. That kiss had been hungry and grasping, born of fear and the need to claim something before it slipped away.

This was different. This was a man who had already lost her and gotten her back, and who knew the cost of both. His mouth moved against hers with the unhurried attention of someone who intended to remember every detail. The shape of her lips, the soft sound she made when his hand slid into her hair, the way her breath caught and then released against his mouth as if she had been holding it since the break room.

She kissed him back with the clarity of a woman who made a decision and wasn't interested in half measures. Her fingers found the front of his shirt, not pulling him closer but anchoring herself there, and the contact sent a current through him that was entirely, unmistakably her.

She kissed him in a chapel, surrounded by broken glass and fallen beams, and neither of them pretended that the setting was romantic or that the timing was ideal or that either of them was in any condition to be doing this.

They were exhausted and grieving and covered in plaster dust and hospital residue. And it was the most honest kiss of his life, though he didn't have the words for that yet. He felt it in the way her mouth molded against his, in the way the world beyond the two of them went quiet and distant, in the way something that had been cracked open in his chest began, impossibly, to mend.

When they separated, Brandon pressed his forehead against hers. His breathing was uneven, coming in shallow pulls that he couldn't seem to steady. He could feel her breath on his lips, warm and sweet. He closed his eyes for a moment just to hold the feeling of her there.

"I don't want to change you," he said.

"And I don't want to fix you," she replied.

He gave a faint smile, his lips still close enough to brush hers if he leaned forward a fraction. "Then what do we do?"

Grace drew back just enough to look at him, and the sight of her in the thin emergency light hit him with a strange, painful tenderness. She looked tired, bruised by the night. Her hair was escaping from wherever she'd pinned it hours ago, and there was a smudge of something dark on her collar. Still utterly herself. He wanted to memorize the way she looked right then, in this moment before the world rushed back in.

"We do what we've both been doing all along," she said. "We show up. We stay. And we figure out the rest as we go."

Brandon looked at the two silver feathers resting on the pew. He picked up his and put it in his pocket. Grace picked up hers and returned it to her bag.

"We should go," he said. "The hospital needs us."

Grace stood, and Brandon rose with her. Both of them looked spent. But when she turned toward the chapel doors, something in her face had steadied, and the sight of that steadiness moved through him like grace he had done nothing to deserve.

They walked out of the chapel together, stepping over the debris, ducking under the caution tape, and emerging into the hospital corridor where the real work was waiting. Brandon's hand held hers as they walked, and neither of them let go until they reached the point where the corridor split, the ER to the left, the chaplain's office to the right.

"I'll see you," he said.

"You will."

He turned left. She turned right. And the hospital, battered and understaffed and running on generators and the stubbornness of the people inside it, kept doing what hospitals do. Healing. One patient, one family, one impossible hour at a time.

Chapter 24

For the first time in almost a week, Brookside was soaked in warm, golden sunlight, making the devastation appear both more severe and somewhat easier to bear. Under the cloak of darkness, the wreckage had taken on a monstrous quality, as if the storm were still lurking nearby, ready to finish its destructive job. But in the light, it transformed into lumber, brick, and glass. It looked like work. A grueling and sacred kind of work, but work nonetheless.

Grace stood in the shell of Cottonwood Faith Community Center's fellowship hall with a phone wedged between her shoulder and her ear, squinting at her notes. The sanctuary was gone, but the fellowship hall had survived, with its roof intact and its plumbing operational, making it the obvious staging ground for the community recovery effort that had been building momentum since the tornado sirens ceased.

"Carmen, we're running low on supplies at the temporary clinic on Fifth Street," she said. "The Presbyterian congregation brought gauze and antiseptic, but we're almost out of pediatric medications."

"Already on it." Carmen sounded tired, but she was still running at full capacity. "The Methodist church is running a supply drive with their sister congregation in Atlanta. Father Vargas from St. Catherine's is personally driving the delivery truck. He should be here within the hour."

Grace scanned the fellowship hall. Baptists sorted clothing donations along the far wall while Pentecostal volunteers stirred enormous pots of soup in the kitchen that Meghan and Aaron had designed for Meghan's cooking education program less than a year ago.

Catholics mapped transportation routes for homebound seniors whose houses had been damaged. Presbyterian youth hauled boxes alongside Episcopalian elders. Individuals who worshipped separately their entire lives now worked collaboratively, as though they had always been part of the same congregation.

A week ago, Grace would have said that this kind of cooperation was possible in theory but complicated in practice. But the tornado had stripped away the complications right along with everything else that wasn't essential.

"Grace, there's a call for you," a volunteer said from behind the makeshift information table, her hands dusty from hours of sorting.

She picked up the portable phone. "This is Grace," she said.

"Grace, it's Pastor Morrison. We've just received confirmation that the temporary morgue at Eternal Light Funeral Home needs more chaplains." His deep baritone bore the weariness of too many calls like this one. "Families are arriving to identify loved ones, and they shouldn't have to go through this alone. Can you coordinate coverage with Pastor Wilson and Father Vargas?"

"How many are we expecting?"

"There are forty-three confirmed deaths so far, and eight people are still unaccounted for. Most of the missing are from the trailer park and the senior housing complex."

She closed her eyes. Forty-three. The number landed hard, and then harder. It was too immense to grasp in its entirety, so her mind did what it kept doing these days. It broke the grief into pieces small enough to manage.

She had sat with some of them at the hospital. Others were strangers to her. It didn't matter. By the time they walked through the doors of that funeral home, they would all fall under her care in some small, trembling way. They were coming to look at the faces of people they had eaten breakfast with a week ago. People they had expected to see at supper, at church, at school pickup, and at choir practice. People who had been ordinary and full of life... until suddenly they weren't.

"I'll have chaplains there within the hour," she declared. "No one goes through that process alone."

"Amen to that." Pastor Morrison paused. "You know... right now, denominational pride seems like the most foolish thing in the world right now. When children are missing, and families have nowhere to sleep, nobody cares which church you belong to. They just care that you showed up."

She ended the call and began arranging the chaplain rotation for the morgue, her pen gliding through the names of people she trusted to walk families through the worst room they would ever enter.

Brandon entered the fellowship hall with a medical bag in one hand and a clipboard in the other. Grace felt his presence before she fully turned to look at him, as if some part of her learned the shape of him so thoroughly that it recognized him even in motion, even across a crowded room. The dark circles under his eyes were more pronounced, and his scrubs remained wrinkled from a hospital locker rather than being fresh from home.

But his posture had shifted. The rigid control he normally wore had abated. He looked as if he had set down a load he had carried for years and was still figuring out how to walk without it.

He approached Grace at the coordination table and gave her the medical update. Thirty-seven patients had been treated at the community center's temporary clinic since yesterday. Most injuries were minor, involving cuts, bruises, and respiratory issues caused by dust. But the emotional trauma experienced by the children was significant. Sebastian suggested that the clinic add a counseling component.

"How are you?" Grace asked. She could ask that now without the question pulling everything unspoken between them to the surface. It was a question of a woman who loved a man and wanted to know how he was doing.

"Better than I should be, all things considered." Brandon set the clipboard on the table. "There's a story from this morning I want to tell you about."

Grace waited. She had the odd sense that he wasn't only presenting a report. He was handing her something delicate and newly discovered, something he still wasn't sure how to identify.

"We were at the medical station in the community center. A father came in with a deep laceration that needed stitches. His wife was showing early signs of shock. Their seven-year-old daughter was standing beside the treatment area, and she wouldn't stop crying. She was so scared. Her father was bleeding, her mother was shaking, and she was watching all of it from a few feet away."

Grace could visualize the scene as he recounted it. The bright medical lights, the smell of antiseptic and dust, and the little girl frozen in place because fear had rooted her there. She had experienced such situations countless times before.

"Sebastian knelt beside the girl. He didn't explain the procedure. He didn't try to distract her or send her to another room. He looked at her and said, *Would it be alright if I prayed for your daddy before the doctors help him?*" Brandon paused. "She nodded and took his hand, and Sebastian prayed. Not a long prayer... maybe twenty seconds, or so. He asked for wisdom for the medical team, for healing for her father, and for peace for their family."

"What happened next?" she asked.

"The girl stopped crying. She held Sebastian's hand while I sutured her father's wound. Twenty-seven stitches. The girl watched the entire thing without flinching because Sebastian was holding her hand, and he had prayed. It seems that was enough for her to feel safe."

Brandon looked at her, and Grace understood it clearly then. This wasn't merely admiration for Sebastian. It was a sense of disorientation as if he were carefully rearranging his inner landscape while still standing inside it.

"I've dedicated my entire career to believing that those two aspects are separate. Medicine operates here, and prayer exists separately. The two aren't supposed to mix or interfere with each other." He gave a slight shake of his head, more in wonder than disagreement now.

"But they weren't separate in that room, Grace. The prayer didn't interfere with the sutures. The sutures didn't compete with the prayer. We were two people doing two different actions for the same family at the same time... and the little girl was calm because both were taking place."

Grace didn't say anything. She didn't need to. She could almost feel the idea flowing through him, transforming him even as he attempted to speak it aloud. It reminded her of watching the effects of medicine beginning to take hold in a patient. There was no sudden drama, just the slow, undeniable proof that something inside the body had begun to respond.

"And then, yesterday, before a complex surgery on a teenager with internal injuries, Sebastian asked if I minded if he prayed,"

Brandon went on. "He didn't make a fuss about it. He didn't ask me to participate. He just bowed his head for about thirty seconds."

A quality entered his tone that she hadn't heard before, as if he were acknowledging a truth he could no longer brush aside.

"The procedure went flawlessly. Every decision was crystal clear, and every movement felt precise. I can't prove that his prayer made a difference... but I can't say it didn't either."

"What did that feel like?" she asked.

He drew in a deep breath. "It felt like perhaps the categories I've used to understand healing are too limited. Like maybe the realms of mystery and medicine can live in the same space without one undermining the other."

A commotion at the entrance of the fellowship hall redirected their attention. Daniel and Samantha came through the doorway, leading a team of volunteers hauling boxes of medical supplies. Behind them, Aaron and three members of his construction crew maneuvered a truck loaded with lumber into the parking lot.

"Supply drive from New Hope Baptist," Samantha announced, picking her way through the debris with a box balanced on her hip. Her face perspired from exertion, but there was a sparkle in her eyes. "Dr. Martinez sent extra antibiotics and wound care supplies. She said to tell you that the hospital is finally operating at normal capacity again. The last critical trauma case was discharged this morning."

Relief moved through the room as if it were visible.

"One more thing." Samantha placed her box on the table. "The sheriff's department confirmed this morning that all eight missing persons have been located. Three were found at a Red Cross shelter in Harris County. The others had been transported to hospitals outside the area during the first wave and weren't in our system." She hesitated, and for the first time, there was a tremor in her voice. "All eight are alive. Every last one of them."

Grace pressed her hand against the edge of the table. Forty-three lost... eight found. The numbers didn't cancel each other out. They never would. Tornado statistics were cruel that way, always with more devastation than healing in their wake.

But this piece of it mattered. Eight families who had endured a week trapped inside the prolonged nightmare of not knowing had just been pulled back into the world of the living. Somewhere in Brookside, phones were ringing with news that would bring mothers to their knees and cause grown men to bow their heads, thanking God through tears of relief.

Daniel set his box down and turned to Grace. "Aaron's crews have finished emergency repairs on twelve homes. They prioritized families with young children and the elderly. The Methodist church is coordinating volunteer housing for families whose places aren't livable yet."

Daniel said it the way he said everything, with measured calm, as though the logistics of disaster recovery were simply another version of the quiet competence he brought to everything he touched.

She looked past him and watched Aaron cross the parking lot with a bundle of two-by-fours on his shoulder, speaking with a crew member about a roof repair on Cedar Street. The community center he constructed, the one designed for Meghan's cooking program, had become the epicenter of Brookside's recovery.

The commercial kitchen that the couple spent months designing now produced hundreds of meals daily for displaced families. Willow and Anna had been alternating shifts alongside Meghan since the storm, and the kitchen hadn't stopped running.

Samantha reappeared beside Grace. "Principal Watkins and some of the other teachers set up temporary learning centers at three churches. It will keep the kids in a routine while parents deal with insurance claims and repairs." She softened a bit as she smiled. "Meghan's been incredible in the kitchen. She and Willow figured out how to feed four hundred people from a space designed for sixty, and Anna's been overseeing the volunteer rotation, so nobody burns out."

What they were witnessing wasn't a coordinated disaster response. It was a community revealing itself. It was people who knew each other's names and children and histories, doing what neighbors do when confronted with a catastrophe. The scale was greater than anything Brookside had faced, but the underlying instinct was the same one she had always cherished in this town.

Willow pressing free scones into tired hands. Carmen organizing childcare before anyone had to ask. A retired firefighter who kept showing up even when his body told him to rest. Love, not as sentiment, but as labor. Love with work gloves on. Love expressed through casseroles, clipboards, soup ladles, and pickup trucks. Love designed to meet the crisis.

A scripture rose in Grace's mind, and she spoke it spontaneously. *"By this everyone will know that you are my disciples, if you love one another."*

Brandon, who had been watching the volunteers move through the hall, turned to her. "What was that?"

Grace allowed her gaze to sweep over the hall once more. She saw people who typically worshipped in separate buildings and held different theological views, now sorting socks together, stirring soup, and outlining transportation routes as though they had always belonged to one another.

"In John 13:35, Jesus told His disciples that love in action would be the hallmark of authentic faith. Not doctrinal agreement or theological perfection. Just love, manifested through showing up."

Brandon looked at the hall for a long time.

"I've never seen anything like this," he remarked.

"Me either." Grace paused, and the gravity of that statement settled deep. She had spent her life inside churches, watching theologians disagree and defend their boundaries. But she had never seen them like this, stripped down to the one essence that apparently could not be stripped away.

"Me either," she murmured softly to herself.

Sebastian arrived in wrinkled scrubs, indicating he had come directly from the hospital. He approached Brandon and Grace at the coordination table and gave them a surgical update. A woman who was hit by flying debris had successfully undergone surgery. Her family had been holding a prayer vigil in the waiting area for the past two days.

"When I told them the surgery was successful, they asked if they could offer prayers of thanks in the chapel." Sebastian's tired face folded into a faint smile. "I had to tell them that the chapel was still under repair. They said that the God they were thanking is bigger than any damaged building."

Brandon let that sit between them for a moment. "Sebastian, can I ask you an honest question?"

"Always," his friend replied.

"When you pray before surgery, what exactly are you praying for?"

Sebastian took a seat on a bench assembled from salvaged pew wood. "I pray for wisdom beyond my training, clear decision-making, healing for the patient, and peace for the family." He looked down at his hands... hands that had spent the past week cutting people open and working to put them back together. "And I pray that, regardless of the outcome, love will be present in the operating room."

"Does that ever distract you from focusing?"

"I believe it enhances my focus. Recognizing my limits and asking for help doesn't make me less capable. It makes me more careful... more humble. I'm more conscious that I can't control every result."

Sebastian met Brandon's eyes. "I've lost patients after praying, Brandon. Prayer isn't a guarantee. But it's an acknowledgment that what I do matters beyond the surgical result. The people on my table are more than the sum of their injuries."

Brandon absorbed that without answering right away. Grace stayed quiet, close enough to hear, but far enough not to intrude. This wasn't her conversation to guide. It belonged to two doctors. Two long-time friends. Something in her knew it needed room to unfold without being helped along.

"Sebastian," Brandon said at last. "You mentioned that you have a surgery scheduled for tomorrow morning, right?"

"Yes... it's a cardiac case."

"I'd like to be there for it." Brandon paused, and Grace felt the hesitation like a suspended breath. "I'm not saying that I'm ready to pray, but I'd like to be in the room when you do."

Sebastian looked at him. The expression on his face was so fleeting that Grace almost missed it. Relief, maybe. Gratitude. The careful restraint of a man who had waited six long years for his friend to take this small step, and loving him enough not to make too much of it when he finally did.

"I'd like that," Sebastian said hoarsely. "Five-thirty tomorrow morning at the pre-op suite."

Brandon nodded. "I'll be there."

The afternoon wore on. Grace coordinated chaplain assignments for the morgue, the shelters, and the three churches operating as temporary learning centers. Brandon alternated between the medical station and the hospital. Carmen appeared periodically with updates, each one unveiling another layer of the community's response. The Red Cross was facilitating family reunification at the high school and emergency housing had been arranged for thirty-seven families. Counseling services were being developed through the school system.

By evening, the golden light had softened to amber, and the fellowship hall quieted to the rhythm of a day's work ending. Volunteers packed up. The kitchen wound down, and the soup pots Meghan and Willow had been tending since dawn were finally empty, their metallic sides scraped clean.

Grace strolled alongside Brandon toward the parking lot, their fingers entwined as they maneuvered over the uneven ground. The contact was simple, warm, and so natural it felt less like a choice and more like a recognition. His hand enclosed hers as if it inherently understood its place.

"Sebastian asked me to pray with him before the cardiac case tomorrow," Brandon said.

Grace's step faltered slightly for just a moment. Brandon's grip grew firmer, steadying her to prevent a stumble. Once she regained her footing, they resumed walking. "What did you say to him?"

"I told him I'd like to try." He looked at the sky, which was clear for the first time in a week, stars twinkling for the first time since the tornado. "I still don't understand everything about prayer or divine intervention. And I certainly don't understand any of it the way you and Sebastian do. But I can't ignore what I've seen."

Grace squeezed his hand. She didn't push or dress the moment up in church language that might make him feel scrutinized instead of heard. She wanted to let his fragile honesty breathe, giving it a chance to take root.

"Whatever questions you're carrying, I want you to know that I love you for who you are in this moment," she said, "Not who you might become, but this version of you... the one who's willing to be in the room."

Brandon stopped in his tracks, and she halted beside him. The parking lot was nearly deserted, and the evening air smelled like sawdust, the last remnants of soup, and the distinctive sweetness following a week of rain.

"I love you too," he replied. "I love that you haven't tried to rush this. I love that you've allowed me to come to terms with everything at my own pace."

He turned to face her. "I don't have a theology, Grace. I may never have one. But I have you, and I'm surrounded by people who showed up for each other because love inspired them to. Plus, I have two silver feathers in my pocket that I can't explain." He drew in a breath. "Maybe that's enough for now."

She swallowed once. "It's more than enough."

They stood together in the parking lot as the last light faded from the sky. Around them, the town was still broken. Trees were strewn across the roads. Power lines still dangled from tilted poles. Roofs were still missing, and families still slept in church basements. The toll of forty-three lives lost still hung heavily in the air, and the sorrow wouldn't disappear anytime soon.

But the people were still here. They worked, cooked, rebuilt, and prayed. They treated wounds, held hands, and engaged in the slow, unglamorous, vital work of reconstructing a community one family at a time.

Grace leaned her head against Brandon's shoulder. He laid his chin on her hair. They stood there, two weary souls in a battered parking lot, clinging to each other.

Chapter 25

THREE WEEKS AFTER THE tornado, the hospital's east wing smelled more like primer and sawdust than smoke and stagnant water. Brandon ducked under the caution tape still blocking access to portions of the corridor. He followed the orange tape that the construction crews had marked to guide their efforts across the patched floor.

New drywall covered the torn sections, and the hallway ceiling tiles had been replaced. The emergency lights that had flickered ominously for weeks had vanished, replaced by standard fluorescent fixtures that hummed softly, creating a familiar sound that hinted at the hospital's gradual return to normalcy.

Brandon was on his way to the chapel at six o'clock in the morning, having just finished praying with Sebastian before a cardiac bypass. He had expected to feel self-conscious, restless, or even out of place. Instead, it had felt strangely natural, as though he had stepped into a moment that had been waiting for him longer than he understood. He craved a quiet spot to sit with that feeling before the ER swept him back into the whirlwind of the morning.

The chapel doors had been rehung. Scaffolding still braced the repaired ceiling in the far corner, and canvas tarps covered areas where restoration work was ongoing. Even so, the transformation that had taken place in the weeks since the tornado was visible in every detail.

Volunteers from across the community had accomplished this. Wildflowers in mason jars decorated the makeshift windowsills that would one day house stained glass. Candles in glass holders lined the renovated ledges. Fresh paint brightened the walls, and the floor had been swept clean of the glass and plaster that littered it the night he and Grace sat on the only surviving pew, sharing secrets they could never reclaim.

In the far corner, where the altar would eventually be refurbished, someone placed a small, rough wooden cross. Crafted from salvaged wood, it still bore the scars of the storm, exuding a rugged elegance as if built by someone who needed it to exist without the luxury of time for beauty.

He sat on one of the refinished pews and dropped his elbows to his knees, pressing his hands together while his thoughts moved in slow, unsteady circles. Three weeks ago, he had told the woman he loved that her life's work was worthless. The memory still stung with humiliating clarity. Two weeks ago, he stood in a pre-op suite, listening to Sebastian pray over a cardiac patient.

Last week, a nine-year-old boy asked him if the doctors were going to pray before fixing his broken arm, because the doctors at the tornado clinic had prayed, and it helped him feel brave.

Brandon had hesitated only a second before asking, "Would you like that?"

The boy had nodded eagerly.

So Brandon bowed his head and said, in his own awkward, unpracticed words, a thing that wasn't quite a prayer but wasn't nothing either. He asked for steady hands, a good outcome, and for the boy to feel safe. The boy smiled and held still for the entire procedure.

Brandon hadn't disclosed that to anyone. He still struggled to define it for himself. Some stubborn part of him insisted on categorizing it before embracing its reality. Yet another part of him, one that was becoming harder to ignore, was starting to recognize that perhaps the label mattered less than the experience itself.

The chapel door opened, and Grace entered holding two cups of coffee. She wore a blue dress that accentuated the gold in her hazel eyes, and her hair hung loose around her shoulders in a way that told him she hadn't been at the hospital long enough to pull it into its usual bun arrangement.

She didn't seem surprised to see him. After handing him a coffee, she settled beside him on the pew.

"Sebastian told me you were here," she said. "He said you came to the pre-op suite this morning."

"I did," he replied.

"How was it?"

Brandon looked down at the coffee warming his hands, pondering the question. A month ago, he would have dodged it, diverting the conversation to the patient's vitals or the details of the surgical approach. Anything concrete that wouldn't lay him bare. But Grace had changed him in ways he was still discovering. Not by pushing him... she never pushed. Instead, she made honesty feel safer than avoidance.

"It felt... right," he finally admitted. "Not in the sense of a dramatic conversion or some sort of religious epiphany. It was simply me being fully present for something important and choosing not to be a bystander."

Grace sipped her coffee. She didn't push or say, *"I'm so proud of you,"* or *"God is working in your life,"* or any of the well-intentioned phrases that would have turned his private, tentative step into something he wasn't sure he was ready for. She just drank her coffee and allowed the chapel to hold the silence.

"There's a story that's been on my mind all week," he continued. "Last week, a nine-year-old boy in the ER asked me to pray before I set his broken arm. He said the doctors at the tornado clinic prayed, and it made him feel brave."

Grace set her coffee down, attentive.

"I told him that I would. I wasn't sure what I was doing. I just asked for steady hands and a positive outcome. I wanted him to feel safe."

He lifted his gaze to the wooden cross in the corner. Looking at it somehow made the words flow more easily.

"The boy smiled. He held still for the entire procedure. And I've been thinking about it nonstop since then. I don't know if it was truly prayer or just a man trying to comfort a scared child. But I do know that the room felt different afterward, and I know the boy felt that difference too."

Grace's eyes shone with unshed tears, but her words were steady. "You don't have to know what it was, Brandon. You just have to know it was real."

They sat together in the tranquil space. The candles flickered. Morning light began filtering through the temporary windows, laying pale rectangles on the restored floor. The chapel smelled like paint and flowers, the scent a reflection of a place being rebuilt out of love and care.

"I have some news," Grace announced. "Janet Crawford called me yesterday. The hospital administration has approved the expanded chaplaincy program. They want to incorporate spiritual care into every department. Not just during times of a crisis, but as a permanent aspect of the treatment model."

Brandon turned to look at her. "Sebastian and I submitted a proposal for that two weeks ago. It included evidence-based protocols for integrating spiritual care alongside medical treatment. We provided patient satisfaction data from the tornado response, metrics on staff burnout, and the family support outcomes from your chaplain teams."

He stopped, suddenly aware of how significant this was. Not only for the institution but for him and her personally.

"I cited your work, Grace. I used the tornado response as a case study to demonstrate how spiritual care positively influences medical outcomes."

Her eyebrows lifted in astonishment. "You wrote a medical proposal citing chaplain work?"

"No... I wrote a medical proposal citing *your* work specifically. Because the data supports it, and because it's the right thing to do. And because I watched Wilbur Danes die in peace because you told him his family was alive and prayed with him while my team tried to save his life."

He met her eyes without flinching. "I couldn't save him, but you gave him the last thing he needed. And the hospital administration should understand that what you gave that man was as crucial as anything I did with a scalpel."

Grace stared at him for a long time. "Do you have any idea how far you've come?"

He gave a huff that almost turned into a laugh. "I have some idea. Mostly because you didn't give up on me when I was at my worst."

He reached for her hand. "What if we build this together? Not just the program, but the model itself. What if Lakeside becomes a place where medicine and spiritual care work together rather than separate entities? What if every action taken in the ER, OR, and consultation room is seen as part of the same mission?"

"That's the vision I've had since I became a chaplain," Grace said. "I just never imagined I'd share it with a man who used to tell me that prayer was a distraction."

A wave of shame coursed through him, but it no longer had the power to make him hide behind walls of defensiveness. "I'm a former skeptic and, currently, a work in progress." Brandon squeezed her hand. "And for the record... I was wrong."

Grace stood and walked to the wooden cross in the corner. She knelt next to it and touched one of the flowers at its base, a yellow wildflower still glistening with morning dew.

"I've been thinking about a verse," she said. "Colossians 3:14. *And over all these virtues put on love, which binds them all together in perfect unity.*"

Brandon came to stand beside her. "What does it mean to you right now?"

"It signifies everything we've endured... the tornado, the losses, the fight, the reconciliation, all the different people from all the different churches who showed up and worked together... all of it's held together by one thing. Love. Not doctrinal alignment or identical beliefs. Just love, expressed through the willingness to support each other."

She looked up at him and her words moved through him with tenderness.

"That's what I see when I look at us, Brandon. Two individuals with their own questions and fears, united by the decision to love each other anyway."

Brandon looked at the cross, then at Grace kneeling beside it, and then at the chapel being rebuilt around them by a community that had lost so much yet continued to rebuild. The morning light brightened the floor. The candles, unnecessary now, still burned.

"Yesterday, Carmen told me that they're establishing a memorial garden at Providence Park," Grace said, rising and wiping dust from her knees. "It's going to be on the site where the tornado first touched down. The town council approved it last week. Forty-three trees... one for each person we lost. And they're placing a fountain near the gazebo. A dedication service is scheduled for August."

Brandon wrapped his arm around her shoulders. "I heard. Pastor Morrison asked if I'd speak at the dedication."

"What did you say?"

"I said yes."

He looked at her and then out toward the corridor beyond the chapel doors.

"I still don't have a solid grasp of theology... but I have a story about a community that persevered through a terrible tornado. And I have a story about a doctor who spent twelve years building walls against faith and was brought back by a chaplain, a surgeon, an eight-year-old girl, and a man with silver hair and a wooden cane who left behind feathers that defied explanation."

He paused, but this time, the hesitation felt less like resistance and more like honesty catching up to itself. "I think that story is worth telling."

Grace leaned into his side. "I think so too."

They walked out of the chapel together into the hospital corridor. The morning shift was beginning, and the day's first patients were arriving, signaling the continuation of healing in all its forms. The caution tape still hung in the east wing, but beyond it, the hospital was alive, functional, and full of people who had chosen, again and again, to show up.

His silver feather rested in his shirt pocket. He knew Grace's was in her bag. Two small, warm, inexplicable objects carried by two people who had stopped trying to rationalize everything and instead, learned to be grateful.

The summer ahead held a memorial service, the gradual work of rebuilding a town, a relationship, and a faith that looked nothing like the polished certainty he had watched his mother carry so effortlessly when he was a boy. His version was rougher than that, constructed from salvaged wood, enduring love, and the cumulative evidence of months spent showing up.

It would suffice.

Chapter 26

Grace fastened the fine gold chain and let the pendant settle against her collarbone. The small silver feather, commissioned by Brandon from a jeweler in Atlanta, shimmered in the light streaming through her bedroom window, scattering tiny reflections across the ceiling. It had been three months since the tornado. Three months since Brandon walked into the wreckage of the hospital chapel holding a feather he couldn't explain and professed his love to her.

Warm August breezes wafted through the open window, bringing with them the scent of honeysuckle and the faint sound of church bells. Every rebuilt church in Brookside was ringing them tonight. The memorial service for the forty-three lives lost would unite congregations that had spent the past three months learning lessons they should have grasped long before disaster compelled them into action.

Grace studied her reflection in the mirror. The woman looking back wore a rose-colored dress with her hair loose around her shoulders. She looked different, and it wasn't because of the dress. Somewhere between the storm and the rebuilding, she had released the need to sound certain when certainty was impossible, and oddly enough, it had made her more productive at her work.

The doorbell rang. She opened the door to find Brandon dressed in a navy suit and a silver tie. The sight of him still sent a thrill through her that she had given up trying to articulate. Three months of mornings, evenings, and late-night conversations about everything and nothing had only intensified it. He stood in the threshold, just as he had in the ER, fully occupying the space, his presence outwardly serene yet charged beneath the surface.

"You look stunning," he said, his voice low and warm. The words settled over her like a caress. Not the polite kind of compliment men usually gave, but something deeper, something that felt like truth.

"And you look pretty sharp yourself." She grabbed her purse. "How are you feeling about the speech?"

"A little nervous." He extended his arm. "Sebastian reminded me that I'm sharing what I've seen, not preaching a sermon. That helped."

They walked to his car beneath a sky washed in amber, the color that came just before a summer sunset gave itself over to evening. The oaks along the street were lush with leaves again, whole and green, almost defiantly resuming life after the tornado had stripped them bare. New growth was everywhere.

Providence Park had undergone a remarkable transformation. The memorial garden occupied the section where the tornado first touched down, the same ground where Brandon had sat on a bench at three in the morning, discussing loss and purpose with a silver-haired stranger.

Curved pathways wound between forty-three flowering trees, one for each life lost. Bronze plaques at the base of each tree bore a name and a date. Near the white gazebo, the fountain shimmered softly in the evening light, the same spot where Aaron proposed to Meghan last year.

Families were gathered in clusters. Grace recognized faces from the hospital, from the relief center, and from the long, aching nights spent beside gurneys, holding hands and whispering prayers when explanations felt useless. She spotted the Robinsons standing beneath a small dogwood tree, Emma's name etched on the plaque at its base.

Mrs. Fletcher sat alone on a bench near the fountain, cradling a photograph of her husband in her lap, her fingers spread across his image as if she could still feel his warmth beside her. The Harmon family stood together further down the path, Rebekah walking independently now, her father's arm around her mother's shoulders.

"Grace! Brandon!" Carmen waved from near the fountain. Sofia stood beside her in a pale pink dress adorned with white ribbons and tiny flowers woven into her curls.

Sofia dashed away from her mother and wrapped her arms around Grace's waist. "Miss Grace, you look like a princess. And Dr. Brandon looks like a prince who rescues people."

Grace laughed and knelt, wrapping the little girl in a hug. "Thank you, sweetheart. You look lovely."

Carmen joined them, her eyes shifting between Grace and Brandon with the warm assessment of a woman who watched their relationship withstand trials that should have torn it apart. "How are you both holding up?" she asked. "This evening will touch every person here."

"We're ready," Grace answered. She glanced at Brandon, and the steadiness in his expression confirmed it.

The crowd gathered around a small platform near the fountain as the sun touched the horizon. Grace and Brandon took their seats near Sebastian and Sloane. Pastor Morrison stepped to the podium, his deep baritone quieting the murmurs of several hundred attendees who had come to reflect on their losses and celebrate the new beginnings they had discovered.

"We are gathered tonight to grieve what was taken from us. And we come to honor what was given to us in the taking. This garden stands where the tornado first struck our town. Three months ago, this ground was covered in rubble. Tonight, it's home to forty-three trees, each one dedicated to a life that helped to shape us. And it surrounds us, the survivors, standing together in a way that wouldn't have been possible if we hadn't first been broken."

Grace felt Brandon's hand find hers. She held on tightly.

"Tonight we'll hear from Dr. Brandon Lawson." Pastor Morrison looked toward their row. "A man whose work alongside our spiritual leaders has changed how Lakeside Community Hospital serves its families and its community."

Brandon stood. Grace watched him walk to the podium with the measured gait of a man accustomed to performing under pressure throughout his entire medical career, now channeling that discipline into unfamiliar territory. He placed his hands on the edges of the podium and scanned the crowd.

"Three months ago, I stood in this park when it was a field of debris."

His voice traveled easily through the still evening air, low, steady, and unmistakably his own.

"I'm an emergency physician. My training involves fighting death, preserving life, and gauging success by whether my patients walk out of the hospital. By that standard, the tornado was a defeat. We lost forty-three members of this community despite everything medicine could provide."

The garden was silent, save for the steady spill of the fountain.

"I stood in the rubble, and I was angry. Angry at the storm. Angry at a God I wasn't sure I believed in. Angry at my own inability to control the outcome."

Grace could see the faces looking back at him, open, attentive, and expectant.

"In the weeks that followed, my anger gave way to a different kind of perspective. Not because I found answers, but because I watched people. I watched a retired firefighter named Julian Dawson volunteer at the hospital every day because he couldn't stop showing up. I watched a social worker named Carmen Delgado organize childcare for hospital staff families so that parents could focus on saving lives without worrying about their children.

I watched nurses, doctors, and chaplains working side by side, sacrificing sleep, because the individuals in those beds mattered more than their own exhaustion."

Then his gaze locked onto hers, and that single look nearly unraveled her.

"And I watched a hospital chaplain, named Grace Winslow, sit with families during the most devastating moments of their lives. She didn't promise them miracles. She didn't tell them that God had a plan. She simply sat beside them, held their hands, prayed with them, and stayed. Long after the surgeries were over and the doctors had moved on to the next patient... she stayed."

She gripped her knees to keep her hands from shaking.

"I used to believe that healing was the exclusive territory of medicine," he continued. "I believed that the only instruments that mattered were those I could hold in my hands." He paused. "The tornado showed me how mistaken I was."

His voice deepened, gathering momentum. "True healing happens when a community rallies for its members. When churches that usually worship separately share kitchens, pews, and volunteers. When a surgeon takes a moment to pray before an operation, and a skeptic finds the strength to stand by his side. When a man who's spent years running from hope finds the courage to embrace it."

He turned toward the rows of trees.

"We lost people we loved. We can't bring them back. But we can pay tribute to them by becoming the community they helped create. A community that treats the whole person, body and spirit, doubt and faith, science and mystery. A community that shows up." He paused, and Grace saw his hand flex slightly against the podium. "That's what I've learned from all of you. And that's what I'll carry with me for the rest of my life."

The applause began slowly, almost reverently, then swelled. Grace watched as he returned to his seat. The pride that surged within her felt too intimate to resemble victory. He hadn't hidden her from that truth. He had honored her within it.

The service continued with readings from the clergy, a combined choir from six churches singing a hymn written specifically for this night by the music director at New Hope Baptist, and testimonies from family members who shared their small, gradual steps toward healing.

As twilight deepened, Pastor Morrison concluded with a prayer and invited the crowd to walk the memorial paths. Families drifted toward the trees planted in memory of their loved ones, while others headed to the reception tables. Grace watched Mrs. Fletcher lay a hand on the bronze plaque beneath her husband's tree and stand there, motionless, for a long time.

Brandon touched her arm. "Would you walk with me?"

Grace slipped her hand into his and let him lead her away from the gathered crowd. They followed a curving path deeper into the garden, leaving the soft murmur of voices behind as they moved toward the restored gazebo. Solar lights illuminated the pathway, and the flowering trees arched overhead, their branches creating a living canopy that turned the last of the evening light into a golden, private tunnel.

As they walked, she began noticing the little details. Fresh flowers adorned the base of the gazebo. The climbing vines were restored and lush. The path itself looked swept and tended with special care, as though someone had intentionally made this walk perfect for tonight. For the two of them.

A tremor of awareness swept through her. She slowed her pace. "Brandon... where are we going?"

"Almost there." The words were steady, but she could feel a new tension in his hand, tighter than the nerves he had shown before his speech. This was different... deeper. Her pulse stumbled into a quicker rhythm.

By the time they reached the gazebo, her breath had grown shallow. The white octagonal structure had been repaired, and in the fading light, it looked almost surreal, too exquisite and carefully lit to be part of the ordinary world.

Brandon stopped at the foot of the steps and turned to face her.

He looked at her, and whatever he saw in her face must have given him the confidence he needed. He reached into his jacket pocket and slowly, deliberately, lowered himself to one knee.

Her hands flew to her mouth.

He opened a small velvet box. Inside was a ring. A center diamond framed in delicate silver metalwork, fashioned into tiny feathers that curved around the band. The design was so unmistakably theirs, infused with all the sacred moments they had endured together, allowing her to comprehend it before her thoughts could fully materialize.

Brandon Lawson was kneeling before her in a memorial garden with a ring in his hand.

"Grace Winslow." His voice was rough, and that roughness somehow made it more genuine. "Before I met you, I was a man who believed that control was the only thing that could protect me from losing what was important. I thought my skepticism made me strong. I thought keeping people at a distance equaled keeping myself safe."

His eyes didn't leave hers. Somewhere in her peripheral vision, she was dimly aware of movement. Figures approached along the path, but she couldn't have looked at them if she tried.

"You proved me wrong about all of it. You loved me when I was at my worst. You stood by me when I almost destroyed everything. You showed me that hope isn't the absence of doubt. It's the decision to love even when the outcome isn't guaranteed."

His free hand reached for hers, and she took it. His fingers shook against her skin. Brandon, who often exuded strength, now knelt vulnerable before her, and witnessing him lay bare his soul in such a public moment was heart-wrenching.

"I don't have it all figured out, but I have a story about a woman who sat with me in my darkest room and refused to leave. And I want to spend the rest of my life striving to be the man who's worthy of that kind of love."

He lifted the ring from its box.

"Will you marry me? Will you build a life with me that has room for hard questions and sacred mysteries? Will you let me stand beside you while we figure out the rest together?"

"Yes." The word came out almost soundless, a breath more than a voice. Then it grew. "Yes, Brandon! Yes!"

His hands were steady now as he slid the ring onto her finger. The silver feathers nestled against her skin, warm as living things, in that impossible way that no longer startled her the way it once might have. She didn't attempt to analyze it. Some gifts thrived in their enigmatic nature, and this one was no exception.

She pulled him to his feet and kissed him. This kiss wasn't the tentative exploration they had shared in the parking lot. Nor the raw, aching connection in the chapel. This kiss was a declaration, a manifestation of her commitment, a promise resonating with every fiber of her being.

His arms came around her, strong and sure, and she slid her fingers up to the back of his neck, curling them into the collar of his jacket. Surrounding them, the garden was shrouded in darkness, broken only by the soft glow of the lights. In the distance, she heard the murmur of the crowd shift, then swell into applause as people realized what was happening.

When they parted, Grace looked at the ring on her hand. The feathers reflected the light from the nearest solar lamp. She looked at Brandon, and the expression on his face was one she had never seen there before, a relief so profound it resembled an awakening, as if he had finally broken the surface after being underwater for far too long.

"I love you," he confessed, his voice rough with emotion. "More than I knew was possible."

"I love you too." She laced her fingers through his. "And I already love the sound of Grace Lawson."

The rest blurred gently after that in a blend of happy tears, congratulations, and laughter. Carmen hugged them both, crying, but then denied it with such fervor that Grace laughed through her own tears. Sofia proclaimed that Brandon was now officially a prince. Sebastian shook Brandon's hand with a quiet, deeply satisfied smile... the look of a man who had been waiting years for this moment and didn't need words to express it. Pastor Wilson took off his glasses to clean them, never quite managing to hide his smile.

When the garden was nearly empty, they strolled toward the gate, their footsteps quiet on the gravel path. Just as they were about to exit, Grace noticed a flicker of movement near the towering oaks that lined the garden's periphery. She felt Brandon's grip tighten around her hand.

A figure stepped into a patch of moonlight. Silver hair. The silhouette of a wooden cane. A face she couldn't clearly see, yet recognized with an odd certainty. It was like recalling a melody that lingered in the recesses of her memory, familiar yet elusive.

The figure raised one hand, but it wasn't a casual wave of greeting. It felt more like a benediction, a silent blessing offered by someone who understood more than words could hold. Then he receded back into the shadows beneath the oaks and was gone.

No footsteps. No rustle of leaves. Only the empty space where he had been, and that mysterious stillness that followed Liam's departures, a silence so profound it felt as if the very air was holding its breath.

She turned to Brandon. He looked back at her.

"He was watching," she stated.

Brandon nodded, his voice soft and untroubled. "I believe he's been watching us right from the beginning."

They walked to the car, Grace's ring catching the light with every step, her silver feather pendant resting against her throat. Behind them, the memorial garden held its forty-three trees and the memory of a proposal made by a man who had spent twelve years in darkness and had finally, at the exact right moment, stepped into the light.

The drive home was peaceful. Brandon steered with one hand on the wheel and the other wrapped around hers, his thumb tracing the feathers on her ring.

At her door, he kissed her goodnight. The kiss was unhurried and tender, as if he knew he no longer had to rush now that the future he once feared losing was a promise they could create together.

He pulled back just enough to lean his forehead against hers, their breaths mingling in the small space between them.

"I should let you go," he murmured, his voice a low rumble lacking true intention.

"You should," she whispered back, her fingers curling into the fabric of his jacket to keep him exactly where he was. A soft, giddy laugh escaped her. "Though I was thinking... it would be a shame to wait too long for the next part."

His brows arched in a blend of surprise and curiosity, a slow warmth igniting in his soulful eyes. "The next part?"

She tilted her head, happiness making her daring in the loveliest way. "A Christmas wedding. I think it would be wonderful. All the lights, the music... the cold outside and all that warmth inside. Just picture it."

A slow smile spread across his face, one that reached into the depths of his eyes. He lifted his hand to cradle her cheek, his thumb brushing away a tear she hadn't realized she had shed.

"Then we'll have a Christmas wedding," he replied. "I promise you lights, music, and all the warmth I have to give."

He kissed her once more, a seal on the vow, before finally, reluctantly, stepping back.

Grace closed the door and leaned against it, her hand raised in front of her face, turning the ring in the hallway light. The silver feathers caught every angle, breathtaking and extraordinary.

She pressed a hand against her heart and closed her eyes.

Lord, thank You. For the storm. For the ruins. For the man who walked through all of it and chose to stay. For feathers that shouldn't exist and for a love that defied the odds we placed upon it. Thank You for not giving me the life I planned. Thank You for giving me this one instead. Amen.

Chapter 27

Four Months Later

GRACE STOOD ON THE elevated platform at Brookside Bridal Boutique, consciously forcing herself to unclench her fingers one by one. The ivory silk cascaded around her feet in soft liquid folds. As she gazed into the three-way mirror, she was struck by the image of a woman she was still getting used to seeing. She wasn't merely the composed chaplain with her hospital badge and her hair neatly pinned up, nor was she the woman who had always believed that certain chapters of life belonged to other people. She was a woman who was three weeks away from becoming Brandon Lawson's wife.

"Grace, if you keep fidgeting, I won't be able to finish the hem." Carmen knelt beside the platform, a cushion of pins strapped to her wrist and a tape measure looped around her neck. Her eyes narrowed in concentration on the silk. She insisted on handling the alterations herself, and Grace hadn't objected. Having Carmen's hands tailor this dress made it feel less like just fabric and more like a blessing.

"Sorry." Grace tried to hold still. "I can't stop worrying about the chairs. Have we confirmed the number yet?"

"Yes, and you need to stop stressing over them," Carmen slid a pin into place. "Your only job between now and Christmas Eve is to show up and say *I do.* Everything else is already taken care of."

Sofia peeked out from behind a rack of bridesmaids' dresses, carrying an armful of lavender tulle that was almost as large as she was. At ten years old, she approached her junior bridesmaid duties with a solemnity that belied her age, treating her responsibilities as if they were sacred. Sofia had weathered the tornado, spending nights in a church shelter while her mother worked tirelessly. She emerged from it filled with love and bravery. Grace understood that resilience could be both a beautiful trait and a heavy burden for a child.

"Miss Grace, I practiced walking in my dress again. I took tiny steps so I wouldn't trip." Sofia's face glowed with determination.

"Let me see, sweetheart."

Sofia stepped forward and twirled in the lavender silk, her skirt flaring around her knees. She beamed with such unguarded joy that Grace felt tears unexpectedly prick her eyes.

"You look stunning," Grace said, meaning it with her whole heart.

Carmen rose and brushed stray threads from her slacks. "Grace, look in the mirror. Tell me what you see."

Grace turned back to the glass and paused. The gown, the gentle waves of her hair, the softness in her own features... it all came together in a way that felt almost surreal.

"I see a woman who's ready to be a wife," she said quietly. "One who doesn't have to stop being herself."

Carmen's eyes sparkled with approval. "Perfect answer."

The heavy doors of Cottonwood Faith Community Center opened with a creak that Grace had encountered countless times before. The sanctuary smelled like fresh lumber and paint. Winter light slanted through the newly installed stained glass, casting vibrant colors across the polished floors. The renovation had taken months to complete, funded by donations from every church in the county and executed by Aaron's construction crew, who worked hand in hand with volunteers from six congregations.

Brandon walked beside her, his hand at the small of her back. Pastor Wilson greeted them in the hallway, his cardigan speckled with glitter from assisting the children's ministry with Christmas decorations. Pastor Morrison was already in the office, his notes sprawled out on the desk.

"Today, our discussion will center on partnership," Pastor Morrison stated once they were seated. "More specifically, we'll delve into the dynamics of a marriage where both people are coming from different spiritual backgrounds."

Grace felt Brandon shift beside her. It wasn't so much a withdrawal as it was a preparation for full transparency.

"Pastors, I need to be upfront." Brandon leaned forward, his elbows on his knees. "I've grown in my understanding of faith. I've even started praying with my patients in the emergency department. But I don't have Grace's theological foundation. I don't know scripture the way she does, and I'm still working through questions that she's answered for herself years ago."

He paused, and Grace felt the seriousness of what he was trying to say. "How do I lead in our home when I'm still finding my way in what I believe?"

Pastor Wilson removed his glasses and polished them. "Tell me, Brandon... what does leadership mean to you?"

"It means having answers... knowing scripture. And making decisions based on biblical teachings." A thread of genuine uncertainty ran through his words. "Those are areas where Grace is far ahead of me."

Pastor Morrison interjected. "Son, leadership in a marriage isn't about holding a degree in theology. It's about creating a home where your family can cultivate a loving relationship with God."

He looked at Brandon with the directness that had made him a cornerstone of New Hope Baptist. "You've spent your entire career making life-and-death decisions in high-pressure situations. Your experience has prepared you to confront difficult questions. You serve others, even when the outcome is unclear. And you love a woman without insisting she change to accommodate your doubts."

A lump formed in Grace's throat.

"That's the heart of a shepherd, Brandon, whether you have the vocabulary for it yet or not."

Pastor Morrison leaned forward, his large hands clasped between his knees. "There's a man in scripture I want you to think about. His name is Thomas, and he was one of Jesus's disciples. After the resurrection, every other disciple believed because they had seen the risen Christ. But Thomas hadn't been in the room when Jesus appeared. He told them he wouldn't believe unless he could touch the nail marks himself."

The warmth in Pastor Morrison's voice felt like a truth he had carried for decades. "And do you know what Jesus did when He appeared again? He didn't shame Thomas for doubting. He walked straight up to him and invited him closer. In John 20:27, Jesus said, *'Put your finger here. See my hands. Reach out your hand and put it into my side. Stop doubting and believe.'*"

Brandon went very still beside her.

"Jesus met the skeptic on the skeptic's terms," Pastor Morrison continued. "He provided the evidence that Thomas needed. He didn't condemn the question. He honored it."

The pastor held Brandon's gaze. "You've been Thomas for much of your life. And God hasn't been waiting for you to stop asking questions. He's been placing the evidence in front of you, one piece at a time, just waiting for you to reach out to Him."

Grace turned her head slightly and looked at Brandon. She couldn't read everything behind his expression, but she could feel that the pastor's words were finding a place deep within him.

"Leadership can look like suggesting that you read a devotional together, even if you're not sure which one to pick," Pastor Wilson added. "It can be praying for your wife, even while the mechanics of prayer still feel unfamiliar. It can be saying, *I don't have this figured out, but I want to figure it out with you.'* That's honesty. And honesty is the bedrock of everything else."

Pastor Morrison turned and spoke to Grace. "How do you feel about Brandon's approach?"

Without missing a beat, Grace replied. "He keeps me grounded. He challenges me to step outside my comfort zone and confront the truths of my faith. Instead of simply reciting what I've always heard, he asks questions that push me to explore my beliefs deeper. Because of that, I feel I've become a more effective chaplain, and hopefully, a better partner too."

She turned to Brandon. "I'm not looking for a spiritual mentor. What I need is a partner who's committed to growing alongside me. I want you to ask questions that differ from mine and to point out what I might miss. I need you to call me out if I become complacent in my faith."

She held his gaze and felt the tenderness of the truth rise between them. "That's what you've been doing since the day we met. You just didn't know it had a name."

The relief on his face was unmistakable, an easing of a tension he had been carrying into this room with him.

"A partnership in discovery," he said slowly, as if savoring the idea. Then he gave the smallest nod. "That I can do."

On a chilly December afternoon, they drove to the Miller home, the sun hanging low in the sky. The previous evening, Tobias Miller had sent a brief and somewhat perplexing text. Gabrielle had been having dreams again. She claimed the messages were intended specifically for Brandon and Grace, and she insisted they be delivered before the wedding.

The house was adorned for Christmas, with smoke drifting from the chimney and a wreath hanging from the front door. Tobias opened it before they had a chance to knock.

"Thanks for coming." He stepped aside to let them in. "Denise and I are a bit puzzled by what Gabrielle has been telling us, but she was adamant that she wanted to see the both of you."

The living room smelled like hot chocolate and pine. Denise sat in an armchair with an expression of a mother trying to balance wonder and parental protectiveness. Gabrielle perched on the couch and bounced excitedly when she spotted them.

"Dr. Brandon! Miss Grace!" She launched herself off the couch. "I knew you'd come today. The angel man said you would."

Grace knelt to Gabrielle's level. "Your parents told us you have news for us."

Gabrielle nodded with the grave seriousness of a child entrusted with important information. "The nice man with the silver hair has been visiting my dreams again. He told me stuff about your wedding."

"What did he tell you?" Brandon asked. He sat next to Grace on the couch while Gabrielle squeezed between them, as if that were the most normal place for her to be.

"He showed me pictures," Gabrielle said. "You'll be wearing the prettiest white dress with sparkly bits on it, Miss Grace. And Dr. Brandon will wear a dark suit with a silver tie."

She looked back and forth between them. "And there'll be purple flowers on the wedding cake. And people from all the different churches will come."

Brandon exchanged a glance with Grace. The details about the dress had been shared only with the bridal party. His silver tie was in his closet, chosen to match the feather metalwork on Grace's ring. The lavender buttercream on the cake had been Willow's suggestion, inspired by flowers harvested at the memorial garden. Gabrielle had access to none of this information.

"He had special messages for both of you," Gabrielle continued. She turned to Brandon first, placing a small hand on his sleeve. "He said to tell you that your questions make God happy. He said grown-ups sometimes think asking too many questions is bad, but he said it really means you care about getting the right answer."

She patted his arm with solemn approval. "And he said you do two kinds of healing at the same time now. You fix people's hurt bodies, *and* you help them not be so scared. He said that's very special."

Then she turned to Grace, her young face reflecting a tender understanding of grief that seemed far beyond her years.

"He had a really important message for you, Miss Grace." The words came out hushed and reverent. "He said Mr. Anthony smiles when he sees you being happy with Dr. Brandon. He said Mr. Anthony doesn't want you to be sad anymore. And he said that when you love more people, it doesn't make your love for Mr. Anthony any smaller. It makes your love bigger."

Grace's hand found Brandon's and gripped it hard. Gabrielle kept going, exuding the serene certainty of a messenger who is too young to grasp the doubt that often weighs on adults.

"He said your wedding is going to be special because it'll show everyone that different kinds of people can love each other and help each other grow." The little girl looked between them, radiant with confidence. "And he said he'll be watching to make sure everything is beautiful."

"Does the man have a name?" Brandon asked.

"Liam." Gabrielle said it without hesitation. "He said his name means strong warrior in the old language. He said he's been helping people for a really long time."

The living room was quiet. The Christmas tree lights blinked in their slow, repetitive pattern. Tobias had his arm around Denise, both looking at their daughter with a mix of bewildered awe and acceptance.

"Thank you, Gabrielle." Grace had to work for every word through the thickness in her throat. "These messages are more precious than you know."

Gabrielle gave a small matter-of-fact shrug. "I don't have to tell him you said thank you. He already knows."

They said their goodbyes and walked down the stone pathway to the car. Grace held Brandon's hand, and they remained silent until they reached the vehicle. Brandon opened her door, but she hesitated before getting inside.

"Anthony's name," she said. "It came in a dream about a man she calls Liam." She looked at the sky, which was turning to that distinctive winter-blue hue typical of December afternoons in Georgia. "I shouldn't be surprised anymore. But I am."

Brandon stroked his chin. "I've given up being surprised. I've moved into a state I can only describe as grateful confusion."

Grace almost laughed. "Grateful confusion, huh? That might be the most honest theological position I've ever heard."

They got in the car. Brandon started the engine but didn't pull away. He sat with his hands on the wheel, looking through the windshield at the house with its Christmas decorations and smoke rising from the chimney into the cold blue sky.

"Three weeks," he said, breaking the silence.

"Three weeks," Grace echoed. "Christmas Eve."

"I'll be the one at the altar looking scared, grateful, and completely certain, all at the same time."

She turned toward him and reached across the console for his hand. "I know exactly how that feels." Then she smiled, because joy was there too, threaded all through the mystery and the ache and the wonder of it.

"Take me home, Brandon. We have a wedding to finish planning."

He backed out of the driveway, and the December sun threw long shadows across the road as they drove toward Christmas and toward the rest of their lives. In Brandon's shirt pocket, the silver feather rested warm against his heart. On Grace's left hand, the feather ring caught every angle of light. And somewhere behind them, in a ranch house decked out for Christmas, an eight-year-old girl with impossible dreams was telling her parents that the angel man was smiling.

<h1 style="text-align:center">Chapter 28</h1>

"Hold still." Carmen adjusted a pearl-tipped pin in the veil. "If you fidget one more time, I'm going to pin this to your actual hair."

She stepped back to examine Grace in the full-length mirror, tilting her head as her gaze scrutinized every detail with the same meticulous care she applied to everything she worked on.

"Sorry." Grace pressed her palms flat against the ivory silk at her hips, doing her best to remain still. The gown fit exactly the way it had at the final fitting, as though it had always been meant for her and she had only just caught up to that fact. The silver feather pendant Brandon had given her rested against her collarbone, and the engagement ring with its intricate featherwork flashed in the light from the dressing room vanity.

"Sebastian says he's been pacing for an hour," Meghan reported from the loveseat, her hands resting on her rounded belly. The baby was due in January, and Meghan moved with the deliberate care of a woman nearing the final weeks of pregnancy. "He says Brandon keeps checking his watch every thirty seconds, asking if afternoons always take this long."

Carmen smoothed the train of her gown with a soft sigh. "Men think they're prepared for marriage right up until the moment it asks them to hand over their whole future."

Just then, Grace felt a tug at the hem of her gown. Sofia stood there in her lavender dress. "I practiced everything just like you showed me. I won't drop any petals until I'm supposed to."

Grace knelt gingerly, the beading on the gown pressing into her knees. "You're going to be amazing. And even if something goes wrong, it's still okay. Today is all about love."

Sofia let out a delightful giggle. "What if Elijah decides to crawl instead of walk?" The young girl clearly found the idea of the seventeen-month-old ring bearer abandoning his role amusing.

"Especially then." Grace stood and smoothed her skirts. "Love turns even the unexpected moments into the ones you cherish the most."

Carmen checked her watch. "It's time. Are you ready to become Mrs. Brandon Lawson?"

Grace picked up her bouquet. White roses and silver ribbon, arranged with sprigs of lavender from the memorial garden at Providence Park, the same garden where Brandon knelt on one knee and asked her to build a life with him.

"I've been ready since he held me in that broken chapel and promised to grow alongside me."

Carmen touched her arm gently. "Come on, *amiga*. He's waiting."

The sanctuary doors opened and Grace momentarily forgot how to breathe.

White roses and silver ribbon bedecked every pew. Candles lined the aisle, their flames steady in the still air, casting warm light across polished wood and gleaming brass. The Christmas tree beside the altar sparkled with white lights and silver ornaments. The new stained glass created colorful patterns on the floor that hadn't existed just six months prior.

Every congregation in the community had a hand in this room. The Methodist women's circle arranged the flowers. The Baptist youth group placed every candle with the mathematical precision that teenagers apply to tasks they consider important. Catholic families donated the silver ribbon. Presbyterian volunteers polished the pews. The sanctuary that a tornado had leveled was restored by the very community that would fill it tonight.

She spotted Brandon instantly.

He stood at the altar in a charcoal suit and silver tie, his eyes already fixed on her. Those brown eyes had been one of the first things she noticed about him, all those months ago, during a midnight encounter in an emergency department supply closet. The intensity in his eyes hadn't changed, but everything underneath it had.

Sebastian stood beside him as best man, a warm smile on his face. Pastor Wilson waited at the altar in ceremonial robes, his silver-rimmed glasses reflecting the candlelight. Pastor Morrison stood beside him, his tall frame and graying hair completing the interfaith alliance that anchored Brookside through the worst year in its history.

Pachelbel's Canon floated from the organ. Sofia began her careful journey down the aisle, scattering rose petals with a concentration so fierce that several guests smiled through their tears. Behind her, Naomi Grant walked hand in hand with Elijah, guiding the wobbly seventeen-month-old as he clutched the ring bearer pillow in both fists.

Carmen glided gracefully down the aisle and took her place at the altar. Meghan followed, one hand resting on her belly and the other holding her bouquet, moving with the careful elegance of late-stage pregnancy.

Then, the music shifted to the traditional wedding march. Grace had made the choice to walk alone. Not because she had no one who would have been honored to accompany her, but because walking alone represented both her independence and her desire to join her life with Brandon's under her own power and on her own terms.

She strode forward, step by step, past the faces of those she loved. Samantha and Daniel sat in the third row, Daniel's arm around his wife's shoulders. Willow and Anna were a bit further back, with Willow already reaching for the tissues she had tucked into her purse. The Miller family sat near the middle, Gabrielle's eyes wide with the wonder of a child witnessing a dream she already knew the ending of, come true in front of her.

Hospital colleagues occupied two rows. Dr. Martinez offered a slight nod, a gesture that carried immense respect from a woman who valued every moment. Hanna dabbed her eyes with a handkerchief. Jessica pressed both hands to her mouth and then clapped silently as Grace passed.

Grace kept her focus on Brandon. With each step, she watched as the careful control he had likely been holding all day crack open, revealing a torrent of raw, unguarded emotion filled with love that transformed his face. His jaw loosened, his eyes widened, and his lips parted. For one beautiful, vulnerable moment, he looked like a man who had completely forgotten everyone else in the room.

When she reached the altar, he stepped forward. His hands trembled as he helped adjust her train. The familiar shaking mirrored the first time he touched her face in the parking lot, nearly breaking her composure entirely.

"Dearly beloved," Pastor Wilson began, his words resonating through the sanctuary. "We gather on this blessed Christmas Eve to witness the union of Brandon and Grace. They've chosen to begin their marriage on the eve of our Savior's birth, recognizing that their love, like the Christmas story itself, represents new life rising from broken places."

Pastor Morrison's deeper voice joined the liturgy. "Brandon and Grace have walked a road that tested everything they believed about love and about God. They stand before us tonight not because they have all the answers, but because they chose each other anyway. That is the kind of love worth celebrating."

Brandon's fingers intertwined with Grace's and held tight. Around them, candlelight danced against the windows. Their community, composed of every denomination, every volunteer, and every family they served throughout the toughest months of their lives, witnessed two people vowing their futures to one another in a space they rebuilt together.

"Brandon," Pastor Wilson continued. "Do you take Grace to be your wife, to love and cherish in sickness and in health, in joy and sorrow, for richer or poorer, as long as you both shall live?"

"I do." The two words rang clear and confident.

"Grace," Pastor Morrison carried on. "Do you take Brandon to be your husband, to love and cherish in sickness and in health, in joy and sorrow, for richer or poorer, as long as you both shall live?"

"I do." Her voice held even, as the rest of her did not.

Pastor Wilson nodded. "Brandon and Grace have prepared personal vows they wish to share."

Brandon turned toward her. He drew a folded paper from his pocket, but once he began speaking, it was obvious the page was merely there for comfort. His eyes stayed on hers.

"Grace Blair Winslow." The way he said her full name sounded like a blessing. "Six months ago, I was a man who believed that control was the only thing keeping me normal. I trusted what I could measure and dismissed the rest. I was convinced that keeping people at a distance was the same thing as keeping myself safe."

The sanctuary held the stillness like a vessel.

"You proved me wrong about all of it. You loved me when I was at my worst. You never demanded that I change as a condition of your love. You just showed up, again and again. There you were... in supply closets, parking lots, broken places, and during the toughest emergency department shifts I've ever worked, and you stayed."

Tears welled up in Grace's eyes, and she let them come.

"I promise to support your calling. I promise to encourage your service to others and walk beside you through questions I can't answer and mysteries I don't understand. I promise to grow with you. I promise never to ask you to change to make me comfortable."

His voice dropped lower on the last lines, and the intimacy of that made her chest ache. "And above all, I promise to do everything in love. Every decision. Every hardship. Every moment of joy and sorrow. I choose love, Grace. I choose you."

Grace unfolded her own paper. Like Brandon, she discovered that the words came from a place deeper than the page.

"Brandon Desmond Lawson." Each syllable rang clear, despite the swell of emotion surrounding them. "You've shown me that trust doesn't hinge on perfection, just honesty. Your questions have only strengthened my convictions, and your integrity has made my beliefs more real. And your willingness to stand in rooms where you didn't have the answers, and to stay there anyway, has taught me more about courage than any scripture I've ever read."

Brandon's eyes were bright as she watched him swallow.

"I've watched you fight for every patient, even when the odds were impossible. I've seen your heartache when medicine fell short.

Your dedication to healing shows me the heart of God more clearly than any sermon ever could."

She reached for both his hands. Their fingers laced, and the ring on her left hand caught the candlelight.

"I promise to be your partner and your companion. I promise to support your calling and welcome your growth at whatever pace is right for you. I will never rush your questions or pressure you for certainty you don't feel. And I promise to do everything in love... every prayer, every conversation, every moment of doubt, and every celebration. I choose to grow alongside you, Brandon, for the rest of our lives."

Pastor Wilson's words sounded thick when he spoke again. "Brandon and Grace, you have each, independently and without knowing the other's words, made the same essential promise. *'I will do everything in love.'* This promise has a name."

He opened his Bible and looked at them over the top of it. "First Corinthians 16: 14 tells us, *'Do everything in love.'* These four words encapsulate the entirety of the Christian life in one simple sentence. You've just spoken them to each other without needing to be told." He closed the Bible. "That's how I know this marriage will endure."

Sebastian stepped forward with the rings. Simple platinum bands inlaid with thin silver threads, the design honoring the feathers that marked their journey from the beginning.

"These rings represent the unending nature of your commitment," Pastor Wilson said as Brandon slipped Grace's band into place beside the engagement ring. "May they serve as daily reminders of the promises you've made and the life you're building together."

Grace placed Brandon's ring on his finger. The band settled against his skin, and she held his hand for an extra heartbeat, appreciating the solidity and permanence of their union.

Pastor Morrison's voice boomed with authority as he proclaimed, "By the power vested in us by the state of Georgia, and in the name of the Father, Son, and Holy Spirit, we pronounce you husband and wife."

Pastor Wilson's eyes crinkled behind his glasses. "Brandon, you may kiss your bride."

Brandon stepped closer, his hands tenderly framing Grace's face, his thumbs gently brushing along her cheekbones. The touch was soft and reverent, resonating with the depth of all they had endured together.

When their lips finally met, it felt almost sacred, a prayer of love spoken without words.

The sanctuary erupted in applause. Cheers rose beneath the organ's final notes. Their community, the same community that had rebuilt these walls, now celebrated within them as though joy itself had become part of the stones and beams surrounding them.

"Ladies and gentlemen," Pastor Morrison announced as they separated, both slightly breathless. "It's my profound joy to present to you, for the very first time, Dr. and Mrs. Brandon Lawson."

Chapter 29

The reception hall was radiant with white linens and silver centerpieces. Willow's lavender vanilla cake sat at the center like something from a dream, surrounded by platters of Southern food that made the whole room smell like home. Fried chicken. Macaroni and cheese. Green bean casserole. Cornbread. These dishes weren't elegant in a magazine sense... they were better than that. They were familiar and generous, a meal that conveyed a sense of belonging, and an invitation to sit down and enjoy.

Sebastian raised his glass. "To Brandon and Grace." He chose his words the way he chose surgical instruments, with precision and care, each one placed deliberately.

"I've watched this man transform from someone who trusted nothing he couldn't quantify into someone courageous enough to love the unexplainable. And I've watched Grace become even more fully herself beside him. May your marriage be as strong together as both of you are on your own."

Glasses lifted as the toast echoed through the room. The evening unfolded like every jubilant reception does, with overlapping conversations, laughter, delightful food, and music. Grace moved through the crowd on Brandon's arm, accepting embraces that carried years of shared history.

Mrs. Patterson took both of Grace's hands. "Seeing you this happy feels like watching a Christmas miracle."

Julian shook Brandon's hand and said nothing. His face did the rest.

Dr. Martinez informed them both that the hospital was a better place because of what they had created together, and then promptly excused herself to search for more cornbread, which felt so exactly like her that Grace laughed.

They danced. The first dance was slow, and Grace rested her head against Brandon's shoulder. The music played, the candles burned, their friends watched, and outside the tall sanctuary windows, snow began to fall, blanketing the world in white on Christmas Eve.

During a turn in the dance, Grace's eyes drifted toward the rear of the reception hall. A figure stood near the entrance, half-concealed by a decorated pillar. Silver hair captured the chandelier lights. With a wooden cane in one hand and a weathered face she had never seen clearly, she felt an instinctive recognition.

"Brandon." She kept the word low, meant only for him. "Look."

He followed her gaze. They both saw Liam at the same moment. He stood watching them with an expression Grace could only describe as content, as if he had been following a long, challenging story that had finally reached its destined conclusion.

Liam raised one hand. The gesture was simple. An acknowledgment. A farewell. A blessing spoken without words.

Then he withdrew, and the space where he had been standing was empty. No footsteps. No door closing. Just the candlelight, the music, and the snow cascading beyond the windows.

"He came," Grace whispered.

"Yes, he did indeed," Brandon acknowledged.

His arm tightened around her waist. They continued to sway across the dance floor, the music still playing. In that moment between the tangible and the intangible, a silver-haired man with a wooden cane had witnessed the marriage he had quietly been guiding toward its fulfillment ever since that night he sat on a park bench and asked a broken doctor whether bearing witness might be its own kind of healing.

The reception wound down in the way that the best gatherings do, with guests lingering over the final cups of coffee and the last slices of cake, reluctant to let the evening come to a close.

Carmen hugged Grace at the door and whispered, "You did it, *amiga*. You chose love."

Sofia told Brandon he was officially the best prince in Brookside.

Pastor Wilson adjusted his glasses and said, "Well done, both of you." It was the highest praise he had ever given anyone in Grace's memory.

When the last guests departed, they stood near the Christmas tree. The sanctuary was serene. The candles had burned low. Snow still fell outside, visible through the stained glass in the leisurely, unhurried way that snow falls, as though the sky was savoring each moment.

"Merry Christmas, Mrs. Lawson," Brandon murmured.

The words sent a fresh thrill coursing through her.

"Merry Christmas, my love."

He pulled her close, and she rested her head against his chest. For a while, they stood there in the candlelight while the snow accumulated on the windowsills.

Grace thought about the year that had brought them here. A supply closet at midnight. A cup of coffee offered without expectation. A skeptic and a chaplain, circling each other in a hospital where both were trying to heal people with different methods.

A tornado that tore apart everything they thought was solid. The hospital chapel, stripped bare by the storm, where they confessed their worst fears and their deepest love on the same night. Silver feathers, defying logic, left by a man who appeared without explanation and vanished without a trace, and somehow altered everything by asking the right questions at the perfect time.

She didn't understand all of it. But she understood that she was standing in a rebuilt sanctuary on Christmas Eve with a ring on her finger and her husband's arms around her. She now had knowledge that love, the stubborn, imperfect, terrifying, beautiful kind that required showing up every single day, was the only answer she had ever needed.

Outside, Brookside slept under its first real snow of the season. The memorial garden at Providence Park held its forty-three trees under the thin, white hush. Hospital lights glowed against the night sky, constant as ever.

And somewhere in the quiet space between what could be seen and what could only be believed, the silver feather at Grace's throat rested against her skin while another rested in Brandon's pocket, and the mystery they carried was not solved or explained.

It was simply loved.

Epilogue

Six Months Later

Grace dried her hands on her apron and peered out the kitchen window. Six months of marriage had taught her that Brandon tackled backyard barbecues with the same exacting focus he applied to the ER. He was outside measuring the distance between picnic tables for the third time, adjusting grill temperatures with a meat thermometer in one hand and a timer in the other, timing each dish as though a patient's life depended on the corn turning at exactly the right interval.

"The corn rotates in fifteen minutes!" he called through the open sliding door. "Sebastian just texted. They're bringing dessert."

Grace smoothed the collar of her yellow sundress. The warm June evening carried the aroma of charcoal, cut grass, and the jasmine she planted along the back fence. They had purchased their house in March, chosen because Brandon stood in the empty backyard, pointed toward the memorial garden's flowering trees, and said:

That's where I want to drink my coffee every morning.

The house sat on a spacious lot that backed up to Providence Park, allowing Grace to see the memorial garden's trees from the kitchen window. Forty-three trees. Every morning while sipping her coffee, she admired their beauty, grateful that something so lovely could grow from a night so devastating.

"Of course they are. Sloane never shows up empty-handed."

The doorbell chimed. Grace crossed the living room, noting, as she always did, signs of their blended lives. Brandon's medical journals were stacked beside her theology books. The photograph from their Christmas Eve wedding was displayed next to the certificate for the hospital's interfaith chaplaincy program, which they had designed together. A small wooden cross rested on the mantel, carved from reclaimed storm wood Brandon had brought home one afternoon and casually placed down, as if he always knew it belonged there.

Carmen stood at the door with a casserole dish. Sofia rushed forward before Grace could say hello.

"Miss Grace! *Mami* made her *tres leches cake*. Dr. Brandon asked for it special."

Grace took the dish and bent to hug Sofia, breathing in shampoo and sunshine and the sweetness of childhood. "How are you both? Sofia, did you make the honor roll again?"

"Math is way easier since Dr. Brandon started helping me." Sofia beamed. "He explains it using how he figures out medicine stuff at the hospital, and it just clicks."

Carmen followed Grace through the house toward the backyard. "How are his theology classes going?"

Grace glanced through the sliding door to where Brandon was adjusting a platter by fractions of an inch. Love swelled within her at the sight of him, still so himself and yet so changed.

"He loves them. His seminary professor told him he's never had a student ask more thought-provoking questions." She paused, warmth filling her voice before she could temper it. "He isn't aiming for ordination, just delving into deeper meanings. Honestly, watching him dig into questions he used to be afraid of is one of the best parts of being married to him."

Sebastian and Sloane arrived with their teenagers, Nathan, fifteen, and Rachel, fourteen. Daniel and Samantha came through the back gate, chasing Elijah, who was twenty-three months old and fascinated by the sprinklers Brandon had set up. The toddler squealed as the water splashed him, prompting Samantha to laugh as she gave up on keeping him dry.

"Sorry we're late," Samantha said. "Someone wanted to play with building blocks until the very last second."

"No apologies needed." Grace scooped Elijah up as he barreled toward her, his curls damp and his grin enormous. "How are the almost terrible twos treating you?"

"He keeps us on our toes." Samantha watched her son grab Grace's necklace with wet fingers. "Daniel says it's good practice for when he's a teenager."

Aaron and Meghan arrived through the back gate with Naomi pushing a stroller. Their baby was born in January. He slept soundly, blissfully unaware of the lively backyard around him. Naomi, at seventeen, managed the stroller with the confident ease of a young woman embracing her big-sister role.

"Sorry we're late," Meghan said. "We had a diaper emergency right as we were heading out."

"No worries!" Brandon called from the grill. "The chicken needs another ten minutes."

Sebastian clapped Brandon on the shoulder. "I see you're still overthinking everything. How many varieties of tomatoes did you plant?"

"Only six," he replied, mock offense coloring every syllable. "And for your information, they're thriving. Grace has been enjoying fresh salads since last month."

Naomi sought out Grace near the drink table. "Mrs. Lawson, I've been thinking about what you said about college. Do you think studying psychology would be a good fit for me?"

"Absolutely. You have natural empathy, and you're a wonderful listener." Grace set Elijah on her hip. "Have you spoken with your guidance counselor?"

"Uncle Aaron's helping me look at programs. He thinks I should consider combining medicine with social work, the way Dr. Sloane does." Naomi's eyes were bright with excitement. "I want to help families, just like you and Dr. Brandon helped ours."

Grace felt the words land in her chest. This was the ripple, and what love did when it continued to spread. It traveled from the giver to the receiver and then outward again, widening into lives not yet touched. "Whatever you choose, you'll do extraordinary things. You already do."

Pastor Wilson and Pastor Morrison arrived together, carrying notebooks and looking slightly disheveled, clearly having been in the middle of a debate that they weren't finished with.

Pastor Wilson hugged her. "How's the chaplaincy program? I heard a hospital in Atlanta is interested in implementing a similar model."

"It's better than we hoped. Brandon and I are presenting at a national conference in September." Grace looked across the yard to where her husband was arranging grilled chicken on a platter. "Hospitals are starting to recognize that spiritual care and medicine work better together than apart. Brandon's data from the tornado response became the backbone of the proposal."

"His medical perspective has been invaluable," Pastor Morrison added. "His questions push us to articulate our faith in ways that make sense to scientific minds. It can be uncomfortable, but it's absolutely necessary."

"Speaking of which," Pastor Wilson said, cleaning his glasses with the twinkle that meant he was about to stir the pot. "Jameson and I have an ongoing debate about the theological implications of quantum physics, and I believe Brandon would find it fascinating."

"You're overcomplicating it," Pastor Morrison said, a hint of affectionate exasperation in his voice. "Some mysteries don't need a theological footnote."

Brandon appeared with the chicken platter at exactly the moment his name was spoken. "Did someone mention quantum physics? Because I do, in fact, have thoughts."

"Please don't encourage them," Grace said. "The last time they started this conversation, it went on until midnight."

Willow and Anna arrived carrying enough food to feed the entire block. Willow surveyed the table layout with a discerning eye and immediately began rearranging things. "Grace Lawson, don't you dare lift another finger. We've got this. You just sit down and enjoy time with your friends."

Anna set a dish on the table. "Willow made her famous snickerdoodle cookies and I brought banana pudding. With everything everyone contributed, we could probably feed half of Brookside."

"That's the idea," Willow replied with a grin.

As the sun began to set, Grace stood at the edge of the patio and watched.

Sebastian and Brandon stood by the grill, engrossed in a discussion that was either about a complex case or the Braves' pitching rotation. Carmen and Sloane sat in lawn chairs, organizing a game for the younger children while exchanging experiences on balancing work and motherhood. Daniel and Aaron leaned against the fence, arguing with the comfortable familiarity of men who spent enough time together to enjoy their disagreements. Naomi cradled the Grant baby on her lap while Rachel showed Sofia photos on a phone.

A year and a half ago, most of these people barely knew each other. A tornado introduced them, but shared grief bonded them. The slow, everyday process of rebuilding their town turned them into a family gathering in each other's backyards out of desire, not obligation.

"Penny for your thoughts?" Brandon joined her, resting his hand on the small of her back.

"Just watching." Grace leaned into him, letting his nearness complete the moment. "I was remembering how hard you fought against getting to know any of them."

He gave a soft laugh. "I really thought keeping my distance would protect me from disappointment." He looked at the yard full of people. "Turns out, staying closed off was the actual risk."

Sofia called from across the yard. "Dr. Brandon! The baby's crying. Does that mean he's hungry or tired?"

Brandon kissed Grace's temple and headed toward Meghan and the fussy infant. Grace watched as he took the baby in his arms and began to rock gently, his movements perfected through months of experience. The same hands that sutured wounds and performed chest compressions now cradled an infant against his shoulder with the tender patience of a man who was discovering, at forty-four, that showing vulnerability wasn't a flaw.

Carmen appeared beside her. "He's good with them."

Grace nodded, still mesmerized by Brandon as he strolled in slow circles with the baby. "He really is. Sometimes I catch him reading child development books the way he reads medical journals. Last week, he spent an hour explaining aerodynamics to Sofia so she could understand how airplanes fly."

"Any thoughts about children of your own?" Carmen asked.

Grace pondered the question, letting the evening ambiance envelop them. The sounds of laughter, a baby's soothing hiccups, and the clinking of dishes created a comforting backdrop.

"We're not actively trying, but we're not preventing it either. Brandon says he wants to feel settled in what he believes before he takes on the responsibility of guiding a little person's spiritual development."

Carmen smiled. "That sounds like him... wanting the map before he starts the journey."

Grace watched Brandon hand the now-calm baby back to Meghan. The infant grabbed his finger and held on. "Except, now, he's learning that faith isn't about having the perfect map. It's about trusting the guide, even when you can't see the road." She smiled to herself. "I think he's more ready than he realizes."

Their guests left in waves as twilight deepened, exchanging hugs, leftovers, and promises to do this again next month. Carmen texted that Sofia had fallen asleep on the way home. Sebastian and Sloane were the last to go. He shook Brandon's hand in the doorway, a man who didn't say much, but whose affections always ran deeper than his words.

Then it was just the two of them. The fire pit in the corner of the yard still glowed with embers, and crickets had taken over where the conversation left off. Grace reached for a pile of plates, but Brandon laid his hand over hers.

"Leave it. Come with me. There's one more thing I need you to see."

He took her hand and led her to the back of the property, past the flower beds they planted in memory of the forty-three, beyond the fence where the yard bordered the edge of Providence Park. The memorial garden's trees loomed as dark silhouettes against the sky, transitioning from purple to black.

A small structure stood at the edge of the property. Grace had seen Brandon and Aaron tinkering with it for weeks. Brandon told her it was a garden shed and asked her not to inspect it too closely until it was finished.

It wasn't a garden shed.

It was a chapel.

Measuring eight feet square, it was constructed from reclaimed wood, much of it salvaged from the original Cottonwood Faith sanctuary, while some came from houses demolished by the tornado and later rebuilt. A simple wooden cross crowned its peak. Large windows on three sides allowed the moonlight to pour in. The door was made from a single plank of oak, still bearing the faint scars left behind by the storm.

"Brandon..." The whisper escaped her lips.

"I finished it this afternoon." He opened the door and looked almost shy for a second, which still had the power to astonish her. "I thought we needed a place... just for us. A place to pray or to find quiet together. And for anyone else who might need somewhere to wrestle with God." He paused, a small, sincere smile spreading across his face. "Or to thank Him."

She stepped inside. The interior was simple yet majestic. A plain wood altar draped with a white cloth was accompanied by a brass cross that caught the moonlight pouring through the windows. Two kneeling cushions, side by side, stitched from fabric she recognized as remnants from the hospital chapel's original upholstery.

He had saved them and used them here. The realization that her husband kept pieces of a destroyed chapel, knowing they would matter again someday, washed over her, overwhelming her emotions.

Her eyes burned. "It's perfect. Brandon... it's absolutely perfect."

He stood beside her in the small space, the moonlight transforming the reclaimed wood silver.

"I built it because of what Liam told me that night at the park. He said sometimes just showing up is the point. I wanted to create a place where showing up was all anyone had to do. No answers. No theology. No certainty. Just a room, a cross, and cushions for those willing to kneel."

Grace turned to face her husband. In the moonlight, his face displayed the same openness she had first seen in the hospital chapel on the worst night of their lives. He had the honest, unfinished, handsome face of a man who was still becoming.

"I love you," she said quietly.

His expression softened even more. "I love you too." He kissed her forehead. "More than I knew love could hold."

Turning toward the altar for a closer look at the cushions, she suddenly paused.

There, on the white cloth beside the brass cross, lay a single silver feather, as if placed there by careful hands.

She didn't gasp or cry out. She simply stared at it and then at Brandon, who was also entranced, and neither of them moved.

The feather felt warm. Of course it did. All the feathers Liam had left behind carried that impossible quality, the heat of a living thing in a place where no living thing had previously been.

She picked it up and held it in her palm. Brandon put his hand over hers. They stood in the small chapel he had built, holding a feather they couldn't explain, in a room made from wood once broken apart by a storm, on land that backed up to a garden where forty-three trees grew in memory of beloved souls the town would not let fade.

"He's still with us," Grace said.

"Yes... I believe he is." Brandon's voice held no strain or need to understand before believing. Just acceptance.

They knelt on the cushions, their hands linked, the feather resting between their palms. The moonlight streamed through the three windows, turning the little chapel silver.

Grace didn't pray out loud. Neither did Brandon. They knelt in the silence, and the silence was filled. Filled with memory. Filled with gratitude. Filled with everything they had survived. Storms, grief, anger, forgiveness, mystery, and the intentional choice to love one another without any guarantees.

Some things didn't need words to be holy.

Outside, the June sky was laden with stars. The fire pit's last embers glowed orange across the yard. The memorial garden stretched beyond the fence, its forty-three trees standing guard in the dark.

And somewhere in the gap between what could be quantified and what could only be received, a mystery known as Liam rested alongside them, needing neither explanation nor understanding. He was present in the way that grace is always present, whether or not anyone remembers to seek it.

The feather was warm in their hands.

And for that moment, it was enough.

THE END

I hope you enjoyed Running with Grace.
Please consider leaving your review.
Be sure to continue for an EXCERPT from the next book in the
Wings of Faith Series,
Walking in Love.

Excerpt from *Walking in Love*

THE UNIVERSE HAD A cruel sense of humor, and this was its punchline.

"I'm telling you, Kendall, I can't make this up." Londyn pressed her phone tighter against her ear, staring at the endless gray of the March sky through her windshield. "I've been driving for three days. I make it to the outskirts of Brookside, and my tire just... gives up. It's like the universe is sending me a message."

"What message?" Kendall's voice carried the warmth of Jacksonville sunshine, even through the phone line. "That you need new tires?"

"No... that I shouldn't be here."

"Girl, stop." Kendall's tone shifted from teasing to firm. "You're doing a good thing. Your aunt needs her family."

Londyn's jaw locked. *Family.* Such a pretty word others used for love and connection. For her, it represented a duty nobody else wanted to shoulder.

Be sensible, her practical voice urged. *"Roadside assistance said they're coming. You've made it through worse waits."*

A sharper thought pushed back. *You wouldn't be waiting at all if they hadn't volunteered you like a sacrificial offering,*

And then, the quiet reality landed the final blow: *They were justified in volunteering you. You're single, expendable, and your job permits you to travel. Besides, what else were you doing anyway?"*

Kendall's voice broke through Londyn's internal turmoil. "Hey... are you still there?"

"Yeah. Sorry. The tow truck said they'd be here in about forty-five minutes."

"Do you want me to stay on the phone with you?" her friend offered.

Londyn looked at the dashboard clock. It was three-seventeen in the afternoon. Kendall would be leaving for the hospital to begin her evening shift as a nurse in the pediatric ICU. The last thing her best friend needed was to spend her break babysitting a grown woman who couldn't manage to reach town without falling apart.

"No, go ahead. I'll call you later."

Silence rushed in when the call ended, thick and pressing. County Road 47 stretched empty in both directions, pine trees framing a town she had no desire to enter. Somewhere down this road sat a house on Rosehaven Lane. Inside, her Aunt Evelyn waited, a woman she barely knew.

You're the logical choice.

Her mother's words from two weeks ago still stung like iodine on an open wound. Not *"the compassionate one"* or *"the one she'd want"*. Just... logical.

Because what else did she have to offer? She worked in a remote job, guiding others through medical crises she couldn't prevent in her own life. She resided in a studio apartment in Jacksonville that someone else was currently renting, probably filling it with mementos that held significance for them. And her marriage had crumbled under the weight of unanswered prayers and quieter disappointments.

Londyn shoved open her car door and stepped onto the gravel shoulder. The Georgia air was different. It held the damp aroma of pine and earth, heavier than the salty breeze she had left behind. She circled her car, inspecting the flat tire as if she knew what to search for. It was a futile act, an attempt to feel proactive rather than helpless.

"Don't give them more ammunition," she muttered. Calling her Monica now would only earn a lecture about how she should have checked her tires before driving across state lines.

What about calling AAA? Her defeated voice was quieter, more insidious. *Oh, wait, you canceled that membership when you were cutting costs after the divorce... another stellar life choice.*

"Stop it." Londyn leaned against the car and closed her eyes. "Just stop."

The rumble of an engine made her eyes snap open. A silver Ford F-150 slowed, then eased onto the shoulder about twenty feet behind her car. Londyn's muscles tensed. This was a stranger, and she was on an isolated road. Every cautionary news story she ever heard replayed in her mind.

The driver's door swung open. The man who emerged was tall, with a solid frame that suggested he was someone familiar with using his body as a tool. He wore faded jeans and a fitted, gray shirt that stretched across his chest in ways Londyn noticed before she could stop herself. He looked to be in his mid-forties, with close-cropped hair and a face that looked like it had weathered storms and work, and hadn't flinched from either.

He stayed by his truck, making no move to close the distance. "Afternoon. I saw you were having some trouble. Need a hand?"

His voice was a steady baritone, its tone seeking permission rather than assuming she would accept his assistance.

Londyn's practical voice chimed in. *He's keeping his distance. That's a positive sign.*

Or, it's a tactic, her cautious side countered.

"I called for roadside assistance," Londyn replied, keeping the car between them. "They said they'd be here in about forty-five minutes."

"That's optimistic for this stretch of road. They sometimes underestimate the time it takes to reach this area." He gestured toward the flat tire without moving closer. "I can change that for you in ten minutes if you've got a spare. My name's Julian Dawson. I'm local here... a retired firefighter. I still volunteer at the station." He presented it as a simple statement of fact.

A firefighter. That should have been reassuring. Londyn's patient advocacy work meant she dealt with first responders regularly and knew most of them exuded the same calm competence this man displayed. But trusting someone solely because of their profession seemed naive, and she experienced firsthand that naivety could lead to complications.

"I have a spare," she heard herself say. "It's in the trunk."

He gave a single nod and turned to his truck bed, retrieving a jack and tire iron. His movements were economical, devoid of wasted energy. He approached slowly, then knelt by the tire, respecting her space, even as he intruded on it.

"Are you moving to Brookside or just passing through?"

"I'm moving here... temporarily." Londyn watched his hands as he positioned the jack. "I'm here to take care of my aunt. She's... she needs help."

"That's kind of you." He glanced up, his eyes meeting hers for a brief moment.

Kind. Another pretty word that felt strange to her.

"It's... complicated," she said, then immediately wished she hadn't. He didn't need to know her life story.

"Family tends to be that way." He began operating the jack handle, raising the car with smooth, effortless motions. "What's your aunt's name? I might know her... Brookside's a pretty small town."

"Evelyn Hartwell."

Recognition flickered across his face. "Miss Evelyn on Rosehaven Lane. Yeah, I know her. My church has delivered some meals to her. She's got breathing troubles, right?"

Londyn's spine stiffened. Of course he knew her. Of course he went to church. He was probably one of those steadfast, devoted types who thrived on casseroles and conviction, and couldn't comprehend a faith that had shriveled into ash.

"That's her."

If Julian noticed the tension in her voice, he didn't comment. He loosened the lug nuts with quick, sure twists, his focus absolute. His forearms flexed, corded with muscle, and Londyn forced her gaze away. Not because he wasn't attractive. He was undeniably appealing, but acknowledging his charms felt dangerous. She was here to take care of an ailing aunt, not to admire the physique of a helpful stranger.

He's just changing your tire, the practical voice in her head reminded her. *Don't make it weird.*

Too late. You're already thinking about his forearms.

Great. Now you're objectifying the man who's helping you. Add that to the list of things you're doing wrong.

"You okay?" She blinked. Julian was looking at her, a faint question in his eyes. Londyn realized too late that she had been caught mid-conversation with herself, complete with facial expressions.

"I'm fine. Just... tired. It's been a long drive."

"I bet." He removed the flat tire, his shoulders bunching under the fabric of his shirt. He set it aside and reached for the spare in her trunk. Their hands brushed when she instinctively moved to help. The contact sent an unwelcome awareness through her arm. Julian was the first to withdraw, granting her a wider berth.

See? He's respectful. Not every man is Simon, her practical voice reasoned.

But her heart, that traitorous entity, whispered a reminder: *You thought Simon was respectful. Look how that turned out.*

Londyn watched Julian work. She forced herself to concentrate on the task, trying to ignore the spiral her inner thoughts wanted to create. He aligned the spare tire, re-threaded the lug nuts, and tightened them. Everything about him conveyed competence, dependability, and a willingness to show up without expecting anything in return.

She despised how much that vision tugged at the lonely, weary parts of her. It made her ache for connection, for someone who saw her fractures and offered steady hands anyway.

"All done." He lowered the jack and stood, wiping his palms on his jeans. "You should get that flat repaired or replaced soon. There's a good shop in town called Faithway Automotive. Tell them Julian sent you. They'll treat you right."

"Thank you." The words felt insufficient against the weight of her relief. "I appreciate you stopping to help."

"No problem. That's what neighbors do around here." He walked back to his truck, pausing with a hand on the door. His gaze met hers again. "Rosehaven Lane is about three miles up this road. Take a left at the stop sign. Miss Evelyn's house is the blue one with the white shutters, the fourth one on the right."

"Thanks again," she said.

He lifted a hand in a brief wave, climbed into his truck, and drove away. Londyn watched him disappear down the road, feeling a peculiar mix of gratitude and stubborn resistance. She didn't want to need help. Needing help signified vulnerability, and vulnerability meant, eventually, disappointing someone when she couldn't be what they expected.

Her phone rang, shattering the quiet. Monica's name flashed on the screen, and her stomach dropped.

She answered. "Hello?"

"Londyn." Her sister's voice carried that particular sharpness that signaled trouble. "Mom said you'd be there by now. Aunt Evelyn had another episode. Where are you?"

Each word was a stone dropping down a deep, dark well. Another episode before she had even made it to the house.

"I'm almost there. I had car trouble," Londyn explained, her voice tight.

"Car trouble? Londyn, she's been waiting—" Monica's pitch climbed into a familiar blend of accusation and exasperation. "You know how anxious she gets. You should have planned better."

You should have checked your tires. You should have left earlier. You should be better at this. The unspoken chorus of her life played on repeat.

"I'm getting in the car now. I'll be there in ten minutes." Londyn kept her voice flat, a shield against the forthcoming wave of criticism.

"Fine. Just... hurry, okay? She's asking for you, and I can't—" Monica's voice dropped to a strained whisper. "I can't keep doing this. That's why you're there."

The line went dead before Londyn could respond. She stood on the gravel, phone in hand, watching Julian's silver truck vanish around a bend. A wild, irrational part of her wished she could call him back. Not for the tire issue, but to ask if he knew how to fix the part of her that shattered a little more with every family interaction.

But he was gone. She was alone. And Aunt Evelyn was waiting.

With a resigned sigh, Londyn got back into her car, started the engine, and drove toward Rosehaven Lane. Toward a house that wasn't a home, a relative who was a stranger, and another chapter of her life that resembled one more flat tire in a long series of things that deflated when she needed them most.

The blue house with white shutters came into view. Her hands clenched the steering wheel.

You can do this. You've tackled harder things.

The defeated voice sighed in response. *Like what? Survive a failed marriage? Bury the dream of a fulfilling life? This is just more of the same.*

But at least you showed up, the practical part of her insisted. *That has to count for something.*

Londyn pulled into the driveway, put the car in park, and sat staring at the front door. Behind it, Aunt Evelyn waited for a niece who was the *'logical choice'.* Meanwhile, Julian Dawson was likely pulling into his own driveway, washing his hands, and moving on with his day. His good deed was completed, and his thoughts were doubtless elsewhere.

Deep inside, all three of Londyn's inner voices fell silent. For once, there were no disputes and no debates. There were no words left for what lay in front of her.

Taking a deep breath, she got out of the car, grabbed her bags from the back seat, and walked toward the front door. The tire was fixed. One crisis was resolved.

Now, for the rest.

Please continue reading Walking in Love: Julian and Lyndon's Story

A Love Letter in Lumber: Running with Grace Bonus Chapters

The story isn't over yet.

THANK YOU FOR READING **Running with Grace** and for walking alongside **Brandon** and **Grace** through the storms, the ruins, and the love that rebuilt it all.

But there's one more story I wanted to tell... one that didn't quite fit inside the novel, yet felt too important to leave untold.

In **A Love Letter in Lumber,** an exclusive four-chapter bonus, you'll discover what Brandon was really building in the backyard all those Saturday mornings. You'll see Grace find the sawdust on his collar and the lumber receipts in his pockets. You'll watch a man who once refused to kneel create something worth kneeling in, with his own two hands and a little help from Aaron Grant.

This bonus is my gift to you for joining my newsletter, where I share updates on the Brookside series, behind-the-scenes glimpses into my writing life, and first looks at what's coming next.

Get your free copy here: A Love Letter in Lumber: Running with Grace Bonus Chapters

He couldn't write her a love letter. So he built one instead.

The storm took the chapel. Love built it back.

Also By Barbara Jane Oliver

ALTHOUGH THESE NOVELS ARE part of a series featuring inter-connected characters, the main romance centers on a unique story-line with its own arc and resolution. Each book can be enjoyed as a standalone novel, making it a pleasurable independent reading experience.

WINGS OF FAITH SERIES

- Before the Blessing: A Bristol Heights Novella (Colton & Nicole): Download FREE When You Subscribe to My Newsletter

- Renewing His Hope Book 1: Daniel & Samantha

- Soaring in Faith Book 2: Aaron & Meghan

- Running with Grace Book 3: Brandon & Grace

- Walking in Love Book 4: Julian & Lyndon: TBA

BRISTOL HEIGHTS SANCTUARY SERIES

- Sanctuary in His Arms Book 1: Joshua & Simone: TBA

- Sanctuary of Truth Book 2: TBA

About the Author

Barbara Jane Oliver is a faith and inspirational based author who lives in the beautiful state of Georgia with her loving husband and partner in all non-crimes, Ronald. She has been an avid reader from an early age, often hiding in her parents' closets to finish reading her books. Her love of reading nurtured her creative mind and sparked a passion for writing. She is also a U.S. Army Veteran and has been a registered nurse for over 20 years. Barbara and Ronald have a wonderful, blended family that includes two daughters, three grandsons, and two great-granddaughters.

I hope you enjoyed this novel. If so, please visit my website for a list of my current and upcoming publications.

Author Web Page: https://barbarajaneoliver.com/

Instagram: https://www.instagram.com/barbarajaneoliver-author/

TikTok: https://www.tiktok.com/@bjoliver7

CLICK HERE for **Free Novella** and **SIGNUP** for my Newsletter.

Thank you so very much.
Barbara Jane Oliver

She thought love always left.
Until he chose to stay.

Some things are more beautiful
after they've been restored.

Visit Author Website For Additional Information

Thank You For Your Support

A MONSIEUR MIGNERET,

préfet du Bas-Rhin.

— — ·

Monsieur le Préfet,

Nous avons l'honneur de vous présenter le premier volume des travaux du Conseil de salubrité du Bas-Rhin.

Ce recueil comprend une période de neuf années, de 1849 à 1858; il contient d'utiles matériaux pour l'histoire de l'hygiène publique en Alsace; c'est le premier document de ce genre qui ait été imprimé à Strasbourg. Ce travail forme un point de départ qui permettra d'apprécier les progrès que l'avenir réserve à l'hygiène publique dans notre contrée.

Le département du Bas-Rhin s'est toujours distingué par ses institutions sanitaires; il a eu l'initiative pour des questions importantes; c'est dans le Bas-Rhin qu'a pris naissance la médecine cantonale; vous avez contribué, Monsieur le Préfet, à compléter et à consolider cette institution, en organisant la pharmacie cantonale qui assure à la population indigente la gratuité des médicaments.

Le Conseil de salubrité saisit cette occasion de vous remercier, Monsieur le Préfet, de la sollicitude que vous avez témoignée pour les grands intérêts de l'hygiène publique et de la bienveillance avec laquelle vous avez encouragé ses travaux.

Recevez, Monsieur le Préfet, l'assurance de notre respect,

Le secrétaire,   *Le vice-président,*
G. TOURDES.   V. STOEBER.

MEMBRES DU CONSEIL DE SALUBRITÈ.

MM. **Migneret**, préfet du Bas-Rhin, *président ;*
Stœber, professeur à la faculté de médecine, *vice-président ;*
Tourdes, ʻ　　　id.　　　*secrétaire ;*
Schützenberger,　　id. ;
Lereboullet, professeur à la faculté des sciences ;
Aroussohn, professeur agrégé à la faculté de médecine ;
Willemin, médecin en chef de l'hospice des Orphelins ;
Oppermann, directeur de l'École de Pharmacie ;
Oberlin, professeur à l'École de Pharmacie ;
Hepp, pharmacien en chef de l'hôpital civil ;
Heydenreich, pharmacien ;
Imlin, vétérinaire ;
Kœnig,　　id. ;
Connes, ingénieur en chef des ponts et chaussées.
Daubrée, ingénieur en chef des mines, doyen de la faculté
des sciences ;
Morin, architecte du département.

NOTICE HISTORIQUE

SUR LES

INSTITUTIONS SANITAIRES DU BAS-RHIN.

Le département du Bas-Rhin, un des premiers en France, a été doté par ses administrateurs d'institutions relatives à l'hygiène publique.

L'exemple de l'Allemagne démontrait toute l'importance de ces institutions. La présence d'une faculté de médecine à Strasbourg assurait à l'autorité un concours utile.

Le 15 messidor an IX, M. Laumond, préfet du Bas-Rhin, sur les observations de l'école spéciale de médecine de Strasbourg, concernant l'inoculation de la vaccine, institua un comité médical, chargé de faire pénétrer dans le département une méthode préservatrice, dont les bienfaits commençaient à être reconnus par tous les hommes éclairés.

Les membres de ce comité médical, première ébauche du Conseil de salubrité, ont été MM. FLAMAND, COZE et NOEL, professeurs à l'école de médecine, et le docteur SPIELMANN.

Le 31 octobre 1810, un préfet, dont le nom est encore vénéré en Alsace, M. Lézay-Marnésia, fonda, dans le département du Bas-Rhin, les institutions d'hygiène publique qui ont existé jusqu'à nos jours ; il organisa, par deux arrêtés qui parurent en même temps, la médecine cantonale et le Conseil de salubrité.

Ces arrêtés avaient pour but d'organiser la police médicale, les vaccinations, les secours en aliments et en médicaments à distribuer aux malades et aux indigents des campagnes.

Les considérants des deux arrêtés indiquent une con-
naissance approfondie des besoins auxquels il s'agissait de
pourvoir ; ils précisent le but des institutions d'hygiène
publique. Aujourd'hui encore la question est posée dans
les mêmes termes.

« Voulant maintenir dans le département l'exécution des
lois relatives à la médecine et à la pharmacie, régler les
divers objets qui tiennent à la salubrité publique, étendre
à toutes les classes les bienfaits de la vaccination, assurer
aux malades des campagnes les secours qu'ils sont en droit
d'attendre de la sollicitude de l'administration, et faciliter
par leur réunion dans un seul arrêté et par leur établisse-
ment simultané les dispositions que réclament ces parties
importantes du service public ; considérant que la plupart
des mortalités n'exercent leurs ravages que parce qu'on a
moins pourvu aux moyens de les prévenir qu'à ceux d'y
remédier ; que l'habitation du pauvre est le berceau le
plus ordinaire des épidémies les plus désolantes ; que les
maladies les plus habituelles sont fréquemment causées
par la misère ; qu'une bonne nourriture est le moyen le
plus efficace pour les combattre, et qu'attendu les faibles
moyens d'une grande partie des établissements de bien-
faisance, il faut suppléer à leur insuffisance par des res-
sources nouvelles, si l'on veut satisfaire à ce que l'huma-
nité réclame à cet égard de l'autorité publique ; que la vaccination gratuite par trimestre et par commune, effectuée
de bras à bras et suivie trois mois plus tard de la revue
de tous les enfants vaccinés, est le moyen le plus sûr
d'étendre à la génération naissante le bienfait de cette
opération.... » Tel est l'exposé sommaire des motifs des
deux arrêtés.

Le titre Ier se rapporte à l'exercice de la médecine